I0623135

Once Upon A Tear

The Land of Dreams, Volume 1

Amy Sousa

Published by Patchwork Press, 2018.

Published by: Patchwork Press www.patchwork-press.com
Cover by: Katzilla Designs www.katzilladesigns.wordpress.com
Editing by:
Abi Pearson
Philippa Attwood
Rachel Schmidt
Felicia Correa
ISBN: 978-1-988902-20-3 Ebook: 978-1-988902-21-0

I dedicate this book to my mother, who has always taken my writing seriously. I also dedicate this to my family, who always believed they'd hold my book in their hands one day, and to Wattpad for providing me with a wonderful platform to share my stories and improve my writing.

Prologue

When Annabella Tompkins wished to become a princess one day, she never thought her life would turn into a fairytale.

"Happy birthday to you," the children chorused, before Annabella blew out the five candles on her birthday cake. Her long, brown hair flowed with the light summer breeze as her mother helped her cut the first piece of the chocolate and lemon cake. Annabella smiled brightly, showing off the new gaps where future adult teeth would take their place, as she held up the first plate to her next-door neighbour, Zach.

"I want the first plate to go to my best friend," Annabella announced with her high-pitched voice.

Zach smiled down at the five year old with a huge grin. "Thanks, Annie!" he exclaimed before giving her a hug and taking the piece of cake from her mother. He had just turned six years old a few weeks earlier and Annabella had received the first slice then. Zach took his first bite, moaning at how delicious the cake was. He gave Annabella a thumbs-up before she dug into her own piece that was just cut.

"Happy birthday, Princess," Annabella's father, Joe Tompkins, said with his arms spread out. Annabella giggled and ran straight into them.

"Thanks, daddy. After everyone's done eating cake, can we open presents?" Annabella was visibly anxious.

Her father chuckled and nodded his head. "Of course we can. What's the point of a birthday party without opening any presents and showing them off to the guests?"

When the time finally came to open presents, Annabella was beyond excited. A majority of the presents she received consisted of dolls, clothes and stuffed animals.

The five year old looked towards the kitchen when she felt eyes on her. Her grandmother stood there with a package in her hand and a small smile on her thin lips. Annabella had no idea that her grandmother had come all the way up to Toronto for her party and felt compelled to go over to her. She followed the woman until they were outside on the back porch.

"Happy birthday, Annabella. I'm here to give you your present," Annabella's grandmother said. Annabella nodded before her eyes widened at the sight of the beautiful book her grandmother pulled out of the box.

"It's beautiful, Grandma, but I can't read very well," Annabella said, embarrassed as she looked down in shame. She had a bit of trouble with reading at school, but the teachers said it was nothing to be worried about at her age. Annabella's grandmother knelt down and held both of Annabella's arms lightly.

"My dear, this book is very special. As long as you truly wish to read it, you shall do so. Do you wish to read it?"

Annabella nodded vigorously before she hugged the book to herself. "I do, Grandma. I wish to read it."

The woman smiled at the little girl before whispering into her ear. "Good. You can read this story every night if you wish. I promise you'll never grow bored of it. Once you're all grown up you can just read it whenever you're sad."

Annabella nodded before she heard children calling her name. "Grandma, can you please put this in my room for me? I want to go play."

"Of course, my little princess," her grandmother replied before going inside and up the stairs. Annabella ran to the backyard where her friends were playing games in the grass.

Annabella's grandmother was nowhere to be seen when everyone began leaving. Her mother said that she was never able to come because she was down in Florida. She explained that it was probably just her imagination, but Annabella knew better than that. She thought her parents were trying to hide that her grandmother had to leave early, so she wouldn't be upset. Showing her parents the book could have easily proved it, but she didn't want to keep pushing and risk getting in trouble. It was because of the book that Annabella was excited for her bedtime to come, which was very unusual for her.

When everyone except Zach and his family had left, he approached Annabella with a sad look on his face. "I need to talk to you about something," he told Annabella as he pulled her towards her bedroom.

"What's wrong, Zachy?" Annabella asked.

"My parents told me this morning that today would be the last time I get to see you ever again," he explained with tears beginning to well in his eyes.

Annabella didn't know how to process this information. "I don't understand," she said, though she knew the explanation wouldn't be good.

"My daddy got a new job and needs to move to America. We're all going with him and we're leaving tomorrow," he said with sorrow. A single tear ran down Annabella's face, which was quickly wiped away by Zach. "Don't cry, Annie. Even if I need to wait until I'm a big kid, I'll come back one day," Zach promised.

Annabella wanted to spend every last second that she could with her best friend. She ran towards the living room and hopped onto Zach's mother's lap.

"Why hello there, birthday girl. You look like you have something to say," Mrs. Carter observed.

Annabella nodded before plainly asking, "When do you leave?"

Mrs. Carter instantly understood what Annabella was asking. "I see that Zach has told you the news. We're leaving at half past eight. The plane leaves at ten o'clock."

Annabella frowned and nodded. "Can Zach sleepover so we can spend a little bit more time with each other?" she asked hopefully.

Mrs. Carter frowned, "I know this was very last minute. We didn't want to ruin Zach's birthday or yours by telling you before. But I don't want to wake you guys up too early. Zach is going to be very tired after the long trip if he sleeps over."

Before Annabella could say anything, her mother butt in. "What if you prepare everything he needs to take to the airport and wake him up after you get there?"

Annabella nodded quickly and hopped up and down as Zach ran to her side.

"Please, Mommy? I really want to spend as much time as I can with Annie," Zach pleaded.

Mrs. Carter sighed, "All right, you two deserve it. I'm really sorry Annabella. This new job is a life-changing opportunity that Uncle Harry can't turn down. He unfortunately lost his old job so we have no other choice. I wanted to tell you before, but I wanted you to be happy on your birthday."

Annabella understood and gave Mrs. Carter a hug before she grabbed Zach's hand, running upstairs towards her new storybook. The two children played until eleven o'clock that night. Their parents wouldn't let them stay up that late for at least another eight years, but they understood their children's love for each other, and made an exception.

When the time came for lights out, Annabella pulled her new book out. "Grandma says it's a special book that I'll be able to read," she explained.

Zach smiled widely and urged her to open it.

Annabella complied and began reading. "Once upon a time..."

Through the entirety of the story Annabella never once struggled while reading. At first she was confused about how easy the words were flowing, but she soon became engrossed in the story and it was evident that Zach was as well.

"And they lived happily ever after. The end," Annabella finished reading before she realized that Zach was now crying. "Zachy, what's wrong?" she asked with her own tears filling up her eyes.

Zach pulled her into a tight hug. "I don't want this to be the last story we read together," he said. The two children cried over the book while holding on to the embrace. Every tear that hit the book would evaporate in a tiny puff of colourful smoke, but Zach and Annabella were too preoccupied to notice. Tears from both children began falling. They landed in the same place causing a silent ripple along the page, but neither Zach nor Annabella noticed. The book went back to normal a mere second before Annabella looked down and closed it.

"I love you, Annie," Zach said and hugged her once more.

Annabella smiled at him. "I love you too, Zachy. We should go to sleep now. I can barely keep my eyes open anymore," she said. Annabella thought it was weird that she was suddenly tired, because she had been wide-awake while reading the story. The children quickly got underneath the covers and put a pillow between them, as that was the rule their parents gave them, before Annabella clicked the light off.

"When you wake up in the morning I want you to check inside of your nightstand," Zach told Annabella. She looked at him questioningly, but it was dark so he couldn't see her expression.

"Why?"

Zach smiled at her, knowing that she wouldn't be able to see it. "I used my allowance to buy you a present, mommy helped too. I need you to promise me that you'll never get rid of it," he said quietly, but still seriously.

Annabella was really excited to see what it was, but held back as she was too tired to even try and convince Zach to let her see it. "I promise, Zachy. I'm going to miss you so much. Please don't forget me," she said before he gave her a quick peck on the cheek. She was confused at the action. Annabella had always seen her parents doing that with each other, and they would always kiss her on the cheek, but didn't understand why Zach had done it.

"I'll see you again one day," Zach promised before he returned to his side of the pillow, and the two best friends fell asleep.

Chapter One

Annabella flopped down on her bed as she giggled. Zach had sent her yet another silly picture of them that was over a decade old. The picture showed the two children with dark hair making funny faces, while what looked like chocolate icing was smeared all over their faces. It would be an understatement to say she was curious to know what Zach looked like now. Had his teeth grown in straight? Had his eyes and hair gotten lighter or darker? How did he sound in person?

The years had treated Annabella well. Her hair was still the same caramel colour as it had always been, except the sun had naturally lightened the ends over the years. Her big, almond-shaped hazel-green eyes, which Annabella claimed to be boring, had such warmth to them that people always complimented. Annabella had a minimal amount of acne, which was normal for any sixteen year old, but she still cursed that she didn't have perfect skin like the many pretty girls at her school. Annabella also had perfectly straight teeth due to three years of braces.

Though—like many teenagers—Annabella only seemed to notice her imperfections, such as her legs touching, that she was small chested, and many other things a teenager would worry about.

'Can you send a picture of yourself so I can see how much you've changed? It's only fair considering you know how I look,' Annabella texted Zach. She pouted slightly at his response.

'You're just going to have to wait and see for yourself.'

It was no surprise that Annabella was excited about Zach and his parents moving back to Toronto in just three days. She wasn't too disappointed at his response because ever since they started texting, Zach had wanted it to be a surprise. His Facebook profile was a picture of himself when he was young, and he didn't care about or use social media enough to change it.

The last time Annabella saw Zach was on her fifth birthday. The best friends however, didn't lose contact for many years. Besides the constant phone calls, Annabella's mother helped her write letters to Zach up until she was finally allowed to get her own email account in the fifth grade. Once Annabella had her first cell phone, her father agreed to pay for a plan that would allow her to text the states. Annabella and Zach would text each other once in awhile to say happy birthday, or Merry Christmas, but it was only in the past few months when Annabella heard that Zach and his family were moving back that they started talking with each other every day again.

Annabella played with the necklace that she kept in her nightstand—a habit she had developed many years ago. The morning after her fifth birthday, she followed Zach's request and looked for his present in her nightstand. Annabella found a beautiful necklace of a white-gold heart that hung on a delicate chain. For weeks, the five year old would cry while holding onto the necklace, wishing that Zach would come back or that it was all just a nightmare. She barely ever wore it, as she was afraid that she would lose it, but always kept it safe and swore that she would wear it again when Zach returned.

Annabella continued texting Zach about random things while she set up his part of the room. His parents' lease wouldn't be starting for two weeks after they arrived, so Annabella and her parents offered their guest room to their old friends, and the daybed in Annabella's room to Zach.

Annabella's room was painted a light violet colour that complemented the white furniture. The walls were covered with photos of family and friends, so Annabella didn't worry much about it being too girly. Zach's daybed was set up against the wall on opposite to Annabella's bed. It was one of those day beds that is a bit too big to be a real couch, but still looked like one when decorated accordingly.

After a few hours of watching random movies, Annabella decided to call her parents. They were supposed to be on their way home from a week-long work trip, to spend Annabella's birthday together, and welcome their old friends home. After waiting a few seconds the call ended before it even started to ring. *That's strange,* Annabella thought. *They must have run out of battery.*

Instead of just sitting around and doing nothing, Annabella decided to check the weather. She wanted to know what the forecast for the week would be, so she would know where to take Zach out. Annabella was excited at what her weather application was reading; it would be sunny for the entirety of the weekend, meaning everything would be perfect.

Annabella jumped when a knock sounded from the door. It was already dark outside, so she felt a bit uneasy and decided to look outside through the window first. Annabella was surprised to see a police cruiser parked in front of the house and two officers waiting at the front door. *That's weird,* she thought, as she slowly made her way down the stairs and towards the front door.

"Are you Annabella Tompkins?" A male police officer asked the second the door was open.

Annabella nodded. "Yes."

"Is it ok if we come inside and sit down?" This time it was the female police officer who spoke.

Annabella looked between the two and considered their uneasy expressions. "Is it that serious?" Annabella was beginning to feel anxious herself. "Did I do something wrong?"

The two officers looked at each other and the female sighed. "My name is Officer

Patterson, and this is my partner, Officer Blake. Yes, it is very serious, but you didn't do anything wrong."

Officer Patterson looked behind Annabella at the sofa. Annabella moved out of the way, and the officers both made their way in. The heavy clack of their shoes made Annabella flinch until they made it to the carpet and sat down.

They can at least take their shoes off.

Annabella closed the door after noticing that a few neighbours were observing from their windows. They quickly stepped away when they noticed that she'd caught them.

"What's this about?" Annabella asked the police officers.

"I think it would be better if you sat down for this," Officer Patterson said.

Annabella sat down in the love seat that was located diagonally from the couch. She grabbed one of the pillows and placed it on her lap—a habit that she had adopted after years of trying to cover up her stomach.

"This is about your parents. Do you have any relatives that live nearby?" It was Officer Blake that spoke this time.

Annabella shook her head. "My grandmother lives in Florida in the summer, and my aunt and cousins live in Vancouver. What happened to my parents?"

Officer Blake quickly whispered something to Officer Patterson, who then turned to Annabella.

"I'm very sorry to be telling you this, but they were involved in a fatal car accident."

Annabella felt a pang in her heart, but sat there completely still, in silence. The only movement coming from her was the occasional blinking.

"They were driving on the 427, their car rolled over several times. It looks like your father may have jolted the wheel, but it's still being investigated with all of the witnesses and accident reconstruction.

They were already gone when a witness ran to check on them. We haven't gotten any other details yet, but we're going to take you to the hospital so you can learn more there."

Annabella didn't move a muscle, but continued staring at the officers as her heart started racing at the possibility.

"You should call someone that you're close with to go with you. We can pick them up as well so you're not alone," Officer Blake continued.

"I'm not going to the hospital," Annabella stated.

"Annabella, I know this is hard, but-"

"No..." Annabella shook her head. "They're not dead. There's no point of me going. They're going to be home soon anyway, so you should probably leave so they don't think I did anything illegal."

Both officers had a look of confusion on their faces. "Annabella, please listen to us. This is not a joke. Your parents are gone, and you should come with us to the hospital to see them while you still can. We're very sorry."

Annabella once again shook her head, but this time she stood up and made her way towards the door. "I already said no. Now can you please leave? I'm feeling tired and would like to relax until my parents get home."

"Please, Annabella. I know this is really hard. I lost my mother when I was very young and I remember being in denial about it. Just, come with us," Officer Blake pleaded.

"We'll stay with you, and we can call whomever you'd like," Officer Patterson put in.

Annabella sighed. "I'm going upstairs. Feel free to stay here, but I'm not leaving. You'll see. Soon enough my parents are going to get home and freak out when they see you guys sitting there." She trudged up the stairs, not giving the officers a chance to say anything more.

Annabella quickly closed the door to her room before making her way towards her bed and laying down. "They'll see," she said to herself with her heart still beating extremely fast. *I'll just have to kill some time until Mom and Dad get home so I can see the officers' faces.*

Annabella reached for the storybook that her grandmother had gifted her for her fifth birthday, and began to read as she did every time she needed to feel better. Whenever she was in a bad mood, she would read her storybook to distract herself. Annabella always felt better after reading it, and would always think back to her grandmother telling her to read it when she was sad. Annabella grew up on many fairytales, and slowly transitioned into the originals and the Grimm versions. She also loved reading mythology, but fairytales were definitely her favourite.

Annabella loved her storybook because it was one of a kind. She researched it and nothing ever popped up about it. Princess Annabella, the main character, and the Land of Dreams seemed to be an original fairytale and Annabella often wondered if her grandmother had it made specially for her, or if it was just a coincidence. Annabella loved the happy ending and how the characters had to work hard to achieve their goals in her book. After what felt like half an hour, Annabella was on the last page where the Princess is finally being crowned as queen with her new husband by her side and parents watching her proudly.

Annabella had never cried while reading the book except for the very first time, when she found out Zach was moving away. However, what the police officers had said was beginning to bother her, and a few tears slipped out. Annabella wiped them away and quickly closed the book, failing to notice the tears evaporating in a puff of colourful smoke on the last page. She stuffed the book under her pillow before sitting up and sighing.

Annabella had a feeling that she wouldn't sleep as comfortably as she normally did when she read the book. She had never once had a nightmare the same night she read from the storybook, but she wasn't so sure about tonight. She really wanted to wait for her parents to get home, but a feeling of exhaustion quickly came over her. Annabella was breathing deeply in a matter of seconds, a wheezing sound coming from her slightly stuffy nose. She was sleeping so deeply that she didn't hear Officer Patterson walk in and sit on the futon in her room.

Everything froze except for Annabella. Her pillow slightly lifted up before her storybook slipped out and floated to the middle of the room. The book was glowing and blasts of shimmery colour flew around the room in different patterns before the book's pages started turning.

Annabella's bed started to levitate, the colourful sparkles flying around it several times before they turned into one long, transparent rainbow-coloured strand that continued circling the bed. Annabella was still sound asleep and unaware of the events taking place in her own bedroom. The colours had covered her entire room when her bed started to spin counterclockwise, and everything began to change.

If Annabella were to wake up, she would likely pass out immediately from all of the strange things happening around her. After several hours of strange events, the book closed and the room became completely silent and dark. The book gave one last twitch and quietly crept its way back underneath Annabella's incredibly soft pillow. It settled down and remained quiet, waiting for Annabella to wake up well-rested and to the surprise of a lifetime.

Chapter Two

The sun shone through the gaps in the curtains into Annabella's room. She slept still in her bed, completely unaware of the changes that had occurred just hours before. She finally began to stir.

Annabella was confused the moment she opened her eyes. The door was in a different location, and it didn't have the cracks from when she fell into it while trying on her highest heels. It now looked brand new and more ornate than before. There was a beautiful chandelier hanging in the centre of the room instead of her normal light, and in the place of the light bulbs there were white candlesticks. The walls were painted a pretty crème colour and had crown molding around the room.

Annabella sat up quickly, only to observe her blankets felt different, and her head was throbbing. She was wrapped up in a warm duvet that was covered by a crème coloured cover a few shades darker than her room, with its border outlined with designs made out of what looked like golden thread that Annabella had read about in fairytales. Annabella herself was wearing a long baby pink robe that was made of what seemed like extremely expensive silk, embroidered with the same golden thread that ran along the entirety of the duvet.

"Where am I?" Annabella asked out loud as she started to get out of bed. She almost tripped on a pair of fluffy, pink slippers that were on the edge of the soft rug that sat under the colossal bed. Annabella stood up straight and looked around the huge room. The furniture all looked Victorian, yet brand new. Everything seemed to be in its own perfect place.

Annabella was about to open the curtains when a light knock made her jump.

"Breakfast is ready, Princess. May I come in?" an unfamiliar voice of a woman asked from outside.

Confusion struck Annabella. *Am I dreaming about some random princess?* "Uh... Yeah. I mean, yes, you may come in," she answered warily.

The door opened slowly, an unusually tiny woman who looked to be in her early thirties, walked in with a cute little cart.

"I brought your favourite," said the strange woman with a perfect smile.

Annabella was about to ask what was going on, when the smell of cinnamon and french toast hit her. She observed that there was also a small bowl which looked like it was filled with maple syrup on the side of the delicious looking plate. She smiled at the woman when her stomach growled, thanking her. Just as the woman was leaving, Annabella realized that she still did not know what was going on, and she wanted an answer quickly.

"Wait," she called after the woman desperately. The woman quickly turned around and wore a confused expression. Annabella cleared her throat softly before speaking.

"Where am I?" she asked.

The strange woman began to laugh. "Oh Princess, you are inside of your bedroom. Have you not woken from your dreams?"

Annabella shook her head slightly. "I mean where in the world am I? Why do you keep calling me Princess? My name is Annabella," she informed the woman.

"You are inside of your castle, located north from the centre of The Land of Dreams. I know you do not like being called Princess, but you are the Princess, so it is hard for me to call you anything other than that. But if it is what you truly want, I will call you by your first name," the woman said before she started laughing to herself again and walked out of the room.

Annabella wanted to close the door so she could inspect the room once again, but as she walked towards it and reached for the doorknob, her hand began to glow pink and the door closed on its own with a slight gust of wind.

"What on earth? Maybe it was just the wind," Annabella guessed as she slowly backed away from the door. She observed that the windows were all closed, so she shook her head to forget about it. She walked towards the cart of delicious looking food and decided to eat it before going back to reality, trying to figure out what was going on.

Why is she saying that I'm a princess? she questioned herself. *Better yet, why did she say the Land of Dreams? The only Land of Dreams I know of is inside my book.*

"Maybe this is just a dream," she said out loud before starting to eat. After finishing up her delicious food, Annabella decided to go back to the wall with the large curtains. Annabella was skeptical about moving the curtain out of the way. The thought of a nightmare starting and something popping out from behind them scared her. She just wanted to wake up quickly.

When Annabella moved her hand up, she let out a yelp as the curtains started to move themselves with another gust of wind. She quickly looked at her hand to see the soft pink glow getting smaller and smaller.

"This is just too weird," Annabella said, as her hand went back to normal after shaking it quickly. A gasp left her lips as she finally turned to look ahead of her. A perfect-looking version of Annabella was wearing the same nightgown and staring right at her.

"Oh my God. I'm sorry, I didn't know you were there." Annabella's hands were covering her mouth at the surprise. "I don't know where I am, but I'm sorry if I'm not supposed to be here," she said before putting her hands back down. She was extremely confused and waited for the other girl to do something.

"Can you hear me?" she asked, only to realize that the girl was mimicking her actions right in time with her. Annabella took a step closer in sync with the girl and realized that she was definitely looking into a mirror.

"Oh my God..." she started saying before quickly fumbling with her tied up hair. She saw it was in fact the same silky hair as the reflection, noticing that she seemed to be a bit taller and thinner. She felt the skin on her face and noticed the lack of bumps or blemishes. She inspected her face closely in the mirror and saw that her skin tone was even, her eyes looked much greener and brighter. She looked a little less like a teenager. Lastly, she put her hands up to her breasts and felt that they were larger than before.

Annabella couldn't believe what was happening. First she wakes up in a completely different room, then she gets told that she's the princess of some dreamland and now she looks completely different.

This is *impossible*, she thought before she reached to close the curtains, only to realize that her palms were glowing pink once again. Annabella decided to not waste her time in the crazy dream and moved the curtain without touching it.

"Now that's awesome," she whispered before she started to explore her room. Curiosity took over Annabella, who spotted another door on the right side of the bed. She was prepared to use whatever magic her imagination gave her, so she held her hand up and just as she thought, the door opened on its own. The room was about the size of her living room back in her real house. The walls were filled with hundreds of beautiful dresses on long rails that seemed to be organized by colour and style.

"Whoa," Annabella said as she walked through the room and ran her fingers over the expensive dresses. "This looks way too real," she said when she reached the other side of the room, which walked through into a bathroom.

There was a beautiful antique soaker tub that looked brand new. As pretty as the bathtub was, Annabella was confused at the lack of a faucet from where the water would come. In the place of the sink, there was just a large glass bowl decorated with intricate glass designs which contained clean-looking water inside of it. Annabella walked back towards the bedroom, waving her hands in the air before the French doors closed themselves quietly. She started making her way over to the windows so she could see what the view was from the strange room. She signalled towards the drapes to open, gasping at the beautiful view.

Annabella was high up and could see the beautiful land in front of her. The sun was shining brightly against the huge castle walls, making the grass look unrealistically green—almost as if someone had turned up the saturation on a picture. Adorable birds that she had never seen were flying around happily, they seemed to greet her by flying in little circles, chirping excitedly. Annabella smiled back at them every time they flew by.

In the distance, a long, thin lake, ran under a small bridge that looked like it led out of the castle into the pretty forest. Annabella could also see a village on the other side of the forest.

"This is incredible," Annabella said as she took it all in. *If this were real mom would be freaking out*, she thought to herself.

Annabella instantly felt something strange inside of her. It wasn't a pleasant feeling at all. Her stomach churned, and she felt anxious. She couldn't seem to remember what had happened the night before. All she could remember was that Zach would be coming back to Toronto in a few days after her parents arrived home, and that they would all celebrate her seventeenth birthday together.

"Aw man," Annabella sighed as she continued looking outside. The view looked familiar. Annabella had a feeling that she'd dreamt about this before. "I love dreams like these," she said out loud. *I can do whatever I want, for as long as I want, and the only people who can wake me up are my parents when they get home later.*

Annabella could go explore her crazy and magical dream. She could eat like a pig and not gain a pound. She could even attempt to try on all of the dresses in that insanely sized ensuite. Annabella was taken out of her thoughts when she heard knocking at the door again. She snapped her fingers towards the door while concentrating on it and it opened quietly. After a few seconds the sound of small feet walking echoed from the hallway before a small figure entered the room.

"Good morning, Princess Annabella." It was a different woman than before, though she was the exact same height as the lady with the breakfast.

"Good morning," Annabella said with a smile.

The lady walked up to her and held her hand softly. "I hope you had a good night of sleep. You look very pale, I hope that you are not sick."

Annabella smiled at the woman's concern. "Don't worry, I'm perfectly fine. I'm just a little bit confused and have a bit of a headache."

The woman nodded her head slowly, but still looked concerned. "You are slurring your words quite a bit. If you did not have a good night of sleep, it would explain everything. Anyway, it is time to get ready so you can enjoy your last free day for the next week," she said before leading a confused Annabella towards the large washroom.

"Last free day? I'm- I am sorry, but what are you talking about?" Annabella asked, realizing that the people in her dream spoke without contractions. The little woman laughed as if Annabella had said something strange.

"Oh, Princess, you are so funny. Next week is your seventeenth birthday. Today is your last day to do whatever you would like before you have to start organizing everything," the little woman explained.

Annabella nodded her head as she reached the bathtub. *My birthday really is next week, but why would it also be next week in a dream?*

"Thank you, I can take it from here," she said to the woman, who laughed once again.

"You are being so silly today, Princess. Your powers are not yet strong enough," she informed Annabella.

"What are you talking..." Annabella started, but stopped as she saw the little woman's hands glowed a dark blue colour.

"See? This is what I am here for. My job is to bathe you, Princess, everyday at half past nine so you can enjoy your day," she said to a wonderstruck Annabella, whose mouth was slightly hanging open in awe.

"All right, if you say so," Annabella said as she stepped into the bathtub. She was a little bit uncomfortable when taking off her nightgown, but she felt better when she realized that the body provided from her dream was a bit different, and it was just an innocent bath. After a good fifteen minutes of being scrubbed until she was spotless, Annabella was sitting down in a chair about to get her hair brushed.

"You should probably go to the nurse to get that bump on your head checked out. I do not know how you would have bumped it in your sleep. I really hope you have not started sleepwalking," the woman said when she started to brush Annabella's hair.

Annabella smiled. "Do not worry. I probably hit my head on the nightstand. I do not want to worry my parents either so I would appreciate if you did not mention it. How long have you been working in the castle?" Annabella asked the little woman who was standing on a stool.

The woman looked confused by the question.

"Oh, I am sorry. Is that a bad question?"

The woman shook her head. "Oh, not at all. You have just never asked me about anything or talked very much at that. You are usually quite timid. I have been here since the day the Queen and King announced that they had a baby on the way," she replied happily. "Do not worry, Annabella. I will not mention your injury to your parents as long as you are more careful and get checked out if it gets worse."

Annabella kept asking the little woman questions. She soon found out she was named Maria, and she herself was amazed at how the Land of Dreams worked. She had just learned that Maria loved her job because it gave her all day to spend time with her family and friends, who either worked in the village, the castle, or attended the school located in the village.

Annabella learned that Maria's husband, David, also worked in the castle. He was a nodum, and Annabella learned that it meant he was much taller than average, and he did all of the reaching in Annabella's tower. She also learned that Maria had a son that was only a year older than Annabella and would soon be starting work at the castle. Annabella was excited about this because at least there was someone her age in the amazing dream.

"All done, Princess—I mean, Annabella," Maria said with a smile as she slightly blushed. Annabella had finally convinced her to call her by her first name.

"Thank you, it looks beautiful," Annabella said truthfully as she admired how nice her hair looked in the style Maria had done.

"You are very welcome." Maria curtsied and then left.

Annabella had told Maria to go home earlier because she wanted to pick her dress for the day. She didn't realize just how many choices there were. After half an hour, Annabella finally picked out a baby pink coloured dress that seemed perfect for the summer weather. It was a long, short-sleeved dress, with light fabric to keep her from getting too warm. She picked a pair of cream coloured flats that were so comfortable she felt like she was walking on clouds.

By the time she was completely dressed, Annabella had decided to try and fit the part of 'Princess Annabella' while the dream lasted. Trying to fit in in a strange dream was always more fun for her.

When Annabella walked back into her room she was surprised. The bed was perfectly made without a dent in sight, and her breakfast cart had been cleared. All of the drapes were open wide letting in a great amount of natural light. The curtains on the wall were also open, exposing the beautiful mirror.

Annabella finished looking in the mirror before she heard a knock on the door. "Come in," she called out.

"Princess Annabella, it is now the time for you to go out and enjoy your day," an impossibly tall man said from near the door. His legs seemed to end above Annabella's head, and his head was merely two feet away from hitting the 12-foot tall ceilings. Annabella realized that she was staring in awe and quickly composed herself.

"Thank you," she said to the tall man. "Your name is David, is it not?" Annabella asked him, to which he nodded, smiling with a bit of confusion. She smiled at him and thanked him again before he bowed and crouched to leave her room. When Maria said he was tall, Annabella did not think that he would be *that* tall. It only made her wonder how it was possible to have children. *They probably use magic for that too,* she thought with a small laugh.

Annabella walked towards the perfectly made bed and noticed that there was something poking out from under one of the pillows. Curiosity took over and she made her way over to it and stuck her hand out. Her storybook flew out and landed softly in her hands.

"What is this doing here?" she asked aloud right before the book opened on its own accord. The pages started flipping and she quickly realized that they were all blank. Only the first four words— Once upon a time—remained. "What the-" Annabella started to say, but stopped when her door flung open.

At first she thought it was one of the little women, or perhaps David again, but to her surprise it was a young man that looked to be around six feet in height.

"I am very sorry, Princess!" the man apologized as his hands grabbed onto his hair on either side of his head. "I was using my magic to open the other door, but I accidentally opened yours," he explained.

Annabella noticed how nervous he looked. She could not help but laugh at the fact that an extremely attractive boy was apologizing so much about accidentally opening her door. "It is all right," Annabella assured him. "I am sorry, I am having a strange morning and cannot seem to remember much, including names. Could you please remind me of yours?"

The boy looked up quickly and gave her a surprised look before breaking out into a nervous smile. "I uh... I am actually new here. My name is Jacob. I am Maria and David's eldest son," he told Annabella.

Annabella offered him a big smile. She was expecting a dwarf or a nodum, but was happy that she wasn't the only human in this crazy dream. She already loved Maria, even though she had just technically met her. Now she had a well above-average looking human, or at least human-looking person, with her. She didn't understand how Maria and David could possibly produce a human son, but she mentally assured herself that she would find out before she woke up.

"That is great. What is your job around here?" Annabella asked him.

Jacob smiled at how nice the Princess seemed, happily answering, "I am here to personally assist Your Highness, everywhere you go—to keep you out of danger and do tasks that you request."

Annabella frowned. *Do they really need this many workers for one person?*

"Well I am not going to need you to do tasks for me unless I am too short to do something. It would be very nice of you to keep me company and show me around though," she said to Jacob.

Jacob smiled, but Annabella noticed it didn't quite meet his eyes. "Thank you, Princess Annabella. I appreciate your kindness," he said to her sounding a bit nervous. "However, you probably know more about the castle than myself."

Annabella laughed. "You would be surprised at how little I know," she said in a joking manner. She found the fact that she was royalty in the dream hilarious, considering how awkward she was. "Also please Jacob, do not call me Princess. My first name is all I want," she pleaded. Jacob's eyes widened a little bit before he cleared his throat.

"Are you certain?" he asked unsure of himself. Annabella nodded at him before she grabbed his hand and walked through the same door everyone came in from.

"Everything just seems to be getting weirder and weirder," Annabella said to herself as she stepped out of her room into a short, yet wide, hallway.

There was a very large, rounded staircase for Annabella and Jacob to descend before they reached a long hallway where the walls were filled with doors. The hallways were wider than the average high school hallway, which are already pretty big. The walls were all beautifully decorated with wainscoting, and there were candle lit chandeliers every fifteen steps or so. With Jacob leading the way through the large hallway, they finally reached the end before descending another rounded stairway into what seemed like a gigantic main hall, that Annabella had read about in every fairytale.

"Would you like to say good morning to the Queen and King before I take you wherever you would like to go?" Jacob asked.

Annabella turned to look at Jacob, getting distracted when she looked into his eyes. They were such a beautiful chocolate brown colour that made her feel strange in a good way. She realized that those eyes seemed really familiar, but couldn't remember from where.

Annabella started to get the feeling that she had forgotten something very important. Something deep within her gut was trying to tell her what it was, but she could not remember for the life of her what it was. She did know that it was not a good feeling, and she just wanted it to go away.

"Are you all right, Annabella?" Jacob asked her in concern.

Annabella nodded her head quickly and tried to straighten her face. "I must have been day dreaming. Like I said, I have been having a strange morning, I cannot remember a lot," she said to him so he would believe her. "Can we just say a quick hello and then go to the village?" she asked Jacob, who smiled at her again.

"Of course you can. Let us go find them. They are probably working at the moment, so it will be very quick," he explained before leading her to a different part of the castle that was just as amazing as the parts she had already seen.

When they reached a room, Jacob knocked on the door which then opened slowly, revealing what seemed to be a large library. In the center of the room was a large wooden table where the Queen and King were sitting with a pile of papers in front of them. Annabella was shocked by how much the Queen and King resembled her real parents. Their eyes looked the same and their voices were also similar, but their hair and certain, younger features, seemed flawless even with the resemblance. Annabella wasn't really sure of what to say. These were just her dream parents so she felt kind of awkward acknowledging them as her mother and father.

Why would they look like them?

When Jacob nudged her, she realized that the Queen and King were waiting for her to speak. "I just wanted to stop by so I could say good morning to you both before I go out to the village," Annabella explained.

Her "parents" both smiled at her and said good morning at the same time, just like her actual parents would whenever they were home. Annabella suddenly felt the urge to hug them. She didn't know what had come upon her, but her legs took her to the table where she hugged the Queen and King tightly.

"Annabella Rosalyn, you have not hugged us on your own since you were thirteen. What is with the change of character?" the King asked her surprised, but also seemed to be pleased.

"Um... I am not quite sure. I have been feeling a bit strange since I woke up so that might be it. I will be heading out to the village now, so I will let you carry on with your work," Annabella said before backing away with an awkward smile on her face.

"Have fun, and do not let her boss you around too much, Jacob, " the Queen joked.

"Be careful though," the King said before Annabella left the room.

As Annabella and Jacob walked towards the main entrance to leave the castle, she forced herself to smile. The bad feeling in her stomach had only worsened after meeting the King and Queen.

Annabella was confused as to why she felt such an urge to hug them, but when she did, she felt like it would be the last time she would ever hug them again. She didn't want to let go once she was in their warm and comforting embrace that felt so similar and yet so distant to her. It almost felt like she had not seen her real parents for a very long time.

This is just weird, Annabella thought. *My parents are coming back in a few hours for my birthday. This dream must almost be over. Hopefully it doesn't turn into some weird nightmare. It's probably because I miss them. Yeah... that's it,* she thought as Jacob slowly waved his hand to unlock the front gate of the castle.

Once the gates were fully opened, they revealed the beautiful day that Annabella would be able to explore.

Chapter Three

"**A**re you sure that you are feeling all right?" Jacob asked Annabella when he saw her gawking at the front lawn. Annabella quickly cleared her throat in attempt to compose herself and nodded.

"It is just so beautiful out here. I never seem to tire of seeing it," she partially lied. Jacob chuckled at her answer and led her outside. The two walked through a large garden, with Annabella observing every little thing that surrounded her. There wasn't a single cloud in the perfectly blue sky. All of the flowers were perfectly grown and brightly coloured, and the grass too was perfectly cut and a rich hue of green that she had never seen before.

"I will call the chariot," Jacob said before he did a strange hand signal, the sound of bells reaching Annabella's ears. She had only been on a chariot ride when she was a little girl on a trip to New York with her parents, so she was expecting a beautiful white horse to be leading it, but much to her surprise, it wasn't a horse at all, but a unicorn.

"Jacob, that's a unicorn!" Annabella almost squealed.

She had momentarily forgotten that people spoke properly in this world, and hoped that Jacob hadn't noticed her little slip up. She knew it wouldn't matter when she woke up, but she wanted to make the most of her crazy dream.

"Yes it is. Why do you seem so excited by this? You see unicorns almost every day," Jacob answered her with an eyebrow raised.

Annabella froze at the question. "Yes, of course. They just still seem so extraordinary," she explained quickly, cringing at her explanation. Jacob gave her a weird look as if to say that she was crazy, so she lightly nudged him, causing him to burst out laughing.

Jacob seemed much less tense now.

Annabella could tell that he was nervous about offending the Princess, so she joined in on the laughter.

"Wow, you are pretty strong. I am not sure that I should be the one protecting you, Annabella. I feel safer being near you, so you can fight off any danger with those elbows," Jacob joked. Annabella gave him a smug look, but stopped walking towards the chariot when she processed what he said.

"What danger could there possibly be here?" she asked him. Everything seemed to be so perfect and magical. Annabella couldn't imagine anything possibly being dangerous.

Maybe they consider stepping on sticks and getting a splinter dangerous?

Jacob looked both ways and brought himself closer to Annabella. "The dark forest. If we do not go inside of it, than we are perfectly safe. It is only dangerous if we get caught up in it for some reason, or get stuck outside at night—the magical creatures may take their chances to explore the land and may cause a bit of trouble," he explained quietly to her.

Annabella suddenly felt a chill run down her spine. She stared at the dark forest and swore she heard a snarl. The way that Jacob said that the creatures might cause "a bit" of trouble seemed like an understatement.

"We do not need to worry about that, Annabella," Jacob reassured her with a big smile.

Annabella felt safer just looking at Jacob, so she carried on walking. When they got to the side of the chariot, she started to feel nervous about the ride. Jacob helped her get into the chariot, just like a gentleman would in one of those old romantic movies, and Annabella couldn't help but observe how handsome he was.

After sitting down, Annabella noticed a tiny man who resembled a gnome was in control of the chariot. He was about a foot and a half tall and had a huge smile plastered on his face.

"Good morning, Princess Annabella," he greeted Annabella after he bowed. Annabella smiled in response before speaking.

"Good morning." The unicorn made a neighing sound and began to walk towards the bridge, with the gnome holding onto the air as if he had rope in his hands. As the unicorn began to pick up speed, Annabella began to worry.

"He is not going to start flying, correct?" she asked Jacob nervously. Jacob chuckled at the question before giving Annabella a knowing look.

"Have you not been reading your books?" he questioned. Annabella sent him a look that screamed 'please explain.'

Jacob chuckled again. "Oh Annabella, no one likes to study. I know you have many responsibilities as a princess and as future queen, but you do not have to go to school so you have the time to learn. The unicorns in this land do not fly. You would need a pegasus for that. They are wild so you would need a trainer. You do not have to worry about flying," he reassured her.

"You caught me," Annabella said with her arms raised. "I have not been reading. Thank you for reminding me. I promise to start reading again so I do not have to keep annoying you with my questions," Annabella told Jacob nervously, hoping he would not catch her lie.

"Your questions are not annoying. They amuse me and teach me things about you," he told Annabella. "If you would like books on a certain subject, all you have to do when we get back to the castle is tell me and I will fetch them from the library," Jacob explained.

Annabella was suddenly interested at the new information. She wanted to see how far her imagination would take her in the dream, so she can enjoy her temporary time being as a princess.

"That would be lovely. May I come with you for today?" Annabella asked Jacob and slightly pouted while batting her eyelashes, trying her best to give him puppy dog eyes.

Jacob gulped loudly enough for Annabella to hear, quickly composing himself after he realized that he was staring.

"Of course you may come, only on one condition," Jacob said with a small smirk. Annabella was curious to know and sat closer with wide eyes. "What would that condition be?" she asked him curiously.

"Even though you do not want me doing tasks for you, I want you to at least let me help you," he said. Annabella narrowed her eyes slightly at him and he did the same to her. The two ended up having a staring competition, but when a wheel broke a branch, the noise made Annabella blink.

"Oh all right. I will let you help me out," Annabella finally gave in with a sigh of defeat. Seeing Jacob smile widely made her want to melt in her own, kind of bumpy, seat. She had never met someone his age that was as attractive. Only the actors and models in magazines compared. Not even in the movies were they as genuinely nice as Jacob.

Sadly, this was all a dream, and Annabella believed that she would never meet someone like him in real life. *I would never have the luck,* she thought.

Annabella quickly got lost in the beauty of the forest. She learned that this was not the dark forest, but the Forest of Light. The animals all gathered around as the chariot, which was going at a much slower rate, passed by, and they bowed down to Annabella. She was in complete awe and greeted all of the animals with a huge smile on her face. She especially loved when the fawns came up to her and pranced happily. She watched as they chased after each other and then away from their parents.

When the chariot arrived at the village, Annabella was getting nervous again. Many little dwarfs like Maria and many nodums, were standing in front of their homes and waved to her. Annabella waved back and smiled at each family they rode past. The unicorn stopped when they reached what seemed to be the center of the village. Jacob was the first to get out and helped Annabella step down from the carriage.

"What is the driver's name?" Annabella asked Jacob.

"He has a very strange name. Most of the gnomes do. He is named Fred. I know, it is a strange name, but I think it suits him," Jacob explained with chuckle.

Annabella was confused about how it was a strange name, but smiled to make it seem like she agreed.

"Thank you for the ride, Fred," Annabella told the gnome. Fred tipped his hat in a mini bow, before he started off to a different end of the village. Jacob turned to Annabella and raised his eyebrows.

"So Annabella, what would you like to do today?" Annabella thought for a moment, but came up with nothing.

"What do you like to do in town when you are not busy?" she asked Jacob, who seemed surprised.

"Well, I like to go to the library, but you already have one with every book that has ever been written. I also like to visit my younger siblings when they are on their break in school," Jacob explained. Annabella's eyes lit up instantly. She knew that she wanted to meet his siblings.

"Could I meet your siblings when they go on break today?" Annabella asked Jacob.

"Of course you can. I am sure that my sisters would be very excited to meet you. They are very fond of you," he explained.

Annabella continued to ask a few questions about the school. Break time was at noon so they still had another half hour until then. She also learned that as soon as you turn thirteen, you may choose to either continue with your studies, or train to become a knight—even if you are female. Jacob originally wanted to be a teacher, but when he learned there was no one to assist the Princess for when she turned seventeen and that he fit the description for the role, he started training.

Jacob went through years of training, advancing very quickly. There was something special about him. He was chosen as one of the ten young knights that would have the opportunity to become Annabella's assistant. Jacob had no problem with any of the tasks at hand and passed every test with flying colours. The King immediately decided that he wanted Jacob to be the one to assist Annabella as soon as he turned eighteen, which had only been a week before. Jacob did not understand what it was, but the King saw something special in him that made him decide.

"Wow," was all Annabella could say. Jacob seemed to flush a bit when he saw how amazed Annabella was. "Why did you want the job so badly?" she asked him interestedly.

"Well, this job allows me to be closer to my parents since they both work at the castle. I also enjoyed the free training because I can now protect my family and loved ones if anything were to happen. The pay is also very generous so I can help out at home. Not to mention that I love the way that your parents rule the land. They are very fair individuals and I imagined that you would be too, so, it was a huge honour to be granted with this job."

Annabella was completely speechless. How could such a young man be so brave and thoughtful? He didn't get this job so he could buy what he wanted like the others competing probably would. She could not believe that Jacob was so giving compared to her and everyone else she knew.

Even I would get the job so I can save up to buy things for myself.
"That is very nice of you. I am glad that my father chose you to assist me," Annabella said, which made Jacob blush again.

"I am also very glad. You are very kind, not at all like I imagined you would be. I am sure that your soon to be fiancé will agree," he said with a small scowl. Annabella stopped in her tracks with wide eyes.

"Fiancé?" Annabella screeched, not being able to hide her shock.

"Yes, you will be meeting him at the ball being thrown in honour of your birthday. Have you forgotten about Prince Jeremy?" he asked, sounding concerned.

"I... No. I just do not want to marry someone that I do not know yet. I do not know if I am going to like him or not."

Jacob smiled at this. "He is very powerful and is the future king of our neighbouring land," he explained.

Annabella just shook her head. "I do not care for this. I want to marry someone if I love him for who he is and if we go together well. Not because of his power," she said. Jacob smiled to himself before frowning a bit.

"If you are lucky enough to get out of it our land will continue as it is. We will not be able to expand onto their land, but do not worry. If another prince shows up you may also have a chance there," Jacob explained.

Annabella shook her head vigorously. "I really do not care about the power. All I care is about their personality. I would just like to have the choice not to marry them if I do not like them."

Jacob sighed. "I am not sure what has caused your loss of memory, but I will explain everything once we get back to the castle."

For a few minutes they walked in silence. Annabella was pinching herself to try to and wake up, but had no such luck. She also didn't want to look crazy—people may suspect something. Jacob decided to break the silence.

"We still have a bit of time before we can go to the school. Would you like to eat the best chocolate cupcakes ever made?" he asked Annabella in an elated manner. Annabella's eyes immediately lit up.

"Oh yes, I love chocolate." she said excitedly. Jacob took her hand in his own before he started walking down one of the roads as she hurried along.

"I will bring you to my Aunt's bakery. She makes the best baked goods and pastries in this land."

The bakery was less than a minutes walk away from the town center. A few dwarfs, nodums, gnomes, and other creatures were walking around. A dwarf couple was sitting at the fountain with their little baby while smiling and talking to each other. Jacob led Annabella to a store with a sign that read 'Bakery' above the main entrance.

The bakery was a cute little place that had a few tables on the inside, and a bunch outside for customers to sit at. Much to Annabella's surprise, there were a bunch of male dwarfs. She thought there were more female than male dwarfs around, because she had only seen a few at the castle. From hearing Jacob speak, she learned that they were in fact dwarfs, just like the ones in her storybook.

"Welcome, Princess Annabella. It is such a big honour to have you visit my bakery. Please, help yourself to whatever you would like," a woman that looked very similar to Maria said from behind the counter.

"Thank you. The honour is mine. And please, feel free to call me Annabella. There is no need to be formal with me," Annabella said to the woman who smiled back at her before noticing Jacob.

"Oh, Jacob. I did not even realize that you were here. You have been working so hard that you had no time to visit your own Auntie," the woman said as she grabbed a small set of steps and climbed them before giving Jacob a hug.

"I am sorry, Aunt Beatrice. I should have dropped by for a visit. I wanted to show Annabella how great your chocolate cupcakes are," Jacob said to his aunt.

"Why of course. I have a batch in the oven. It should be done in a few minutes. You two can pick a seat and I will bring a plate out," Beatrice said before walking away. She suddenly stopped and turned around. "Would you like a certain frosting on the cupcakes? Or would you just like Chocolate?" Annabella and Jacob both looked at Beatrice in a way that showed that they obviously wanted Chocolate.

Jacob led Annabella outside to a table with two seats. Being the gentleman he is, Jacob pulled her chair out so she could sit down and pushed it back in.

"I know it may seem odd that I am asking, but are you Maria and David's real son?" Annabella asked Jacob.

"I am. When dwarfs and nodums have children, they come out looking like you and I. I believe the only name for us is humans, but we are not like most. Only some humans are born with powers, but you already know that of course," Jacob explained. Annabella suddenly realized that she *did* already know all of this. It was all from her storybook.

"That is why my family are the rulers of this land. We all have special powers and with every generation the powers become even stronger," she said. Jacob nodded.

"Exactly. That is why your husband will be chosen for you. You can only have children if your husband is also from a strong line," Jacob clarified with a scowl.

Annabella frowned once again. "Is there something wrong with the Prince?" Annabella asked. Jacob didn't seem to enjoy talking about Prince Jeremy.

"I apologize," Jacob said quickly and looked embarrassed. "It is completely unacceptable for me to react in that way. I do not enjoy the presence of the Prince because it feels like he looks down on people, but, it is not my place to judge."

"Do not worry about it." Annabella nodded and tried to remember what happened at the end of her storybook, but she kept drawing a blank.

"The cupcakes are finished," Beatrice sang as she brought out a huge plate full of chocolate cupcakes. The smell was pure bliss. Annabella had never seen cupcakes that looked so delicious in her entire life.

"They look amazing," Annabella told Beatrice. Jacob took the plate and placed it on the table while Beatrice smiled at the two.

"I hope you enjoy them," she said before quickly making her way back into the bakery.

"Well, are you going to keep on staring lovingly at them or do you want to try them?" Jacob joked. Annabella realized that she was only seconds away from drooling.

"I will try them," she stated. Jacob took a cupcake from the plate and placed it into Annabella's hands gently. The cupcakes had a delicious looking chocolate frosting on them with a sugary decoration. As soon as Annabella took her first bite, her eyes rolled back and she moaned in utter joy at how godly the taste was.

"This is just perfect. I have never tasted anything so amazing in my entire life," she told Jacob.

And since this is a dream I can eat as many as I want without worrying about my weight.

"Why does your aunt not show her work to the castle?" she asked him before taking another large bite.

"My aunt is very shy. I am sure that it took her a lot of courage to even speak to you. She prefers working in the village where she knows everyone and where she does not have to be perfect," he explained.

"I understand," Annabella said. "As long as I am allowed to buy baked goods from here I will be perfectly content."

The pair ended up eating every single cupcake on the plate. Jacob went into the bakery to pay, and Annabella watched as coins appeared in his hand. Jacob handed them over to his aunt who kissed him on the cheek, smiling excitedly. Annabella asked Jacob about the money that he gave his aunt. He explained that the King had him link his magic with the royal account so Annabella could buy whatever she wanted. The sound of bells ringing alerted Jacob that his siblings were on break and would be outside within minutes.

"The school is only a two minutes walk away. By the time we get there my siblings and their classmates will be outside. Would you still like to meet them, Annabella?" Jacob asked. Annabella quickly nodded before taking hold of his arm so he could lead the way.

Jacob didn't seem to mind the fact that Annabella held onto him. She actually quite enjoyed the feeling of his muscular arms, but also knew that it meant nothing. He was her assistant chosen for her by her parents.

He could and would never want to be with someone like me. He probably has a girlfriend or something, she thought to herself, dismissing it quickly enough, because she remembered it was only a dream and had a feeling she would be waking up soon.

"Do not run, children. I do not want any of you to injure yourselves," a human-looking woman yelled after a row of running children. There were some humans, gnomes, dwarves, elves and nodums. Annabella even saw a few fairies, but held back her excitement.

"Does the teacher also have powers?" Annabella asked Jacob quietly as they were getting closer to the school grounds.

"No school teachers have powers. All are ordinary humans, but are trained to teach each type of child—magical or not," Jacob answered before the teacher caught view of the two.

"Oh my. Children, line up in your designated lines please. Princess Annabella is coming this way," the teacher said to the playing children who immediately ran into two separate lines of boys and girls. Annabella watched as the boys line bowed and the girls line curtsied. She smiled at them before looking towards the teacher.

"Good afternoon. I hope that you do not mind our little visit." The teacher looked as if she was going to start skipping around.

"I do not mind at all. It is very special when a member of the royal family visits our school," she explained.

"May I ask what your name is?" Annabella inquired.

"My name is Mirabelle, Princess Annabella," she answered.

"You do not need to call me Princess. Annabella is perfectly fine on its own; Especially since we are just stopping by for a casual visit." Mirabelle nodded before Jacob cut in.

"Good morning, Mirabelle. I wanted to introduce Annabella to my siblings and their friends if that is not too much to ask." Mirabelle motioned for them to go towards the children.

"Brother and sisters. May you please come over here so I can introduce you?" Jacob said before three children ran towards him.

"My name is Daniel," a little boy, who looked to be about seven, announced after bowing.

"It is very nice to meet you, Daniel. I am Annabella," Annabella replied and shook his little hand.

"My name is Katarina," said one of the twin girls.

"And my name is Katherine," said the other.

"You can just call us Kate and Kathy," they said in unison, before they both curtsied. Annabella smiled at how adorable they were before she introduced herself and shook their hands. She learned that they were five years old and did everything together, including wearing the same outfit as each other.

Annabella and Jacob spent the remainder of the school break playing with the children. They were all overjoyed that their Princess was playing games with them. Once the bell rang, Annabella said goodbye to everyone before leaving with Jacob.

A few hours passed by after the visit to the school, and Jacob took Annabella to all of the good places in town. Annabella even ended up buying a casual dress and a swimsuit so she could go to a lake that Jacob had mentioned. She caught Jacob admiring a dress shirt many times as she walked around the store, so she asked him how to get the money to appear.

"With the power of the Land of Dreams. Come to me, thy royal funds," was all she had to say for the correct amount to appear into her hands. She learned that only those of her blood and Jacob were descendants of witches and warlocks and were able to cast certain spells.

When Jacob left the store, Annabella ran back in and grabbed the shirt that he was admiring and quickly purchased it, before running back after him.

"Why did you go back?" he asked her, a look of confusion sitting on his face.

"I noticed that I was still holding onto something so I ran back in to return it," she lied. Jacob seemed to believe her and continued on. By the time they reached the center of town the chariot was anticipating their arrival.

"I hope that you did not wait long," Annabella told Fred.

"Oh do not worry, Annabella. I sense when you are looking for the chariot so I only arrived a minute ago," he explained.

The ride back to the castle was as magnificent, maybe even more magnificent as the ride to the village was. The sun was beginning to set so the Forest of Light looked even more magical than it had in the regular daylight. Two nodums closed the gates after the chariot passed. The gates were very tall and seemed to have a thin layer of something that started from them, covering the top of the castle. Jacob noticed Annabella looking at the transparent lining.

"That is a magical protection force that covers the entire grounds of the castle. Since it is nighttime, there is always a small possibility that knights from a different land or creatures from the dark forest may attack. This layer is completely unbreakable, so it would be impossible for somebody from outside of your family to open or break it. Even the other workers or myself can not break it," he explained to her.

"I see. It is nice to be protected even if there is a very slim chance of attack," she said before Jacob helped her out of the carriage.

"Thank you, Fred. Goodnight," Annabella said before walking with Jacob towards the castle.

Since it was still not time for bed, Jacob decided to bring Annabella to the castle's library. Annabella couldn't believe what she was seeing. The library's ceiling must have been at least fifty feet tall. Many nodums were lighting the candles all over the place. There was even a different type of nodum that had the power to snap his fingers and light the chandeliers away from the walls where the others could not reach. David also had this power, but preferred doing everything manually.

"Where do I even start?" Annabella asked out loud. Jacob chuckled and led her to a seating area that had Victorian furniture like the rest of the castle.

"I can start by explaining some things to you," Jacob said to which Annabella nodded.

"Do I have a choice at all in whom I marry?" Annabella asked him immediately. She did not know how long this dream was going to last so she wanted it to play out in her favour.

Jacob scratched the back of his neck nervously.

"It is very complicated, but if the circumstances work out then yes, you do have a choice," he said. "You must marry somebody with strong powers. They must also be destined for you. Basically, if you have a soulmate they will likely be of a royal line and you will be able to have children. The downside to marrying a non-royal would be that you could not become the future queen, that is because you will not be able to procreate. You would have to give the title to one of your cousins. However, you will forever be a princess, so you will not be shunned from your family."

Annabella frowned at the rule.

"How do I know who my soulmate is?" she asked.

"If you have a soulmate, because not everyone has one, fate will do everything to eventually bring you together. You will immediately be attracted to them, but there are no signs of them being your soulmate. All of that "feeling sparks" stuff that you may hear is just foolishness," Jacob explained before taking a few breaths.

"The only way that you would find yours if you have one, is if you met him before your eighteenth birthday when you are to get married and be crowned as queen. It is very unlikely for this to happen since we rarely get visitors from the other lands, and it has been centuries since a family moved here permanently," Jacob elucidated.

"Did you learn all of this in school?" Annabella asked him.

Jacob shook his head. "I learned this from my parents. Do not forget that us with magic do not age as quickly after we turn eighteen."

Annabella's mouth was wide open. "How old are your parents?" she asked.

"My mother is one hundred and ninety eight and my father is two hundred and twenty two.

Annabella couldn't believe what she was hearing. "That is crazy! How long do most magical beings live? And is it rude of me to ask if your parents are soulmates?"

Jacob laughed. "One thousand years seems to be an average. Although it is not uncommon for someone as young as eight hundred or as old as fifteen hundred to perish," Jacob explained. "And it is not rude at all. Yes, my parents are soulmates. My father decided to wait a few years to find her."

"That is very sweet," Annabella smiled. "Was it not risky for your father to wait? What if your mother had been from before him and married somebody else?" Annabella was so intrigued by all of this. She wished that the real world worked this way. Everyone was so nice and the land did not seem to have issues.

"My father tells stories about visiting the good witch. I do not believe him since the good witch has never been proven to exist outside of tales, and is known to live on the other side of the dark forest in a giant tree. He tells me stories of going through the forest and defending himself against the creatures so he could visit her and find out when he would meet his soulmate, if he did in fact have one. I believe that it was just luck that he decided to wait and then fate helped out. Even until this day he claims that it all happened, so I do not know if I should believe him or not."

"Why would the good witch live on the other side of the dark forest if she is good?" Annabella couldn't imagine any good coming out of the dark forest. She imagined an evil witch, but not a peaceful one.

"She is safe since she is at the edge of the forest and so high up. She is just on the other side and far away from this land. The stories say that an evil warlock trapped her inside and made it impossible for her to leave, but there is apparently a way to get in so he does let her help those who make it to her alive. That is how my father supposedly made it back. She magically transports them back by making him sleep in the guest bed so he would wake up back in his own bed safely," Jacob explained.

"Where did the warlock come from?" Annabella asked.

Jacob shrugged. "No one knows. I have never heard a story about who he is, where he came from or why he decided to trap the good witch. The stories only say he that did it."

Annabella was completely dumbfounded. The things that Jacob explained could only be real in books or movies. They were purely fantasy. She had never had a dream this vivid before and was wondering why it had randomly happened during a completely uneventful week.

"Enough about silly tales," Jacob said after slapping his knees playfully. Annabella was taken out of her state of daydreaming. The way Jacob told stories made it seem so real. It also gave Annabella a feeling of déjàvu, but she could not remember how she knew about it.

"What subjects would you like to read about?"

Chapter Four

While in the castle's library, Annabella ended up choosing books on many different subjects. She picked a royal spell book that would help during the royal occasions or festivities, a basic spell book to not look like an idiot while completing daily tasks, and a special skills spell book for her. She also chose many books on the history of the land, and a huge book that had information on every possible creature. Annabella at least wanted to keep herself entertained.

"This will take you at least a month to read. The royal spells should mostly be learnt during this year. You will need to have them memorized by your crowning. I will be helping you with them, so there should not be a problem," Jacob said as he put the last book down on the cart.

"Oh my," Annabella gasped. "That will be hard to do. I am very glad that you are here to help me. At least I can have somebody to have fun with and whom I can talk to," Annabella said and put her hand in Jacobs and squeezed it softly. Jacob put his other hand on top and kept it there. The two looked looked at each other for a long moment, before one of the books fell on the ground and made them both jolt away. Both Jacob and Annabella shyly looked away and avoided eye contact.

"I believe it is time for me to escort you to the dining hall for dinner," Jacob said before getting up and saying a quick spell that made the books disappear.

"Where did they go?" Asked Annabella in shock.

"They should be in your bookshelf by now," answered Jacob before leading the way out of the library.

After Jacob brought Annabella back to her room, Maria quickly rushed her to the washroom. She was given another bath and had a different hairstyle that was much more formal. She couldn't help but wonder how her skin remained moisturized with the constant bathing, but quickly dismissed the thought, considering all of it was her imagination.

Annabella did not have complete authority in what she was to wear for dinner, because the Queen had picked three dresses for her to choose from. Annabella was surprised that the Queen did such tasks, but apparently she wanted to do as much as possible for Annabella before she became queen. Annabella ended up choosing a light blue dress. She loved the dress even though she had to hold the front of the skirt up so she would not step on the hem.

"I see that you have met Jacob today. Did you have fun?" Maria asked as she tightened Annabella's corset. Annabella cringed a bit at how tight the corset felt in comparison to her everyday clothes, but she didn't complain.

"I had a lot of fun with Jacob. He is a very nice young man. He even showed me your sister's bakery. Beatrice's cupcakes were absolutely delicious," Annabella said happily.

"Really? That is very good. I am sure that you and my son will become the best of friends. You two are very similar," Maria said as she finished with the last button on the dress.

"All done. You look beautiful as always, Annabella," Maria admired with a large smile. Annabella smiled back at her before crouching down and holding both of Maria's hands.

"I could not look like this without you" Annabella said honestly. "I do have a question about Jacob if you do not mind," she began. Maria nodded. "I understand he is my assistant, but why would the

King and... Why would my parents want me to have a male assistant that actually spends time with me?"

"That is simple," Maria started. "There are very few humans your age in this land. There are not any human women available, so the King and Queen wanted you to make friends while still being protected. While several other knights were fighting for the same role, they picked my Jacob because they thought you two would get along well and his powers and skills are very special." It was clear that Maria was very proud of her son, but Annabella wasn't surprised.

"So they hired him so I would not be a loner?"

Maria laughed. "I have never heard that term before, but no. All princesses and princes have an assistant that acts as their protector and they are usually older, but your parents thought it would be nice for you to be with someone your age in your last year of freedom so you can have fun." Maria smiled gratefully before excusing herself.

When Annabella walked back into her room she decided to sit down in the chair next to the bed. Jacob said that he would call for her when it was time to head downstairs. She admired the room and mentally noted the differences from her real room. There was no electricity, no computers, victorian furniture, and a lot of space.

How did people stop themselves from going crazy? Annabella then recalled how busy her day had been. *I guess when you're a princess in a made up world there is no boredom.*

Annabella eventually picked up her storybook and analyzed the front and back cover. The book looked brand new, which it wasn't outside of the dream. The ink had no scratches on it and there weren't any dents or imperfections.

It even has a new book smell... Annabella was truly confused. *Why is everything so detailed in this dream? I thought details like these weren't supposed to be a thing.* "Why do I keep getting weird feelings about back home?" she questioned out loud before opening the book to the first page. Annabella began to look at the page when a knock at the door frightened her, making her drop the book in her own lap.

"Come in," she yelled out before the door.

"Are you ready for—wow...You look absolutely marvellous," Jacob said, admiring Annabella as she stood up. She did a little twirl and smiled.

"Thank you, Jacob. You look amazing too," she said when she saw that Jacob was also wearing formal clothing.

"Thank you, Annabella. Are you ready for dinner?" Annabella nodded before taking the storybook and placing it on her full bookshelf.

"Let us go then. I am famished," Annabella said before linking her arm in Jacob's, using her magic to close the door behind them. She could've sworn that the first page now had writing, but she would check once she was back from dinner.

"Annabella, you look amazing," the Queen said as Annabella and Jacob entered the dining room.

"Thank you uh... mother. As do you," Annabella said awkwardly.

"Well then, I shall be going to dine with the others now," Jacob said before he bowed and sent Annabella one last smile as he left the dining hall.

"Tell me, Annabella. How was your first day with Jacob assisting you?" the King asked. Annabella smiled and prepared to tell them about her fun filled day.

"It was great. We went to the village and explored," Annabella answered.

"I am glad you two are getting along well. We are very fond of Jacob," the Queen explained with a smile.

Annabella smiled once again. "How long will he be my assistant for?"

"Until your wedding day," the Queen answered. "I hope you two continue to get along because you will be spending most of your time with him."

Annabella nodded and smiled. *Spending time with Jacob doesn't sound bad at all.*

THE DINNER WAS DELICIOUS. It consisted of several roasted chickens, rice, salad, and other grains. Annabella learned that there were three cooks in the castle. One is a dwarf that does all of the mixing and controls the ingredients, the other is a human who actually prepared the meals, and the last is a fairy who's in charge of adding spices. Annabella hugged the Queen and King goodnight before she left the dining hall to go back to her room. When she walked into the main hall she was completely confused of which direction she had to go.

"Need help?" Jacob's voice asked from the other end of the hall.

"Help would be very nice" Annabella admitted bashfully. Jacob laughed before taking Annabella to a completely different direction.

"Did you tell your parents about your memory loss? I am sure they would be very worried."

"I told them not to worry about it, and that I have not studied like I should have. It is amazing how I can manage to get lost in my own home," Annabella said to make things seem normal.

Jacob chuckled. "If it were possible, I would think that it was your first day here," he joked.

"What if it were?" Annabella asked seriously.

Jacob thought deeply for a moment. "It would not make any sense, but I would help you either way," he answered honestly.

A smile formed on Annabella's face. How can someone be so perfect? *It's a dream that's all made up. That's why,* she thought sourly.

"Can you bring yourself from here?" Jacob asked as they reached the door to Annabella's tower. "Yes, of course. Thank you very much, Jacob. Will I be seeing your tomorrow?" Annabella hoped she would.

"Of course, Annabella. You will probably get tired of me being around all the time." Jacob's expression turned to worry. "If I annoy you, please let me know and I will talk with the Queen and King about giving you more space."

"No, I did not mean it like that. I was just hoping I would see you." Annabella could feel her face heating up a bit.

Jacob smiled and nodded. "I must go to my family so we can return home. I will be here at the same time that I was today, but I promise to knock this time," he said with a chuckle.

"All right. I will see you then. Goodnight, Jacob," she said before giving him a hug. Jacob seemed surprised, but hugged her back softly.

"Goodnight, Annabella. I will see you tomorrow," he said before he returned back to the main entrance.

Annabella began walking up the stairs in the tower. She noticed that there were windows the entire way up, not like regular windows, but openings between the stones. A strange sound made her immediately stop in her tracks. She could have sworn that she heard her name being called. Her *real* name, which Annabella realized that no one in the Land of Dreams knew since Rosalyn was the royal family's name.

"Annabella Tompkins," a low voice called after she started walking again.

"Hello? Is anyone there?" she called out nervously. *Now this is not the time for a nightmare to begin,* she thought before a white owl flew to the window and made Annabella scream.

"Oh my God! You scared the crap out of me," she said to the owl, whose eyes seemed to glow a golden colour.

"I am sorry, Annabella," the owl apologized.

"It is all right" she said dismissively, but quickly squealed, "You just spoke to me." Her eyes were wide and she could feel herself shaking a bit. *This is just a dream, Annabella. Get it together.*

"Yes. I came here to deliver a message," the owl began. "Tomorrow night you must meet me here at eleven o'clock. I have important news for you. This is not a dream, nor a nightmare. This is just your new, hopefully temporary, reality," the owl said before flying away.

"This is definitely turning into a nightmare," Annabella sighed before she ran the rest of the way up and to her room.

After she took off her dress and switched into her nightgown, Annabella went straight to her bookshelf and took out her spell books and her storybook. She thought this was all a dream, but something inside of her was telling her that everything was a bit too realistic. She knew that she would have easily believed everything without a question, if it were actually a dream. It was also lasting way too long.

Annabella started off with her storybook. What she thought she saw earlier was confirmed when she saw that the first page did in fact, have more writing than the first time she opened the book in her "dream." she recognized the words perfectly. She had read them thousands of times because they were the same words that she read every night before going to bed.

"This is exactly what I did today," Annabella realized. "Why can't I remember what happens next?" she said, frustrated as she clenched her fists. "I need to ask Jacob tomorrow if I'm still here. If this isn't a dream I'm either going crazy or something is really happening. I wish my parents were here," she said before another terrible feeling drew upon her.

Something's wrong with my parents. There has to be something wrong. Every time I think of them I feel like something terrible has happened, Annabella thought as a tear slipped down her face.

Annabella decided to read up on basic spells so she could start doing more things on her own, and to distract herself from the bad feeling. After reading for a long period of time the clock struck twelve and Annabella suddenly felt exhausted. She had memorized a bunch of simple spells and a few of the royal ones. It would be enough for people not to suspect anything.

I'll just have to see what happens if I don't wake up.

Chapter Five

The next morning came quickly for Annabella. The same dwarf who had brought her breakfast the day before was back, and had delicious looking pancakes ready for her. They even had maple syrup and every topping she enjoyed. Annabella remembered to ask for the server's name and discovered that it was Madeleine. When it was time for her bath, Annabella asked Maria many questions about the schedule for the day. She remembered that yesterday was her, 'last free day until her birthday,' so she was curious about what she would be doing all day.

"Well to start off you must go to town with the Queen to pick out your dresses for your birthday. After that, I know that you will go with Jacob to select presents that you would like to receive. It is the same process as last year so it should be easy. Jacob knows the rest of your schedule so it would be best to ask him," Maria explained as she started taking out the curlers in Annabella's hair.

"It is very nice having someone to hang out with. Jacob is great company and very entertaining," Annabella told Maria, who smiled brightly.

"I raised Jacob and my other children with a lot of love and taught them how to be good people. It makes me happy to know that you are enjoying his company," Maria expressed to Annabella, a genuine smile on her face.

"Thank you, Maria," Annabella said before Maria began playing with her curls.

The rest of her preparation went by quickly and soon enough, Annabella had left her room to start off her day.

"Good morning, Annabella. Are you ready for a day filled with shopping?" Jacob asked with a bright smile after Annabella met him at the exit of her tower.

"Good morning, Jacob. I am ready, but I am not sure that you are," she joked.

"I am always ready," he said while pouting.

"Children, are you both ready to get going?" the Queen called from the entrance to the main hall.

"Yes, Your Majesty," Jacob said as he bowed. The three made their way out to the garden and into the chariot. Jacob sat with his back facing the front so he could face both the Queen and Annabella.

"So Jacob, has my daughter been giving you a lot of work to do?" the Queen asked Jacob with an eyebrow raised.

"Not at all, Your Majesty," he answered with an honest smile.

"That is good. I do not want Annabella to tire you."

After taking the same route to the village center, everyone except for Fred, got out of the chariot.

"Thank you, Fred," Annabella said after getting out.

"No problem, Annabella," he answered her before driving off. The Queen gave Annabella a questioning look. "Why is everyone calling you by your name and not 'Princess' or 'Your Highness?'"

Annabella smiled meekly at the Queen. "I told them to call me by my name. I do not want to be called anything else until I absolutely have to." The Queen looked a bit surprised, but did, however, look relieved. All of the residents of the village bowed and curtsied as the Queen, Annabella, and Jacob walked by. The Queen had a few seamstresses make dresses for the evening, but also decided that she would take Annabella to a few different shops to see if she liked anything else.

"You do not have to come in if you do not want to," the Queen told Jacob as they reached the door to the first shop.

"I do not mind. If Annabella wants me to go inside I will," he said before looking at Annabella. Annabella nodded at him quickly. She wanted to know his opinion on the dresses. She always trusted her guy friends more than her girlfriends to tell the truth when it came to their opinions on clothing items.

An entire hour had passed before Annabella chose her first dress that she would wear during the day before her party. She had to beg Jacob to give his honest opinion, but she finally got it and ended up choosing the dress that she wanted from the start. After a few more hours, Annabella had all of the dresses for her birthday and was starving.

"I am going back to the castle for lunch. You two may go buy something to eat if you would like. Do not forget to chose your gifts," the Queen told Annabella sternly before laughing and hugging her.

"I will not forget. I will be home for dinner so I will see you then. Goodbye, Mother," Annabella said awkwardly. It felt very strange to her to call someone else her mother. She was starting to get that awful feeling again, so she held onto her stomach. Jacob looked at Annabella and noticed that something wasn't right.

"Is your stomach hurting because you are hungry for more cupcakes?" he asked her. Annabella took the opportunity to mask the strange pain and nodded.

"You got me. Those cupcakes were so delicious that I cannot help myself," she lied.

"Let us get going to the bakery before you chose your gifts," Jacob said before linking arms with Annabella and leading her towards the bakery once again. After arriving, they were quickly greeted by Beatrice who wasn't surprised at their order. Luckily she had a batch ready for the pair, who quickly dug in.

"If I eat another cupcake ever again I think I might explode," Annabella said after eating six miniature cupcakes. Jacob laughed at this and wiped the corner of Annabella's mouth that had a tiny bit of icing on it.

"I highly doubt it. It would be entertaining though," he said and looked like he was thinking. Annabella's mouth opened and she looked at him in shock. "I was just kidding," he reassured Annabella who lightly punched his arm. "Do not worry, Annabella. I do not want to see you explode," he said before they paid for the cupcakes.

"I do not even know where to start," Annabella said as they entered a large shop filled with pretty feminine things. There were all types of jewelry from rings to watches. There were accessories like hats, shoes, purses and even gloves. There were also things Annabella never even thought of.

"This book cover is really nice," Annabella said as she admired a cotton book cover that had a lot of delicate detailing on it. *This must have taken forever to make,* she thought to herself as she ran her finger over the cover.

"You seem to really like books so it would be a great choice for one of your gifts," Jacob said from behind her.

"You are right. I shall add this," she said before she realized that she hadn't learned the spell for picking gifts. Jacob must have noticed the sheepish look on her face and proceeded to quickly teach it to her.

"Now that you have memorized it, all you have to do is think it in your head before touching the object that you desire with your right hand, then poke it with your left index finger". Annabella thought that this was a bit silly, but complied anyway and noticed that the book cover had what looked like a light pink glow around it.

"What is that?" Annabella asked referring to it.

"That is your personal aura colour. Everyone who has all powers instead of specific powers in this land has one. You happen to have a light pink colour, while I have an electric blue colour. Your mother has a red aura and your father a dark blue." Annabella nodded at Jacob, hiding her awe. She found it fascinating that she had her own aura colour.

"What do you mean by specific powers? Is it like your mother having powers to make water appear out of nowhere and blow air out of her hands? Is that why she is the one to bathe me?" Annabella asked.

Jacob nodded. "That is exactly it. My mother was basically destined to work for you. No one has powers without a reason. My father, mother, and aunt do not have unique aura colours because they all have specific powers, so the colour their hands glow correlates with the powers they wield. You and I do because we have powers for many things from opening doors to setting things on fire," Jacob explained.

"Good to know," Annabella muttered with a small smirk. *Setting things on fire could come in handy in real life,* she thought.

"Who else has all powers in this land?" Annabella asked Jacob.

"Other than all of the royals in your family, only I do," he answered. Annabella stopped in her tracks and threw Jacob a confused look.

"What about all of the other men you trained with for this job? What about the knights?" she asked Jacob.

"Well all of them use to have powers like us, but when knights graduate from their training, they lose their extra powers and keep certain ones that help them with fighting. There currently are not any boys or girls that are at the age of training, so we will not know who will gain all or specific powers until they reach thirteen," Jacob informed Annabella.

"That makes sense," she admitted, but quickly wanted to learn something else. "Wait a minute. What about the girls who gain all of the powers at thirteen? Do they become knights?" Annabella asked him.

Jacob cracked another smile. He seemed to enjoy explaining things and telling Annabella stories. "They can train to become knights if they wish, or sometimes they attain special powers used in wars of the past. They were used to trick the opposing knights and seduce them. They are also used as spies that get sent to other lands that may be planning an attack on our home. Other than that, girls can be whatever they want to be, just like the boys—especially if they are granted with really useful powers. If I did not go through training, I would have eventually lost my powers like anyone else with all powers would," Jacob stated.

"Well, that explains a lot," Annabella laughed before she continued walking around the store, choosing things that she really wanted. Annabella felt silly selecting items that she didn't truly care for. *None of it is real anyway,* she thought, but she hadn't forgotten about the strange owl that visited her the night before.

After another few hours, Annabella and Jacob had gone through every store in town. Annabella chose tons of gifts knowing that her family could very much afford it, but she included many for her staff and decorations for the castle. She didn't feel comfortable only selecting gifts for herself, and if the owl was right, she'd be stuck in her dream for a little while.

Of course the owl isn't right, Annabella thought, but she wasn't confident she believed herself.

When it was six o'clock and they could barely feel their legs, Jacob and Annabella decided that it was time to head back to the castle. Unsurprisingly, dinner was amazing yet again.

"Thank you for a lovely dinner, mother and father. I will be going to my room to sleep now," Annabella said to the Queen and King before hugging them both goodnight, and making her way towards her tower. Annabella said goodbye to Jacob as he exited the workers dining hall, then she started up the stairs where she heard her name being whispered again.

"Right. The creepy talking owl again," Annabella muttered under her breath. She had forgotten about him during dinner, but knew she should listen. The owl repeated what he had said the night before and this time Annabella believed him more.

"This is not a dream, Annabella. You must believe me by now. The only way that you will get your explanation is by visiting the good witch. A friend and myself will carry you over to her and protect you on your journey, so she can tell you what you need to learn," the owl explained to an extremely confused and slightly terrified Annabella.

"I know that you feel strange when you think about your parents, but there is an important reason for that, and only the good witch can explain it herself. Please meet me here in about fifteen minutes for it will be eleven o'clock, and the journey will take about an hour," the owl said before flying over to a tree.

This dream has been going on way too long for it to be a dream, Annabella thought to herself. *Nothing else makes sense at this point,* she concluded as she made her way to her room so she could dress in appropriate clothing, and to pack up her storybook, which wasn't making any sense to her anymore.

Chapter Six

"I am ready," Annabella said when she reached the window. The owl nodded before hooting.

"My colleague and I will meet you at the top of the tower. You must use the door on the right to yours. It will appear with a simple spell. Then make your way up the stairs," the owl explained.

"Got it. I remember that one," Annabella said, before making her way back to the doors to her room. "Let the door hidden in the wall appear before me wood and all," Annabella said out loud, while motioning to the empty spot on the wall. Little did she know that her words automatically turned into Latin as they left her mouth. She was amazed that a door was forming on the wall and with a movement of her hand it opened. "So cool," she whispered to herself before she grabbed a candle and made her way up the secret set of stairs.

When Annabella reached the top of the tower, she was met with a gryphon looking right at her, with what looked like a friendly smile on its face.

"Oh my God. I can't believe I'm actually seeing this. I always wanted to see a gryphon," she said excitedly as she made her way over to the magical creature.

"My name is Tom," the creature introduced himself. "I will be bringing you to the good witch," he explained before lowering himself. "You may sit on my back and hold on to the rope for safety." Annabella climbed on and situated herself.

"How are you going to get out of the barrier?" she asked when she remembered the magical barrier that protected the castle.

"We are good creatures," answered Tom. "We are from the good part of the land and have pure intentions, so we can pass," he explained. The owl flew next to Annabella before resting there.

"I hope that you do not mind, Tom," the owl told Tom who growled like the lion part of him before he started flying away from the castle.

I'm going to die... I'm going to die... I'm going to die, was the only thought flying through Annabella's head as she tightly gripped onto the rope.

The fact that she saw a mythical creature was overwhelming enough, but actually riding one? It was *too* crazy. Sudden growls from below made Annabella let out a yelp.

"It is ok, Princess. Those are the creatures of the dark forest. They cannot reach us from down there, nor would they ever attack a gryphon. They may be evil, but they are not suicidal," the owl explained to Annabella, who smiled slightly at his humour.

"Please, you know that I'm not really a princess. Just call me by my name. My *real* name," Annabella pleaded. The owl nodded at her. "Wait a minute," Annabella started, "I never got your name," she told the owl. The owl then looked both ways and sunk into himself a bit.

"Well... my name is sort of... embarrassing," he told Annabella quietly.

"It can't be that bad," she told him.

"All right," he sighed. "My name is Hoot," he said.

Annabella tried her hardest not to coo at the owl, but failed miserably. "Aww," she said with a giant smile.

"This is why I did not want to tell you," he said grumpily.

"It's not embarrassing at all. It's just really cute because owls that don't speak English hoot instead," she assured Hoot.

"Thank you, Annabella. Tom always pokes fun at me because of it," he said.

"You have to admit Hoot, your name is comically ironic," Tom said before he started to descend.

"Are we almost there?" Annabella asked to no one in particular. It didn't matter who answered her.

"Yes. It has been fifty-five minutes and we will be there in less than five. All you have to do is climb down onto Tom's paw, and he will let you off at the good witch's balcony. For now it is goodbye from us both, but if you need help for any reason all you have to do is call for us," Hoot said.

Annabella nodded at him. "Well it was very nice meeting you both. How do I call you?" she asked Hoot before Tom started flying in place and let out one of his paws.

"If you need us you will figure it out," Tom said before he left Annabella on the balcony and flew away. She didn't miss the two waving at her with their paws and wings.

"Now for the hard part," she muttered to herself as soon as the two were out of sight. Annabella turned around and noticed that one of the doors were open. "She must know I'm here," she said to herself before entering the room cautiously.

It was very dark, so Annabella thought about her hand creating a little fire. Thankfully there wasn't need of an actual talking spell for everything, but only the thought of it. Annabella's hand glowed pink before a small flame appeared. The flame was around the size of a matches flame, but that was all she needed to not trip over anything.

"Welcome, Annabella. I was afraid that you would not show up," a voice of an old woman said. Annabella quickly turned in the direction of the voice and gasped.

"Grandma?" she asked the woman who looked identical to her own grandmother.

"Not really. Your grandmother is almost a copy of myself," the grandmother look alike explained.

"Like a reincarnation?" Annabella was confused.

"Not quite. We live in different dimensions where time works differently, but we are the same person." Annabella didn't like the sound of that.

"That means that this is not a dream," Annabella said. The old woman nodded.

"Precisely. You woke up in this world because you activated an ancient spell that can only be done by the women who have the curse in your blood line," the witch explained. Annabella didn't know what to believe anymore, but seeing as this was the good witch and she knew that she was dreaming anymore, Annabella wanted to know the whole story.

"Can you explain how I have this curse and how I activated it?" she asked the witch. "And can you tell me your name?"

The witch frowned. "My name is Caroline," she told Annabella.

"I'll call you that if that's ok," Annabella told her. *They share the same name too.*

"Every few generations of females in our bloodline, one is affected by the curse. There is a very long history to this curse and I am afraid that it is not relevant, nor do I have most of the information. What you need to know is that the storybook your grandmother gave you on your fifth birthday is a magical book," Caroline, started.

"You sleep much better when you read it, and its powers make you feel happier no matter the circumstances. On the night of your fifth birthday you and your friend Zach, I believe that that is his name, read the story together. Both of your tears started the cycle for you. It always takes at least one person's tear to start it, but yours mixed together when they landed on the book, so the result is indeterminate since it has never happened in the past," Caroline explained. Annabella nodded for her to continue.

"You read the book many times until the day that you cast the spell unknowingly. I know you cannot remember the night of the incident, but it was something terrible that caused you to cry on the last page of the book, activating the spell," Caroline explained. The bad feeling in the pit of Annabella's stomach suddenly returned.

"It involves my real parents, doesn't it?" she said, suddenly feeling determined. When Caroline nodded and her eyes started glowing, Annabella felt unstable and sat on the floor, sobbing while holding onto her head. The memories flashed in her mind, letting her see everything that had happened to her parents, including the car accident.

"I remember now," she sobbed into her dress a few minutes later as her body continued to shake. "My parents died in a car crash," she cried uncontrollably. *The cops weren't wrong.*

Caroline waited patiently as Annabella let all of her emotions out. She knew very well that holding things in would make a person, especially a human, feel worse so she waited for Annabella to stop shaking. When Annabella began to calm down, Caroline knelt next to her before placing a comforting hand on her back.

"Yes they did. I am very sorry," she told Annabella. "There is the possibility to bring them back though," she explained. Annabella suddenly looked up and attempted to wipe the tears off of her face, but they kept on coming.

"Tell me! Please tell me. I'll do anything for them to be alive again," she promised distressfully.

Caroline smiled. "You must complete the story. You are inside of your storybook," she explained as it were a perfectly normal situation to be in. "You are the Princess that you have read about for years, and this is your kingdom. You must go through all of the challenges and complete them successfully so you can complete the story in the right way," Caroline explained as she paced around the room.

"If you complete everything successfully you will wake up back in your own room, and you might even have the chance to save your parents. If t you do not complete everything successfully, you will wake up in your bed in the castle and live on as Annabella, future

Queen of the Land of Dreams," Caroline finished. Annabella didn't know what to say. She sat down thinking for several minutes before finally speaking.

"I'll do it," she agreed.

"Are you sure?" Caroline asked her. "There are many things that were not mentioned in the book. The timeline the story goes on for a little over a year so you have to understand that it will take you at least that," she warned.

Annabella gulped. "I'll train for battle, I'll practice my spells, I'll marry the one meant for me, and I'll be crowned as queen," she announced, but remembered something that Caroline had said. "Is there a chance that Zach's tears may have ruined my chance of saving them or completing everything successfully?" Annabella wondered nervously.

"My dear, all I can say is that you have to listen to your heart no matter what. Even when you are afraid of making the wrong decision," Caroline explained. "You are pretty much a reincarnation of the Princess in the story. You are physically identical, but your soul is your own since you have lived different lives, so you must do the right thing based on your own heart, which may be a little tricky because it may change a few things. The story is different every time because of who you are, so there is no way to know the exact outcome. It will be especially difficult since this is the first time someone else's tears have been introduced."

Annabella nodded nervously before asking her last question. "May I return back now?"

Caroline smiled lightly at the girl. "Of course you can. I just need you to remember one important thing from all of this. It may help you understand things that you will discover and do not make sense," she told Annabella seriously. Annabella nodded before Caroline told her a simple sentence. "Things are not always as they seem."

After talking to Caroline a bit more, and being told that she would have to fall asleep in the extra bed to arrive home, Annabella prepared for the journey back.

"Thank you, Caroline, and no offence, but hopefully I will not be needing to see you after the year passes," Annabella joked before quickly falling asleep. Caroline quietly cast her spell on Annabella as soon as she was completely asleep and watched as the young girl started fading away.

"I hope all goes well," Caroline said honestly with a smile on her face that turned into a quick smirk before going to her own bed for a night of rest.

Chapter Seven

Annabella slept through the entire night. It was a dreamless night, but nonetheless, it was sleep and that was all that was needed to be magically transported back into her own room in the castle. The curtains were all closed so what woke Annabella was the smell of her breakfast getting closer.

"Good morning, Madeleine," Annabella greeted the friendly dwarf.

"Good morning, Annabella. Today you have eggs and bacon. I hope that you will enjoy them," Madeleine said before walking towards the door.

"I am sure I will," Annabella called out before Madeleine nodded and closed the door. "At least I can enjoy the food here," Annabella mumbled to herself before digging in. She ate everything as quickly as possible, before drinking her freshly squeezed orange juice. Annabella was in a rush to get her journey started so she could finish it as quickly as possible.

"Good morning, Annabella. I sensed that you were ready for your bath earlier than usual?" Maria asked as she entered.

Annabella looked up from her empty plates. "Yes, sorry if you were busy," she apologized. Maria opened her arms so Annabella could hug her.

"I had just finished my breakfast so I had nothing else to do," Maria said with a smile.

"Can you make it quick today? I was hoping to get some time to myself before rehearsals," Annabella asked Maria.

"Of course I can. You can just wash your face and I will put your hair up. When it is time for rehearsals, I will run you a quick bath."

Annabella smiled at the woman. "Thank you very much. I do not know what I would do without you," Annabella said before heading into the washroom.

Maria quickly helped Annabella freshen up, dressing her and quickly brushed her hair. Annabella used her bit of free time to send for Jacob and practice a few spells, but she was too anxious to stay in her room, so she left after just fifteen minutes.

"Hello, Annabella. How are you doing today?" Jacob greeted Annabella as soon as she arrived downstairs.

"Hello, Jacob. I am good. You seem to also be well," she observed the smile on his face.

"That I am. You sent a dove with a message about making a schedule. I am very interested to know what type of schedule you want to make". Annabella grabbed his arms and ran up the stairs with him and into her room instead of answering right away.

"I want you to train me how to fight." Jacob seemed taken back by the strange request.

"Fight? As in fighting like a knight would?" he asked. Annabella nodded at him. "I uh... well I could, but... I am sorry if this is personal or sounds rude, but... why?" Annabella blinked at him. "What I mean to say is why would the princess of an extremely powerful land with the best knights working for her, want to learn how to fight? Annabella couldn't help but laugh at Jacob's shocked expression. *If only you knew*, she thought.

"Look, I may be safe, but it is always better to be even safer," Annabella explained. "It will not make sense right now. Trust me, if I tried explaining it all right now I would sound like a mad woman," she added.

"You are confusing me even more. I would never think of you as a mad woman."

Annabella sighed. "I am sorry. Believe me when I tell you that you will think it until I show you proof. I will slowly show you a few things, but it will all come together one day. I promise to tell you eventually," Annabella said and stuck out her pinkie finger. Jacob looked at the finger and inspected it carefully.

"Did you hurt your pinkie?" he asked with a concerned look already formed on his face.

Annabella laughed.

Of course he doesn't know what a pinkie swear is.

"It is this thing I made up when I was a little girl," she lied quickly. "I have not done one in a long time, but I feel like this is a good enough reason for one. We shake pinkies instead of hands. Pinkies are delicate so it would somehow make the promise mean more," she attempted to explain.

Jacob gave her a weird look before giving in and wrapping his own pinkie around hers. Annabella shook his to solidify the promise before they both laughed. Jacob must have found it outrageous, but maybe he was the right amount of fun. Annabella looked up at his face and smiled at how his eyes sparkled with amusement. When Jacob looked into her own eyes Annabella started to feel a bit strange, but quickly dismissed it and spoke up.

"I want to show you something." Annabella walked over to her bed that had magically been made in the time that it took her to go downstairs and upstairs again. She took out her storybook and handed it over to Jacob.

"The Magical Land of Dreams," he said out loud. Annabella gave him a questioning look.

"The title of the book," he explained.

Annabella's mouth formed an 'o.' "How do you know that?" she asked him.

Jacob raised an eyebrow at her.

"It is in Latin. We are speaking Latin at the moment, Annabella. Everyone in the land does so.

"Say what now?" Annabella blurted out, forgetting that she had to speak proper English, *or rather Latin*, for no one to suspect that she wasn't who they thought she was. Jacob looked at her with a worried expression.

"I know that you can not remember many things for some strange reason, but this is a bit *too* strange. A few other lands speak languages that I do not know of, but we all hear it as the same."

"I do not understand why there are even other languages if we can understand each other." Annabella's face went blank.

"*Things are not always as they seem,*" Caroline, the good witch's, voice echoed in her head.

Annabella cleared her throat and laughed.

"I was just kidding, Jacob. No need to worry. Of course I know what language we speak," she said with a smile.

Jacob playfully scowled at her, but didn't look completely convinced.

"I knew that. I just wanted to see if you would believe me and you did," he said with his arms crossed. Annabella laughed and punched him in the arm, but he didn't even flinch. What she wasn't expecting, was that Jacob would tickle her. She hadn't been tickled since she was eleven years old and she didn't realize that she had grown to be extremely sensitive to it.

"Stop, Jacob! I will do anything if you stop," Annabella cried out in laughter. Jacob stopped, but didn't remove his hands from her.

"Anything?" he asked with a smirk. Annabella thought for a second, but Jacob started to tickle her again.

"All right, all right, anything," she yelled. Jacob smiled and stepped back.

"After rehearsals let me take you out to dinner," he stated.

Annabella could feel her face heating up. "Will I be allowed?"

Jacob smiled at her question. "I do not see why not. There is no danger in the village or the Forest of Light. As long as you obtain permission from your parents, you will be allowed," he clarified. "Plus, I am no stranger so I am sure it will be fine."

Annabella smiled at the idea. Having dinner with Jacob would be fun. She would be able to tell him all about the rehearsals, and she could discover what he would be doing at the ball. A knock at the door startled both Annabella and Jacob.

"Annabella, it is time for your bath," Maria said from the other side.

"I guess I will see you later," Annabella said to Jacob before giving him a quick hug and running to the washroom as she used her powers to open the door for Maria. Annabella didn't even remember that she was going to show Jacob the inside of the book.

"BE CAREFUL," THE KING called out to Annabella who sent him one last smile. After hours of rehearsing for the ball, Annabella was finally free. During rehearsals she had to practice dancing, which was incredibly difficult at first, but she eventually started to get the hang of it. Other than the dancing, she just went over the invitation list. She was extremely pleased to know that she could invite one person to be seated at her side. She already had the individual in mind, and it had to do with a certain purchase that she had made only a few days prior.

"I see that you were allowed out," Jacob said from Annabella's side. He was dressed differently from the morning. He had on fancier clothing, but still looked casual with his naturally messy hair that practically called for Annabella to run her fingers through it. She shook her head at her thoughts. The blood rushed to her cheeks and she looked away to try and make the blush go away.

"I was," she answered while still looking at the other direction.

"Is everything ok?" Jacob asked her. Annabella looked at him.

"I thought I saw something, but it was just a plant," she said, positive that the flush had toned down a bit now that her face didn't feel as warm.

The two made their way out to the chariot where instead of Fred leading the way, Jacob did. Apparently he had told Fred that he would do just fine.

"I see that you can also control this," Annabella observed as Jacob started driving the chariot magically. Jacob just nodded before using his powers to open the gates and closing them once they passed.

"How were the rehearsals?" Jacob asked Annabella while concentrating on the path ahead of him.

"They were terrible. I can't seem to dance very well," Annabella admitted grudgingly.

Jacob chuckled.

"I am a great dancer, or at least they say I am. I can help you practice until the ball. There are only a few days left, but I am sure that I can get you to at least be decent," he joked.

Annabella huffed at him. "I will be even better than you," she said.

"We will see about that," Jacob said before he stopped the chariot. "I made reservation for the two of us. There is a fair going on tonight so there will be a lot of entertainment," Jacob explained as he got out of the chariot and made his way to Annabella's side to help her off.

"Sounds like it will be fun. Where are we eating?" Annabella asked right before her stomach growled. Jacob chuckled once again.

"Did you not eat lunch?" he questioned.

"I wanted to, but the food that the coordinator brought out looked terrible, and I did not want to bother the cooks," Annabella admitted. Jacob smiled at her happily.

"You are always so thoughtful. You will make an amazing queen. Maybe even more amazing than your parents, but that will be difficult to beat," Jacob told her, which brought a smile to her face.

"We are here," Jacob announced, bringing Annabella back to reality. There was live folk music playing and many different creatures were dancing around. Jacob opened the short steel fence and motioned for Annabella to go in before him. He pulled out a chair that was near the entrance so Annabella could take her seat.

"Hello Jacob and welcome Princess Annabella. It is an honour to have you at my restaurant on this fine evening. Would you like your menus or would you like to try our pasta special tonight?" A male dwarf with a name tag that said 'Mario' spoke to the two.

"Thank you for having us. I will try the special tonight. What about you, Jacob?" Annabella asked.

"Good evening, Mario. I will have the same," he said before Mario quickly disappeared into the restaurant.

Annabella looked around. There were many couples eating at the restaurant. Two humans who appeared to be in their mid-twenties, were sitting on the other side and were gazing into each other's eyes. As if Jacob could hear what Annabella was thinking, he answered her question.

"They do not have magic. The man is twenty-four and the woman is twenty-two. They are soulmates so they will have a happy life ahead of them," Jacob said. Annabella blinked a few times before smiling.

"That is so sweet," she said "I am happy that they met each other and were lucky enough to be so close in age."

Jacob nodded in agreement. "They are lucky. Usually those of pure hearts have a better fate set out for them, so I assume that they are very good people—at least they seem to be," Jacob added in. The food soon arrived and both Jacob and Annabella enjoyed their delicious dinner.

"Seeing as you two are done, I will bring you the complimentary treat," Mario announced.

Annabella quickly stopped him. "I am quite full so I will pass on a treat for tonight, but thank you. How about you, Jacob?" Annabella asked him and received a smile in return.

"I am full as well. Could you please bring us the bill?" Jacob asked Mario, who nodded before heading off.

"There is one more thing that I wanted to talk to you about," Annabella spoke. Jacob raised a brow for her to carry on.

"Well, I have the right to invite one person to sit at the main table with me during my birthday ball. I want that person to be you."

Jacob looked shocked. "Me? But why?" he asked her. She gave him a look which showed that she thought his answer was completely preposterous.

"Because you are an amazing person, you are basically an expert in everything you do, and you are my only friend. That basically means that you are my best friend—even though we have only known each other for a few days," Annabella explained. A large smile formed on Jacob's face.

"I am glad that you think so highly of me. I would love to be your guest of honour, but I will not fit the expectations. I do not own any clothing of the quality that is required. I am not wealthy enough to afford anything as fancy," he stated, obviously embarrassed that he wasn't a royal. Annabella suspected that something like this would happen. She was prepared for this and already had a plan.

"I have something to give you when we get back to the castle," she said.

"Oh no. Do not do anything special for me," Jacob said in a worried manner.

"What is done is done," Annabella said slyly as Mario arrived at the table with the bill.

The pair quickly reached for the bill.

"I am not letting you pay for this dinner. I invited you and you are the woman. Please let me be a gentleman and pay," Jacob said while reaching into his back pocket for a few gold coins. Annabella shook her head, but remembered that she was not in the real world and women would most likely not pay for themselves—especially not the man—in this land.

"Only you, Jacob. Only you," she said before Jacob led her back towards the chariot.

The ride back was slower, since it was extremely dark and casting a big light spell would take a lot of energy. Jacob decided to use his powers to move the trees back slightly so the light reflecting off of the moon would be enough to illuminate the path.

Annabella was enjoying the ride, but was feeling exhausted from her long day, so she rested her head on Jacob's shoulder before she had the chance to overthink it. She looked into the forest as it passed by. Suddenly, Annabella spotted a pair of red eyes looking at her. She almost sat up quickly, but as the eyes came closer she could tell that they belonged to an animal. When Annabella blinked, breaking eye contact, the animal closed its eyes and moved back into the forest and out of sight.

"THIS IS WHAT I WANTED to give you," Annabella said as she held out something wrapped in a white cloth. Jacob carefully took whatever it was before unraveling the cloth. When his eyes widened and a smile made its way onto his face, Annabella knew it was the perfect gift.

"How did you know?" Jacob asked her, baffled that he was holding the shirt that he was eyeing just days ago. Annabella took a step forward and lowered the shirt so Jacob could look at her.

"I saw that you kept going back to it. Your eyes seemed to light up every time you looked at this shirt, so I decided to buy it. It was the reason that I went back in the store," she explained to him.

"This is so expensive, Annabella. Please let me pay you back when I save up enough money," Jacob pleaded, but Annabella just shook her head before giving him a hug.

"Accept this gift, Jacob. It will mean more to me to have you at my side on the day on my birthday. It would make it much more special than this gift is to you," she admitted to him in complete honesty. Annabella actually had someone as a friend while she was stuck inside of the storybook.

"Thank you, Annabella. I have made a few friends during my training to become a knight, but you are different. You are also my best friend," Jacob told her all while still holding her in his embrace.

"I pinky promised you that I would explain everything to you eventually, but I am promising now that I explain a few things after the ball," Annabella said before wishing Jacob a goodnight and making her way to bed. She needed to rest well for another day of dancing.

Chapter Eight

"Are you ready to dance for the next several hours?" Jacob asked Annabella as soon as she opened the door to the ballroom. Annabella groaned at the thought of how much pain her back and legs would be feeling after it was all over.

"I do not think I will ever be ready, but I guess I do not have much choice in the matter," she said with a scowl. Jacob chuckled before he clapped his hands. A quartet of gnomes began playing a waltz and Annabella smiled. It was pretty easy so at least she wouldn't be *too* terrible.

"We will start out with this and move up in levels of difficulty. Today, we will focus mainly on two of four types of dances, but will touch on the other two, which you will be practicing tomorrow." Annabella nodded at him as he took a step closer. He raised his right hand in the air and placed his left on her waist. Annabella took no time to take her position. *At least I remembered that.*

The dance started off with basic steps. Annabella remembered most of what she had learned the day before, but she surely needed to practice so she could look somewhat convincing at the ball. She was concentrating so hard on what was coming next, that she ended up stepping on Jacob's foot.

"Oh my God, I am so sorry," she said with both hands over her mouth.

Jacob laughed at her concern. "Annabella, you are very light. A small step on my foot will not hurt me," he said before pulling her closer again to continue the dance. After about an hour, Annabella was doing much better. The waltz wasn't too hard, but she had improved immensely from the day before.

"Wait, was it my left foot or right foot that steps next?" Annabella asked for the third time.

"Left. Just think about the hand that you do not write with when you get to this part. Other than that, you are doing very well," Jacob said with a large smile.

"I will keep practicing even when I am on my own," Annabella promised Jacob.

"I trust you to. I think it is time that we have a break. Would you like to eat now or after we go over the other dances?" Jacob asked her.

Annabella thought for a minute. Eating now might make her feel full.

"Are you hungry?" she asked Jacob. He shook his head.

"I ate a bit too much for breakfast. I should be good for another hour or so," he informed her before clapping his hands for the music to start again. The pair danced for another hour before Annabella was beginning to feel too tired to continue. They decided to eat lunch and stop practicing for the time being.

"Those were delicious," Annabella said after she and Jacob left the dance hall. She was referring to the tuna sandwiches that were served for lunch.

Jacob nodded in agreement. "That they were."

The two decided to take a walk around the castle's garden. There was a slight breeze blowing through the yard, which made Annabella wonder if it was also August in the Land of Dreams.

"I did not think that it would start getting chilly so soon," Annabella said instead of asking Jacob what month it was. He would surely find it strange considering she should know her own birthday.

"It is the end of summer. Thankfully your birthday is not during the winter months. We still have a few more weeks until the beginning of autumn," Jacob said. Annabella wondered how the winters were here. Were they just colder or did it actually snow?

"Do you celebrate Christmas?" she asked him. She would be very sad if Christmas weren't a thing in this land. Luckily, a full grin was plastered on Jacob's face.

"Christmas is wonderful. Of course I celebrate it."

Annabella was relieved. "What do you do?" Jacob smiled down at her.

"Every year, as you know, the King and Queen have a big party and invite everyone in The Land of Dreams. There is tons of food so everyone can enjoy a delicious feast. There is music playing and people playing many different games with each other. My personal favourite part is the giant snowball fight. I am always in the top three out of the whole kingdom. I have always loved snowball fights," he said with his eyes twinkling.

Annabella felt bittersweet about this. *I've never spent Christmas without my parents, but at least it'll be movie-like.*

"Look," Jacob said and threw Annabella out of her thoughts. She looked at the location that he was pointing in to see a chocolate-brown bunny hopping towards them.

"How adorable," Annabella cooed as she bent down to pet the little rabbit. The rabbit seemed to like Annabella and didn't back away, so she picked it up continued running her hands through the soft fur.

"She likes you," Jacob observed while petting the bunny himself.

"I cannot believe she is letting me hold her," Annabella agreed before setting the bunny down. "Is there anything that I could give her to eat?" she asked. Jacob smiled mischievously before pulling a baby carrot out of his pocket, leaving his hand to return from the glowing blue.

"How did you... never mind," Annabella said. *That's probably another regular spell.*

The bunny took the carrot and hopped away happily.

"I see you like animals," Jacob observed.

Annabella nodded. "If it were up to me I would have many pets. It would be hard to take care of if I did get them."

Jacob laughed. "You have many workers at the castle to take care of them for you. You could always ask your parents to get you one." Annabella thought about this. She always wanted to have dogs or cats for company, but she knew this year wouldn't exactly be *lonely*.

"Maybe later on," she said. "Right now I am going to be busy learning many things, so there would not be very much of a point."

Jacob understood her reasoning. He grew up wanting pets for many years. When his mother got pregnant with his brother, he then understood that he wouldn't be lonely for a long time.

"Shall we go in?" Jacob said after they circled the entire garden. Annabella stopped looking at the roses and turned to him.

"Do you like roses?" Jacob asked.

Annabella nodded. "I usually do not care for flowers, but roses look so different, so... *beautiful*. It intrigues me that something so beautiful can cause pain."

Jacob smiled at her. "Their thorns help protect them from children pulling them all out. Which is your favourite colour?"

Annabella thought about this. "I am not very sure. I love the white ones because they look so simple and pretty, but the red ones make them seem mysterious. The fake ones that were coloured are cool too, I guess," she mumbled the last part.

"Fake ones?" Jacob questioned. "Roses here grow in every colour. Your mother just prefers the red and white ones. My mother keeps purple, blue, green, orange, and even black ones in our garden."

"Black ones? Interesting." Annabella shouldn't have been surprised considering how magical the land was, but things continued to surprise her.

"I would love to see that. I feel like they would be eerie and beautiful at the same time.

Jacob clapped his hands together."Enough talk about roses. I will bring you to our home one day so you can see my mother's garden. There are many flowers that you probably have not seen in your entire life."

Annabella didn't doubt it. *Black and blue roses that are completely natural? I don't even think he's exaggerating.*

THE NEXT DAY CONSISTED of the same activities. Annabella learned the last two dances from Jacob, and they spent time talking to each other and hanging out. She was learning many things about Jacob's personality that made her want to learn even more. He had always been kind and on the quiet side, but he excelled in school.

"After the ball is over I can finally bring you to the lake I was talking about. The weather fairies said that there would be a spark in the temperature on Wednesday, so we can actually go swimming. If it is ok with your parents, you can even come over to my house so I can show you the garden later that day," Jacob told Annabella with a huge smile on his face.

"I would love to. I cannot remember the last time I went for a swim," she replied honestly.

Even in the real world she hadn't been swimming in over a year. She would only go as a child when her parents drove to a beach, but now the water felt too cold her her to enjoy it. She preferred staying indoors for the most part.

Later that evening when Annabella was ready for bed, she decided to open her fairytale book. It wasn't much of a surprise that the book continued to write itself based on what she had done up until that point.

"How is this only two pages of it?" Annabella complained after reading it. She had been there for almost a week and done so many things, but the book had only recorded big events. It didn't even include her dinner with Jacob, or the last two days of dance rehearsals.

"This is actually going to take forever," Annabella groaned. She remembered not reading much about Jacob, but thought that since she was spending so much time with him, that the book would change. "Oh well," Annabella sighed before putting the book into her nightstand and climbing into bed.

For the next half hour, she practiced easy spells like moving objects in the air with her wind powers, growing a small flower in her flower pot with her earth powers, watering the plant with a bit of her water powers, and lighting a candle with her fire powers. Thankfully none of these spells required any words and nothing was destroyed. Annabella took the opportunity of having a few minutes alone to try a few complicated spells that required a lot of energy. She was going to sleep anyway so it wouldn't be a waste.

"Levitate," Annabella spoke out while concentrating on her bed. Ever since she learned that she was speaking in Latin she tried to hear the words, but they always came out sounding like regular english. Annabella's bed began to levitate, so she realized that her spell had worked.

"That is so cool," Annabella marvelled before the bed came back down. "Now I just need to learn how to keep my concentration and multitask," she said before she realized how tired she felt.

I guess Jacob wasn't lying when he said that this really drains your energy, she thought before snapping her fingers at the candle on her bedside table. The pink glow in her hand came and went as the short blast of wind flew by to blow the candle out.

"Time for some beauty sleep," Annabella told herself. The next day was the day of the ball and she had to be ready to face her entire kingdom.

Chapter Nine

The workers were going crazy from the moment the sun began rising. Annabella was rushed to eat her breakfast and straight into the washroom with Maria. There were three times the regular number of workers around the castle making everything perfect because it was a special day.

"I will just be washing it for now and put in a nice treatment," Maria told Annabella as she put on something that looked like a thermal hat on her head.

"Thank you, Maria. So you want me here at eleven o'clock?" Annabella asked.

Maria nodded before bringing Annabella out to her room, which looked completely different. There were people setting things up all over the place. The human woman that Annabella had seen the night of her dinner with Jacob, was setting up a station on the free wall next to her bed. Annabella introduced herself and discovered that the woman was a makeup artist and would be working on her throughout the day.

"Princess Annabella, I will be dressing you throughout the day," a human looking man said in a flamboyant manner. Annabella smiled at him, but was surprised when she saw that he was not a human.

"I am a shifter. Not an animal shifter, but an actual shifter," he explained as he stretched his arm halfway across the room to grab a pin.

Getting Annabella in her dress was very quick since the stylist could literally shrink and stretch every part of his body and bend it around in any way.

"Thank you, I will be back at noon for the portrait dress," Annabella told her stylist before being dragged to the balcony. Much to Annabella's surprise, Jacob was awaiting her arrival.

"Happy birthday, Annabella," he said before giving her a big hug.

Annabella squeezed back with a huge smile on her face. "Thank you, Jacob. You have the day off, why are you here?" she asked him.

Jacob looked around before smiling. "Well, you are not very familiar with anybody here so I figured you would like someone to talk to while you get ready."

Annabella sat down and introduced herself to the nail lady who turned out to be Fred's girlfriend.

"The nails I do now will be your nails for the entire day and night, so you have to make a decision now. Would you like pink, red, white tips, or one of those choices with something cute on your accent nails?" the lady asked.

Annabella couldn't decide. "What do you think would look best, Jacob?" Annabella asked as a joke.

Jacob scratched his head and looked at all of the choices. "Uh... the white tips with a design?" he said in a very uncertain manner.

Annabella smiled before nodding her head. "I agree. I would like the accent nail to be my ring fingers," she said before the nail lady got to work.

"Thank you," Annabella said, before walking over to the other side of the balcony with Jacob. She had to wait a few minutes for her nails to completely dry and didn't want to use her wind powers and risk smudging them.

"Are you excited for tonight?" Jacob asked her.

Annabella inhaled deeply. "I am, but I am also very nervous. I really do not want to meet Prince whatever his name is. I wish I could just have a small birthday with my parents, you, and your parents," she ended off with a sigh.

Jacob put a hand on her shoulder and squeezed it, "I too wish it could be that way, but sadly it must be like this, but I know you will make it through the night. You have a pure heart so I believe you have a chance at finding a soulmate."

Annabella smiled up at him before she carefully hugged him, trying not to ruin her nails. "Thank you, Jacob. You really are an amazing friend," she told him before someone rang a bell.

"That would be for you. Your parents would like for you to open your first gift," Jacob told her. "Just to be on the safe side—the Prince's name is Jeremy.

Annabella nodded, "Thank you. I will try to remember that. I will see you later," she said while skipping off back into the castle.

The King and Queen were standing behind a table when Annabella walked into the room. "Happy birthday," they chimed in unison as soon as they saw her.

"Thank you," she replied before she went up to them for a hug.

"We wanted to give you one of your presents before we got the portraits done," the King explained.

"We also wanted to be the only ones here when you opened it," the Queen added.

Annabella smiled thankfully at them. "Thank you both so much. I already know that I am going to love it."

The King reached into his suit and pulled out a long box that was wrapped nicely, before setting it in front of Annabella.

"Go ahead, sweetie," the Queen urged.

Annabella slowly unwrapped the present and was left with a long, thin box that looked like a jewelry box. Annabella looked up to see the Queen and King looking excited. When she opened the box she let out a gasp. There was a beautiful diamond bracelet in the box. There were different coloured diamonds randomly placed, but a huge diamond lay right in the center. In real life, Annabella's parents would never be able to afford a bracelet like that. Not even the richest person in school would.

"This is beautiful, This must have cost a fortune," Annabella said in awe.

The Queen and King laughed. "Do not worry about that, Annabella. Let me help you put it on," the King said before picking up the bracelet and putting it around Annabella's wrist. As soon as contact was made, a memory suddenly rushed into Annabella's head of her sixteenth birthday.

"I had to work overtime a few days, but it was worth it for this present. I hope you love it," Annabella's Dad said before removing his hand from Annabella's eyes. She looked down and saw the diamond heart bracelet she dreamed of and almost cried.

"Thank you so much, Daddy. I really love it. Can you help me put it on?"

Annabella snapped out from her memory just as the King's hands left her wrist and the bracelet was secured. Annabella felt like a giant knot was forming in her stomach and she tried to mask her sadness. *You need to remember that it's on you to get back to them,* she scolded herself and plastered a smile on her face.

"Oh it just looks magnificent on you," the Queen complimented Annabella before giving her another hug.

Annabella thanked them again before she made her way upstairs so Maria could style her hair for the portraits. After her hair was done, she went through wardrobe and then makeup before finally going to the back garden. There were many portraits that were made in the next few hours. A bunch of fairies quickly painted everything before Jacob showed up to observe.

"Jacob, we have time for one more portrait. You should do one with Annabella," the Queen said while motioning Jacob towards them. Jacob was surprised, but he made his way over to the family. At first Jacob just awkwardly stood next to Annabella and smiled.

The King saw how strange it looked so he yelled out, "Put your arm around her and relax, son. You are not strangers anymore."

Jacob was visibly surprised at the King's request, but nonetheless put his arm around Annabella and relaxed. Annabella also relaxed and smiled like she always did in her old family photos. Jacob really felt like family to her.

"All done," One of the fairies yelled out before everyone made their way to observe the portraits. All of them looked perfect. Annabella especially liked the one with Jacob because her smile looked the most natural, considering it wasn't forced. *I'm so happy the King was ok with us getting a picture together.*

Annabella could be herself, or at least almost herself around Jacob, and it felt nice with what she was going through. The sound of distant trumpets playing hit Annabella's ears before she could say anything about the portraits.

"Ah, our special guests have arrived. Annabella, please head to your room and get ready for the ball. Your dress arrived a little while ago and I am sure Maria has something nice planned for your hair," the King said before kissing Annabella on the cheek.

"See you all at the ball," Annabella said as she rushed inside to prepare for the long evening ahead of her.

Annabella was all over the place even though there were three hours to spare. The stylist wanted everything to be perfect with the dress, so he made sure the tightness of the corset was just right. Annabella soon figured out that just right meant she could still breathe, but couldn't do so comfortably. Maria came up with a beautiful hairstyle that consisted of waves, a beautiful tiara that matched with Annabella's first gift, and intricate braids that gave her hair a hint of glamour.

The makeup artist spent a long time coming up with the perfect look for Annabella. She wanted the Princess to look simple, but resilient so she decided to go with a natural medium smokey eye.

Annabella's face was highlighted in all of the right places and her cheeks were pinched to perfection to accentuate her natural rosy glow. Her lips were glossy, but weren't sticky, which she was thankful for.

"Are you ready to see yourself in the mirror, Annabella?" Maria asked.

Annabella nodded quickly before taking hold of Maria's hand, letting her lead her towards the mirror. Annabella quickly used her magic to remove the curtains and reveal the mirror and couldn't believe what she was seeing.

"Oh my. I look wonderful! Thank you so much everyone who helped out. I feel and look amazing," Annabella said with much excitement. She couldn't believe how amazing she looked. *And I thought I looked great the first time I saw myself.*

Bells rang signalling that it was time for Annabella to go downstairs and greet her guests. She took a deep breath before squeezing Maria's hand.

"You will do great," Maria said before Annabella made her way out of the room and towards the stairs.

As she had practiced many times, Annabella took slow, steady steps down the stairs to the beat of the music that was playing. She stopped after thirty-seven steps, and waited for her name to be announced. After only a few seconds a loud voice echoed throughout the large hall.

"Now introducing your royal highness, Princess Annabella of the Land of Dreams," the voice boomed before Annabella began the different walk she learned. When the room came into view, she heard a loud roar of awe, followed by clapping. Annabella knew that the entire village was there, but it seemed like so much more. There were all types of creatures in the room. Annabella instantly recognized a bunch of people as she got closer, but there were many others she knew that she had never seen before. As soon as the crowd began to quiet down, Annabella cleared her throat and began to speak.

"Welcome residents of the Land of Dreams and guests from neighbouring lands. Thank you all very much for attending this ball thrown for my birthday. It is a great honour for me that you were all able to make it and I hope you all have an amazing night," she said before another round of applause broke through.

Annabella made her way down the rest of the stairs before a bunch of people swarmed her. She said hello to everyone and got complimented on how beautiful she looked by all. After the huge group of people began to converse within, Annabella took the opportunity to get away.

Upon searching the room frantically for the King, Queen or Jacob, Annabella caught a glimpse of the present table. The table could fit at least twenty chairs on either side and it was packed with presents. She couldn't believe how many there were.

"Annabella," the Queen's voice called out. Annabella quickly made her way towards her.

"We have someone very special that we would like you to meet," the King said with a smile.

I guess there's no way of avoiding this and completing the story, Annabella thought. *It's going to be the Prince. I just hope he's nice.*

"This is Prince Jeremy of the Land of Light," the King spoke just as tall man who looked about twenty-five with hair so blonde it was practically white, stepped out. His eyes were bright blue. This man was the definition of perfection when it came to looks. All of the girls in the room were ogling the Prince—well, all except for one.

"Hello, my name is Annabella. It is very nice to meet you," Annabella said as she stuck her hand out. Instead of the Prince shaking her hand he got down on one knee and softly kissed it. The King and Queen were no longer in sight.

"It is a great honour to meet someone as beautiful as you, Princess Annabella," he said with a smooth deep voice that would melt middle school girls' hearts. "It is also a big relief to me. I was worried that you would be ugly."

Annabella lightly bit the inside of her cheek. She wasn't nervous in the slightest. Sure, he was beautiful and every girl's dream, but he reminded her too much of a Ken doll. A narcissistic ken doll with a smile that was clearly not genuine.

"Why thank you," Annabella replied, trying not to seem angry. "I hope you had a nice trip here. I am going to search for my special guest now. It was very nice meeting you. I will see you at the feast," Annabella said before going in search for Jacob.

It didn't take long for Annabella to find him. Jacob was a few meters away from the Prince with his back turned towards Annabella.

"Jacob, I'm so glad I finally found you," Annabella said before Jacob turned around and left Annabella in awe. The shirt that Annabella bought him looked amazing on and showed off just how sculpted his body was. Jacob's eyes contrasted nicely with the shirt and seemingly sparkled. His dark brown hair looked even darker with the way he had styled it to look fancy, but you could still see a bit of natural messiness, which made it perfect.

"You look... wow," Annabella said.

Jacob smirked slightly before breaking out into a full smile. "You look absolutely stunning, Annabella."

Annabella couldn't hold back and gave Jacob a big hug. "Thank you so much. I am so glad that you are here and are my special guest. I would feel so lost if you were not," she told him truthfully.

The two talked for a while before the bells that signalled the feast began to chime. Everyone excitedly made their way into the dining hall, and took their reserved seats. The dining hall had gone through a huge change, and now had a huge table from one end to another that sat at least five hundred guests. Everything looked like it had come out from a medieval movie, but Annabella now knew that it was all in fact real. When everyone was in their seats and their plates were full everyone quieted down. Every single person at the table had a glass of champagne and was holding it up for Annabella, awaiting her to give a speech.

"I would once again like to thank everyone for being here tonight and I trust you are all having a great time," Annabella started off. "This year has been great like all of my others. I would like to dedicate this to one person in specific. Although this person has not been in my life very long, actually a very short amount of time, but I feel like he has been here forever. I would like to dedicate this to my best friend, Jacob," Annabella said before the King took over.

"Cheers," the King yelled out and everyone clinked their drinks together.

Annabella and Jacob clinked their cups together while maintaining eye contact, taking their sips at the same time. Everyone dug into the delicious looking food. There were dozens of roasted turkeys and the gravy was delicious. Annabella loved seeing everyone having a good time. In that moment she actually felt at home and never wanted it to end.

During the meal, there were many stories told about Annabella growing up. Annabella had to laugh along even though she wasn't actually there for it, but she still found it embarrassing.

Finally, after two hours, everyone was finished with dessert and made their way into the ballroom for the dancing to begin. Annabella was nervous, but felt confident that she would do well with all of the practicing she had done with Jacob and on her own. When the waltz started to play, Annabella turned to Jacob to ask him to dance with her, but someone interrupted.

"May I have the honour of having the first dance with the Princess?" Prince Jeremy asked Annabella.

She really wanted to dance with Jacob, but everyone in the room had their eyes on them so she agreed with a smile. Annabella had to admit that it was fun dancing when the room was full. She however did not like hearing everyone talking about the wedding that would take place next year. *At least let me get to know the guy first.*

"I feel very honoured that I have the luck to be marrying you in just one year," Jeremy said to Annabella when a slow waltz came on.

Annabella forced a smile and nodded.

"Fate must be in our favour. Can you imagine how beautiful our children will be? I was worried that you would not be attractive, but luckily neither of us have any imperfections," he said, which made Annabella want to push him away.

Just a few more minutes with this jerk. How can anyone be so shallow?

Annabella stopped questioning things in her head. She knew she would have to marry Jeremy to save her parents, so she would have to let these things slide.

When the last song came up Annabella decided that enough was enough.

"I had a lot of fun dancing with you, but I would like to have the last dance with my best friend," she told Jeremy.

Jeremy smiled at her, but she could see that it was forced and he wasn't happy about it.

"Of course, go have fun with your *assistant*," he said, putting an accent on his last word.

Annabella quickly made her way into the crowd and pulled Jacob into the center of the room.

"Are you not dancing with the Prince anymore?" Jacob asked her in a less than enthusiastic tone.

Annabella shook her head. "I wanted to dance with you for the last dance of the night so I can show off my amazing dance moves," Annabella joked before she placed her hand in Jacob's.

The two began to move together in perfect unison, which had the crowd watching in awe. By the time the song was done everyone was clapping and complimenting both Annabella and Jacob on their dancing skills. Prince Jeremy was the only one who wasn't, but his father nudged him, making him clap.

The rest of the evening consisted of Annabella opening presents. It took about three hours before Annabella and her parents were able to open everything and thank the gift givers. Prince Jeremy had given Annabella a beautiful set of china. It was the greatest gift of the evening, but Annabella didn't care much for it, seeing as it was just a collectable that would never be used, but nonetheless she thanked him enthusiastically.

After saying goodbye to all of the guests Annabella flopped down on the sofa and let out a huge breath.

Jacob chuckled from her side.

"Tired are we?" he said. Annabella punched him in the arm.

"Of course I am. I am so ready for bed," she said with a yawn.

Jacob had a devilish smirk on his face before he picked Annabella up.

"What are you doing?" Annabella laughed.

"I am carrying you upstairs. Seeing as you are too tired to stand up anymore," he said before carrying Annabella up to her room. When they arrived he set Annabella down in front of her door. "I have a present for you in there," Jacob said.

Annabella raised a brow at him before opening the door. Much to her surprise, there was a huge box with a big hole at the top and many holes around it. As Annabella made her way to the box she heard a little cry and looked down. Inside of the box was a little kitten wrapped up in a fluffy blanket.

"Oh, Jacob," Annabella squealed before pouncing on Jacob and giving him a huge kiss on the cheek. "Thank you so much. I love it," she said before she picked up the kitten and carefully held it in her arms.

Jacob blushed slightly and stuck his hands in his pockets. "It was the least that I could do after your gift. I am going to leave you now so you can rest, but I will be back tomorrow afternoon to help you study. Happy birthday, Annabella," he said before leaving the room with an extremely excited, but still exhausted, Annabella inside.

Chapter Ten

Annabella woke up on Wednesday morning as excited as ever. She was finally going to go swimming with Jacob at his secret hideaway. She quickly ran to her balcony and felt that the weather was in fact, much warmer than it has been since she arrived in the land. Maria was happy when Annabella asked for a French braid.

"I have always loved doing these. My daughters do not like them so I never get the chance anymore," Maria said slightly disappointed.

Annabella smiled at her before saying, "Well I love them very much, so whenever I do not require a more sophisticated style you will have the opportunity."

Since her birthday ball had passed, Annabella dedicated her free time to studying and practicing spells. She especially practiced keeping her concentration while multitasking by keeping a small fire in one hand, while keeping her pillow floating in the air. While Annabella was practicing, there was a knock on her door. Surprisingly, the fire didn't go out and the pillow didn't fall when Annabella heard it and told whomever it was to come in.

"I see you are practicing your magic," Jacob said from the doorway.

Annabella smiled used her wind powers to put her pillow back in place before she closed her hand to extinguish the fire.

"Yes. I have been doing pretty well if I may say so myself," she said with a smug smile.

Jacob crossed his arms and chuckled. "From what I see, you are improving quickly. Are you ready to go? I packed us a few small sandwiches should we become hungry."

Annabella nodded and grabbed her bag. She was wearing a very casual dress. Underneath she had her swimsuit and a pajama dress on top, because she had a feeling that people didn't go swimming with just a swimsuit. Plus, she had seen the old fashion in movies where the women swam with their long undergarments, so she figured it wouldn't hurt to be safe.

"Are you the only one that knows about the lake?" Annabella asked Jacob curiously. Jacob nodded.

"Yes I am. Well, at least I think I am. I accidentally cut down a large amount of hanging leaves while training, and saw light peaking through from between two trees that were very close together. I will show you what I mean when we get there."

The two exited the front gates and walked diagonally through the forest, talking about the events over the past few days. Annabella couldn't help but find it funny how Jacob looked while carrying a girly bag. He wouldn't let her carry it on her own, and forced her into letting him hold it. Annabella noticed that the forest was becoming denser the further they walked.

"We are almost there," Jacob said as he moved leaves out of the way for Annabella to pass. After about another minute, Jacob stopped in front of huge amount of hanging leaves. "We are here," he announced before using both arms to move them.

The lighting instantly became brighter, and Annabella was surprised to see that two enormous trees were hiding the entrance to a beautiful lake. Annabella squeezed between the trees and took at her surroundings. The entire lake was completely surrounded by trees that grew side by side, but there were none in the middle. The sunlight was directly above them, making the water sparkle. There was even a small waterfall that made everything look like an oasis.

"Beautiful," Annabella breathed.

Jacob made a sound of approval before setting down a large picnic cloth on the ground, along with several towels. Annabella took off her slippers and put them inside of her bag before she attempted unzipping her dress. The zipper was a mere centimetre away from Annabella's reach, leaving her struggling to grab hold of it.

"You look like you are in need of some help," Jacob laughed when Annabella glared at him, but she finally gave up and moved towards him.

Jacob easily unzipped the dress before he took off his shirt and pants, leaving him in just swim trunks.

"Thank you," Annabella grumbled before turning around and seeing a shirtless Jacob. *Oh baby,* she thought in her head. *If this was a dream I would so jump him right here, right now.*

Annabella quickly composed herself before Jacob noticed her obvious gawking. She hadn't ever been in a real relationship, and would never *actually* do such a thing. He had a perfectly sculpted body including his abs. *I guess his training was really hard.*

"Ready to go in?" Jacob asked Annabella enthusiastically. Annabella nodded before taking off her dress, leaving her in her undergarments that covered her one-piece bathing suit.

Jacob let out a bark of laughter.

"What is it?" Annabella asked him.

"What on earth are you wearing on top of your swim suit?" was his reply.

Annabella looked down at herself. "Is this not what all of the girls wear swimming?" she asked him.

As soon as Jacob shook his head she ripped them off and was left in just her bathing suit. *I'll never understand what is normal in this world.*

The pair made their way over to the water and slowly stepped into it. Much to Annabella's surprise, the water was actually quite warm. She was expecting cold water like she always experienced when she had gone swimming, but at least it was a nice surprise.

"The water is wonderful," she said as she started swimming backwards.

Jacob submerged himself into the water. "Do not swim too far or the sharks might get you," he told her.

Annabella's eyes quickly widened before she frantically started swimming back towards him. "Sharks?" she squealed.

Jacob nodded before he burst out in laughter. "Your face was priceless. Of course there are no sharks here. Only in the Land of the Sea will you find any and they are generally very friendly," he explained to her.

Annabella glared at Jacob, stuck her tongue out at him and swam away.

"Oh come on, Annabella. Do not be like that," Jacob whined before he swam after her and picked her up.

"You are a big bully," she told him pointedly.

Jacob smirked at her. "Is that so?" he said before picking her up, throwing her into the air and letting her land in the water.

"Hey, no fair. You are much stronger than me," Annabella complained after ascending and splashing Jacob in the face. She then began swimming towards the rocks as quick as possible. Luckily, Annabella was able to climb up before Jacob could reach her, and ran towards the waterfall. She looked for the water source, but found nothing.

Things really are magic here.

"Looks like you are trapped," Jacob said with a sly grin when he reached Annabella. She looked behind her, but there was nothing but rock and the water that was too far down for her to jump in. Before she knew it, Jacob grabbed her and jumped into the water.

There wasn't even a second left to spare for Annabella to protest, but she was able to let out a small squeak before hitting the water.

The two were deep under the water when Annabella opened her eyes. Everything was so clear underwater she couldn't even believe it.

Try to use an air spell, she heard Jacob's voice inside of her head.

Surprised, Annabella swam back up after swallowing a bit of water. When Jacob surfaced, Annabella questioned him.

"It is just magic. I just think something and push my thoughts towards you since you are in close proximity." Annabella attempted to try it.

Cat, she thought and concentrated on pushing it over to Jacob.

"Cat? That is the only thing you could come up with?" he asked her unbelievable way.

Annabella shrugged. "I have been having a lot of fun with the kitten, so it makes sense to me," she said before swimming towards the rocks again.

"Where are you going?" Jacob called out. Annabella giggled and motioned for him to come along with her.

"I want to jump again."

"THESE ARE ABSOLUTELY delicious," Annabella said after swallowing her first bite of her second miniature sandwich.

"Did you make these yourself?"

Jacob smiled guardedly. "With a bit of help from my aunt," he told her.

Annabella nodded. "That makes sense."

"So, what did you think about Prince Jeremy?" Jacob suddenly asked.

Annabella swallowed her food and looked up at him. "I am not really sure," she answered warily.

Jacob shot her a strange look. "You are not sure?" he repeated.

Annabella shook her head. "I only talked to him shortly and danced with him for a bit. He seems like a cocky bastard to be frank," she said before quickly covering her mouth. "I am so sorry for my language," she apologized to Jacob, but he just started laughing.

"The way you said that was just comical. I never imagined you saying something like that about anyone," he said after slapping his knee.

"Well, it is true. All he seemed to be interested in was the wedding and how I am 'thankfully' attractive enough to marry him and procreate," Annabella said irritably.

"Well if it makes you feel any better, I also thought he seemed like a cocky bastard. I have seen him a few times since my training started and he seemed immature then, but I thought he would grow out of it. I feel sorry for you having to marry that. You could probably control him well—he seems quite stupid," he said which made Annabella burst out laughing.

"The sun has already dried me," Jacob pointed out after a while as he was putting the wrappers back into the basket. Annabella felt her bathing suit and saw that she was also dry.

"Since we are already dry, do you want to go instead of getting wet all over again?"

Jacob nodded and grabbed his button down shirt. "We can just head over to my house now."

After the two were completely dressed they headed for the village. Right before they exited the secret lake, a blue bunny hopped by, leaving a sparkling trails behind it.

"Wow, what is that?" Annabella asked and observed as the bunny changed into each colour of the rainbow.

"Quick! It is a magical luck bunny. Make a wish," Jacob said before closing his eyes.

Annabella did the same and started thinking. *I wish for Jacob to believe me and that my parents will be saved.*

Annabella often found herself forgetting about her goal in the Land of Dreams—saving her parents. All of the events and everyone's happiness had distracted her from the goal and she knew she would have to take training more seriously.

Annabella was happy to be out of the forest. She loved the nature, but much preferred civilization.

"School will be over in a few minutes. Would it be all right with you if we picked my siblings up from school? My aunt will be done work in an hour, so we will not have to worry about watching them," Jacob explained.

Annabella nodded and walked by his side to the school.

"Good afternoon," Mirabelle, Jacob's siblings teacher greeted the two.

"Good afternoon," Jacob and Annabella replied simultaneously.

"Jacob," both of Jacob's sisters said before running up to him, giving him a hug. Jacob's brother Daniel just waved and began walking home.

"Are you coming over to see our garden?" one of the twins asked Annabella.

Annabella nodded. "Yes Katherine, I am," she said with a smile.

Everyone started laughing. "The one with the blue ribbon is Katherine, this one always wears a green ribbon," Jacob explained.

"I am so sorry, Katarina," Annabella apologized. "Usually I can distinguish between twins better."

The girls both giggled and continued walking. Jacob turned left after the bakery and walked down a road, stopping in front of a fairly large house in comparison to the others.

"We are here," he announced.

The house resembled a gingerbread house. It reminded Annabella of a ski lodge she had been to for her thirteenth birthday.

"This is beautiful," Annabella complimented before Jacob opened the little gate for his siblings and Annabella to walk through.

The inside was well organized with very high ceilings. From the outside, the house looked like a two story home, but it was only one floor. Jacob explained that it was so his dad could comfortably get around inside.

"This is so cute" Annabella said as she observed everything.

"Would you like to see my room?" Jacob asked her.

Annabella nodded before Jacob opened the door to his room. The walls were painted blue, and there were a few portraits hanging from them. Annabella observed the picture of a young boy that definitely wasn't Daniel.

"Is this you?" Annabella asked Jacob, who nodded.

"I was adorable, was I not?" he asked her with a laugh.

Annabella nodded. When Annabella observed the portrait of Jacob she felt strange. *I swear I've seen this face before*, she thought to herself, but couldn't think of where. *Maybe it's from a TV show.*

"Is something wrong?" Jacob asked her.

Annabella shook her head. "You just look really familiar. I probably saw you in the village when I was younger." Annabella also noticed the bunk bed in the room and a few portraits of Daniel.

"You two share a room?" she asked Jacob.

Jacob nodded at her. "Yes. The house is not big enough for a room for each of us, so we share. It is not that bad though. Nowadays I spend most nights at my room in the castle," he explained.

"You have a room at the castle? I did not know about that."

Jacob chuckled. "I only sleep at home when my parents are working late so I can go with them. Otherwise, I have nothing to do here, so it is much easier and functional for me to stay in my room at the castle. It is just a simple room since all I do is sleep in it, but I have a washroom of my own," Jacob explained with a smile.

Annabella found it cute that he was happy about a washroom. *Imagine what you'd feel like waking up in a different world.*

Beatrice soon arrived to watch over the children, so Jacob decided to show Annabella more of the house.

"This," Jacob said motioning towards the backyard, "is my mother's garden."

Annabella was in shock. There were roses of every single colour growing in the garden. What mostly caught her eyes were the black roses. They looked so dark and beautiful to her.

"Here," Jacob said and stuck his hand out. When his hand started glowing blue, a black rose disappeared from the garden and into his hand.

"I made sure to get the thorns out," he said while handing it over to Annabella.

"Thank you," she told him before sitting down at a picnic table.

"Annabella," Katarina called from the doorway. Annabella turned around to face the little girl. "Would you like to stay for dinner?" she asked.

Annabella turned to Jacob who tilted his head with a smile. "Uh, sure," Annabella replied before the little girl skipped back inside.

"Can you send a message to my parents letting them know that I am eating here?" Annabella asked Jacob. Jacob nodded and pulled a sheet of paper from his pocket, making a pen and ink appear on the table.

"Sure thing," he said before writing a quick note and summoning a dove. "Send this to the King," he told the dove before it flew off in the direction of the castle.

"THANK YOU VERY MUCH for dinner, Beatrice. It was absolutely delicious," Annabella said before giving Jacob's aunt a hug.

"It was my pleasure," she said honestly, before waving goodbye to her and Jacob.

The two walked to the town's center where Fred awaited them.

"Good evening," he said to the two, who replied the same.

Annabella was tired from all of the food she ate, so she rested her head on Jacob's shoulder. She enjoyed seeing the brightness of the moon coming through the trees that Jacob made slant to the side. The blue glow coming from Jacob's hands reminded Annabella of jello for some odd reason.

As the chariot was nearing the castle Annabella heard rustling nearby. She turned her head enough to see the red eyes once again. This time she moved a bit to get a closer look and spotted a tail that looked like a wolves before it ran away.

"Is everything all right?" Jacob asked.

Annabella nodded. "Yeah, it was just another animal."

When they arrived at the castle Maria was waiting for her. "How was your day?" she asked the pair.

"Awesome," both replied.

Maria smiled and hugged Jacob.

"Mother, are you trying to embarrass me?" he asked in a joking manner.

Maria pinched his leg and laughed. "You are never too old for a mother's hug."

Annabella's smile faltered at the words, but she did not want Jacob and Maria to notice, so she brought it back quickly.

"You can go home, Maria. I have been practicing and I think I can handle a very quick bath on my own," Annabella assured Maria, who looked pleased.

"Your powers must be getting stronger, and quickly too. How good," Maria said with a smile. "Well, I will be going with my husband. I will see you both tomorrow," she said, giving Annabella and Jacob a hug before leaving.

"Well I had a lot of fun today. If you want, we can start fight training tomorrow," Jacob said while walking towards the door.

Annabella quickly nodded. "I would love that. I had a lot of fun too. Thank you so much for showing me your secret lake," she said before giving Jacob a hug. This hug was different from the others. It was tighter and lasted a lot longer, but Jacob pulled away awkwardly after letting out a cough.

"Well, goodnight then. I will see you tomorrow," he said quickly while avoiding eye contact and left the room.

Annabella stood in place from confusion. "Why am I so awkward?" she complained to herself. *You need to stop crushing on him. He's not the one you need to marry.*

Annabella shook her head before marching into the washroom and giving herself a quick enough bath with her water powers, rinsing off any dirt from her hair and body.

Feeling even more tired from using her powers, Annabella climbed into bed and snapped her fingers to put out all of the candles except for the one on her nightstand. She pulled out a book titled, 'Creatures', and searched for wolves.

After reading for a while, Annabella discovered that wolves with red eyes were either evil werewolves or witches.

"That's not good," she mumbled. *I thought there wasn't any evil in that forest or any witches other than the good witch.* She would bring it up to Jacob if it happened again. Once Annabella finished reading on wolves, she picked her kitten up from the side of her bed.

"You get to sleep on here, Smokey," she said before placing a kiss on the kitten's head and setting him down on the covers by her feet. The little ball of fur instantly curled up and started to sleep. Finally, Annabella used her magic to put out the last candle in the room and go to bed herself.

Chapter Eleven

"**C**an you do another French braid today?" Annabella asked Maria the next morning.

"Sure thing. I am sure you will be needing a bath after you are done training, so I will come back in a few hours," Maria informed Annabella as she braided her hair.

"Thank you very much, Maria. I do not know what I would do without you," Annabella told her honestly. Giving herself a bath every time would mean draining her powers first thing in the morning, even if it only used a bit of energy now. While Annabella missed showers, it did feel nice being pampered every day. She did, however, miss her bath bombs.

"All done. Tell my Jacob not to go too hard on you."

Annabella laughed at Maria. "How will I learn if he goes easy on me? Do not worry. I know he will not hurt me," Annabella said as Maria searched through a clothing rack.

"I found your training gear. It is quite fitting, but it is great for battle since you can move around freely. It is also custom made so your own powers will not destroy it," Maria explained to Annabella as she handed over a black body suit.

There was a short skirt that attached to it with compartments on the belt for weapons. Annabella gawked at the outfit. It looked like it was out of some sort of warrior princess movie.

This is awesome, she thought as she took it from Maria and started putting it on. The inside was made of a silky material that made it easy to slip into. Maria zipped it up the back before helping Annabella put the little vest on. Annabella wrapped the skirt around her before zipping up the sides and tightening the belt. As soon as Annabella was completely dressed, she ran to the mirror in her room and admired the clothing. *I look like a pro fighter,* she thought to herself as Maria ran to her.

"You must not forget your boots. These are very lightweight and flexible so they will not get in your way. They are also magical so they help you run bit faster, jump a bit higher, and make your kicks a bit stronger," Maria explained before handing them over to Annabella. As soon as the boots were on, Annabella's feet she felt stronger. Everything fit like a glove and she loved it.

"Am I all done now?"

Maria shook her head and handed Annabella a pair of finger gloves. "Now you are done."

Annabella gave Maria a quick hug before walking out of her room. As soon as she was out of sight she ran excitedly down the stairs and towards the training room to get started.

"You look prepared," Jacob said as soon as he saw Annabella running into the room.

Annabella smiled and twirled around. "Does the outfit look good?" she asked.

Jacob nodded. "It is the perfect outfit for battle and training. I see you are wearing your magical shoes. Those come in handy while sneaking up on the enemy since they are incredibly quiet."

Annabella looked down and jumped, realizing that the shoes didn't make any noise. "Wow, I did not realize that while running here. I guess that is really good."

Jacob nodded and walked over to a long cabinet. Annabella looked at him questioningly, but when he opened the cabinet she understood. "This is all of your battle gear," Jacob announced.

Annabella saw a sword that caught her eye and began to reach for it, but Jacob stopped her.

"You will not be using weapons for a while. You must first train without them."

Annabella gulped, but agreed.

"The first order of business is learning how to defend yourself. I am going to come at you in different ways, I want you to try and block me. Do not worry; I will not hit you hard. Even if it may seem like I am, I will not."

Annabella nodded and put her arms in front of her, her fingers closed. Jacob stood in front of Annabella and smirked before he started throwing hits. Annabella screeched and flailed her arms around. He was so fast that ended up with her losing her balance and falling on her butt. She scowled at Jacob as soon as he started laughing.

"Annabella, you cannot be afraid. You must concentrate on blocking me, not acting like some sort of bird" Jacob laughed as he helped her up. She stuck her tongue out at him before dusting off her butt.

"I think you are going to need a few pillows to make your falls softer," Jacob said and started walking off towards a sofa.

"Stop. I need to learn the tough way. I give you permission to go harder on me. Just try not to break any bones," Annabella said seriously.

Jacob opened and closed his mouth, but said nothing.

"I am serious. If anything ever happened and I needed to go into battle I would need tough training. Just train me the way you were trained," Annabella pleaded.

Jacob sighed. "Only if you are completely certain. I cannot promise that you will leave without bruises, but I promise to not break anything or do anything to your pretty face," Jacob said and widened his eyes slightly before looking away.

"I am sure," Annabella said, not thinking much about the last part of what Jacob said. She took a deep breath and cracked her knuckles. "Let us start again."

Jacob spent the next half hour showing Annabella a series of blocks and when to use them. She tried her hardest to hit Jacob just once, but he was too fast at blocking. Annabella's arms were tired from throwing so many punches and her wrists were beginning to bruise from the blocks.

"Are you ready for me to go again?" Jacob asked Annabella.

Annabella nodded and raised her arms up before getting into her position, before Jacob started throwing punches again. Annabella was able to block one or two, but she wasn't fast enough for Jacob, getting hit various times. They repeated the same things over and over again for an entire hour. Annabella was once again on the floor from taking so many hits, to which she was getting frustrated. *You can do it;* she heard a voice similar to hers in her head.

A sudden boost of energy filled Annabella and she sprung to her feet before she started fighting back. She couldn't understand what was happening, but her instincts were fighting for her, and she was blocking every one of Jacob's hits. It almost felt like she didn't have control of her own body.

"Whoa," Jacob said as Annabella started to throw in her own hits all while still blocking.

Jacob started to throw in kicks when he realized that Annabella was starting to get out of control, but Annabella blocked every single one, even managing to trip him badly enough that he flipped before falling.

"Oh my gosh!" Annabella gasped as soon as she saw Jacob fall. She was back in control and fell next to him, checking if he was all right. "Jacob, I am so sorry, I have no idea what happened. Are you ok?" Annabella was worried as she pulled Jacob up into a sitting position.

"How did you do that?" Jacob asked astonished at what had just happened.

Annabella shook her head as her eyes began to water. "I have no idea. I felt like I had no control over myself, like it was all my natural instincts. I cannot believe that I hurt you. I am really sorry," she said before hugging him and crying into his shoulder.

"Please do not cry, Annabella. You did not hurt me at all. I am just a bit shocked. That was simply remarkable. I have never seen anyone fight like that since... well, ever really. The men are great fighters, but you moved so swiftly," Jacob said to her before he wiped a tear from under her eye.

Annabella blushed at how close they were and moved back a bit. "Are you ok, though?" she asked him. Jacob nodded and jumped to his feet.

"I am perfectly fine. You are the one with an injury." He pointed to one of her quickly forming bruises.

Annabella laughed, "Yeah, can we go get some ice to soothe our muscles?"

Jacob nodded and helped her off of the floor. As soon as Annabella was up, Jacob threw a quick punch, which she blocked instantly.

"I think you are pretty much ready for battle training. I thought it would take a few weeks, but it looks like your instincts have somehow kicked in. Perhaps we can try fighting with equipment next," Jacob said before leading Annabella to the kitchen.

When they arrived, Jacob went for the water supply and filled up two rubber pouches. He held one pouch in each hand before his hands started to glow blue.

"There, they are now frozen," he said as he handed one to Annabella.

Annabella smiled at him and put it on her left shoulder. "That feels good," she said before Jacob lightly grabbed her and motioned for her to follow him.

"Why are we in the library?" Annabella asked when Jacob led her inside.

"I want to get you a book," he said before walking near the battle section. Jacob's hands started to glow the blue colour Annabella was all too familiar with, before a few books flew out of the shelf and landed on the table next to him.

"I want you to read all of these by next week. These will really help, just like they helped me when I was training for battle. You have the blood of a royal, so you will be much quicker at perfecting these things. The blood is what likely made your instincts kick in today. I have heard of this happening, but have never actually seen it before. Now that it has happened once you will likely be fine, but we do not know for certain until next time. This will just prepare you for the battle training and teach you some helpful battle spells," Jacob explained before he snapped his fingers and the books disappeared.

Annabella opened her mouth to ask where they went but Jacob covered it with his finger. *They are in your room,* Jacob said in her head.

Annabella smirked at him. *Let us go there. I can finally tell you why I have been acting so strange.*

The two made their way to Annabella's room where she locked the door behind them. Annabella picked Smokey up and put the kitten in her lap, patting the spot beside hers on the sofa for Jacob to sit in. Jacob did and Annabella took a deep breath and prepared

"I'm not actually Princess Annabella. Well, I am, but I'm not. I'm basically a different version of her from a different dimension or whatever this is. I was sleeping one second in my room and the next second I woke up here as Princess Annabella, of the Land of Dreams. My real name is also Annabella and I'm actually just a boring teenager with bad skin, boring hair and a bit heavier," Annabella blurted out.

Jacob blinked a few times and looked very confused. "But, you are Annabella. Princess Annabella," he said in a matter-of-fact kind of way.

Annabella groaned and threw her head back. "I know this is going to be hard to believe, but I'm really not her. I don't actually look exactly like this. I'm not actually attractive. The only part of me that's here, is my personality and most of my thoughts. Everything I told you about myself is true when it comes to my favourite colour or my interests or what I find funny, but who I am and who my family is isn't real. I'm from Canada, which is a country on the planet Earth. There is no such thing as magic in my world. There are no such things as dwarves or nodums or fairies or even living gnomes like Fred. Fred is actually a very common name among older adults. We don't live for hundreds of years there. Everyone dies from old age, usually during their eighties. Roses only exist if they're red, white, or pink. Everything is plain and boring. The weather comes naturally without fairies and is different."

"Annabella," Jacob interrupted Annabella's rant. "How do you expect me to believe this? No such thing as dwarfs or nodums? How would I exist if there were no such thing? Have you gone mad?" Jacob questioned Annabella. He was visibly annoyed.

"I'm not crazy, Jacob. Please believe me. Why do you think I couldn't remember anything? The day we met was my first day here as Princess Annabella. Princess Annabella was here before, but the good witch told me that she is basically a reincarnation of me from a different dimension. In my world in my time, there was a big accident and my parents were killed," Annabella was crying and shaking. She desperately wanted Jacob to believe her and saying out loud made the pain from her parent's death even worse.

"They were killed and I was devastated. I have a storybook that I read all the time since my fifth birthday, and I was never able to sleep without reading it when I was little. The night that this happened I was so sad, but I couldn't sleep so I decided to read it. The good witch told me that my tears activated a spell that brought me here, inside of my storybook, to live as Princess Annabella. She also told me that I had to complete the story so I can go back to my own world, where things will be back to normal, including my parents being alive," Annabella said through her sobs.

Jacob grabbed onto both of Annabella's arms and looked right into her eyes. "The good witch?"

Annabella nodded. "Yes, she is a reincarnation of my grandmother. Her name is Caroline. Your father wasn't lying when he said he visited her. She is real and I woke up back in my bed the next morning," Annabella explained.

Jacob rubbed a hand over his face. "This is all too much to believe. I am real! How is this all a fairytale? I have been living here my entire life," he stated.

Annabella grabbed his hands. "I know you're real, Jacob. The storybook is just a story of real events that happened in the past in this dimension. Right now I'm in the past, which is your present. It's really complicated."

Jacob shook his head once again. "How would you have even gotten to the good witch without crossing the dark forest? Your instincts only kicked in today. You would have died within minutes," he said.

Annabella sighed once more. The tears were slowing down, so she tried to speak without her voice shaking. "A gryphon and an owl sent by the good witch came to me and brought me there safely. She's in a tree covered in moss and vines. She told me about everything and how it would be hard for me. I just need to be here until I am crowned queen, then the story will be over and the real Princess Annabella will be back and I'll be back in my own world."

"It is impossible" Jacob stated before getting up.

"You have to believe me, Jacob. You're the only person I've told. You're the only friend I have here and the only person I trust enough to keep this a secret. Please believe me," Annabella pleaded as she hugged Jacob hopefully.

Jacob hugged her back and sighed. "I wish I could believe you, but there is no proof," he said.

Annabella's eyes widened and she quickly ran to her nightstand. "I do have proof. You're going to have to look closely though," she said before placing her book in Jacob's hands.

"You have shown me this before," he said, confused.

Annabella nodded. "I have shown you, but you haven't opened it. Just read everything there is so far and you'll have to believe me."

Jacob set the book on the coffee table in front of him and opened it slowly. Annabella watched closely as he flipped the pages. About three pages in the words started to slowly and magically appear, displaying t exactly what had happened only hours before.

"It is talking about our fighting practice. It is saying what happened to you and your instincts. It even knows what I told you about the battle spells. How does it know?" Jacob was visibly confused as he sunk back into the sofa and rubbed his face.

Annabella sat in front of him on the ground and held his right hand. "I know it's a lot to take in, but this is my storybook. It is writing itself now as my story, but every few generations it erases itself and writes a new story for a new Princess. The good witch once had her own story written. My grandmother had this book before me when it was Caroline's story, and it magically changed to Princess Annabella's story when she was born. I just have to complete the story properly for me to go back," Annabella told Jacob softly.

"You want to go back to that cruel world? You said you were ugly. That cannot be possible if you look anything like yourself. Besides, your soul is beautiful. Your world must have made you feel that way. Why would you want to go back? Why are you talking in that way?" Jacob asked, confused.

Another tear fell from Annabella's face when she smiled. "So you believe me now? I only want to go back for my parents. I just want them to live so I can be with them again. If it weren't for them I would love to stay here forever. This world is so close to perfect. I actually feel pretty here," Annabella admitted quietly. "This is just the way we talk where I'm from. We combine and shorten the words for simplicity."

Jacob lightly cupped her face. "Listen to me, Annabella. If I were from your world, I would still think you are just as beautiful as you are now. You are the same person here as you are there. People must be idiots if they do not think you are the most beautiful person on the planet," Jacob said with so much power and honesty that Annabella believed it.

"Oh thank you, Jacob," she said before hugging him tightly. Annabella had never been complimented like that before.

"Is it certain that you will save your parents?" Jacob asked Annabella after a few minutes of silence.

Annabella frowned at the question. "When I was five and read the story for the first time, my best friend Zach read it with me and we both cried on the book, which did something magical. Caroline said that it might change the outcome so there is a chance that I won't be able to save my parents. She said that it will definitely be harder and it is impossible to know what might happen. I could even be trapped here forever. If that happens, I will still be myself and the future will still have to come, but when my parents have a baby, it won't be me since it'll have a different soul. I have no idea what's going to happen, but I'm willing to do my best if there's a chance I can save my parents," Annabella explained.

Jacob nodded. "I will help you to the best of my ability, on one condition of course," he said.

Annabella nodded, "Anything."

Jacob chuckled before explaining. "You need to go back to talking like I do. You sound very strange slurring the words together, almost like you are drunk."

Annabella laughed and wiped her face once more. "I am sorry about that. We say 'I'm' instead of 'I am' and 'they're' instead of 'they are'. I will go back to speaking this way though. I cannot let the others be suspicious or it could ruin everything. There is a chance that I have already ruined it."

Jacob was going to speak, but a dove flew into the room and dropped off a note on his lap before going to the windowsill.

"Your mother will be here in a half hour. I will try to process this to the best of my ability. But please do not hide anything else from me. It will be too difficult to understand what is happening. I promise I will not tell a soul about this."

Annabella nodded and smiled at him. "Thank you, Jacob. I really appreciate it." It felt as if a giant weight was lifted from her shoulders, but Annabella knew that she would need to be careful. *I can't risk not completing this story.*

"Jacob, time for you to go home. Annabella needs to get ready for dinner with her parents," Maria said from the door, surprising the pair.

Jacob put Smokey down in his playhouse and gave Annabella a hug. "I will be back tomorrow. Have a good night, Annabella," he said and winked at her without Maria seeing before he left the room to go to his home.

Annabella smiled at Maria before they made their way into the washroom.

I've never wanted a bath so badly in my life.

Chapter Twelve

As the days became shorter, the temperature became cooler. Three months had passed since Annabella's birthday ball and it was now the beginning of December. Snow had yet to fall, but the weather fairies had excitedly been telling everyone that it would be coming very soon.

"Excited for the snow?" Jacob asked from Annabella's balcony door. Annabella was leaning over the balcony railing, watching the rising sun. She quickly turned around and smiled.

"Why are you awake so early?" Jacob laughed.

"I want to enjoy as much of the day as I can, now that it is almost winter."

"I saw you from my window, so I decided to come up," Jacob explained before Smokey started rubbing against his leg.

"You have gotten bigger," Jacob said while picking up the purring cat.

Annabella nodded in agreement and scratched her cat's ears. "He has also gotten smarter. The poor messenger doves are terrified of him," Annabella said, which made Jacob laugh.

"I can only imagine."

Since both Jacob and Annabella were up early, they decided to have an early breakfast so they could enjoy the day outside. Jacob waited in Annabella's room and read through the magical storybook as Annabella had her bath. He was slightly annoyed that the book had skipped over many details, especially anything that he and Annabella did together, but understood that it would be impossible to fit everything in, especially when he wasn't the main focus of the story.

"Let us go outside," Annabella said as she walked back out to her balcony.

Annabella and Jacob joined arms and both used a bit of magic for the wind to make their jump smoother.

"I always find that so fun," Annabella admitted when she landed.

"It is quite fun, but sadly it would take way too much energy to make us go in the other direction," Jacob said and Annabella agreed. She had attempted it before and ended up stuck in a tree.

"Annabella! Annabella," a light blue fairy called from close by.

Annabella turned towards the noise and smiled at her. "Hello, Frost. How are you today?" she asked the fairy, who smiled excitedly.

"I am very happy today. There is going to be a huge snowfall in a few minutes so I have to tell everyone to get dressed. I hope you have fun," Frost said before flying away towards the village.

"Yes, it is finally going to snow. I have been waiting for this. We better go get jackets on." Annabella grabbed Jacob's hand and started running towards the castle, but he stopped her. Annabella looked up at him in question. Jacob laughed.

"I have not explained this to you yet, but royals, myself, and those with fire powers do not require jackets. Our magic keeps us from getting too cold," Jacob explained. Annabella was really surprised by this.

"So when it snows it will not freeze us?"

Jacob shook his head. "Not even one bit. We will feel it slightly colder than usual, but it will not be uncomfortable. In the summer when we felt it getting chilly, it was because it was not the proper season for it to be cold, but now it is the end of fall, so we will not feel much different from what we do now."

Annabella's smile only widened. "That is amazing. I always hated wearing so many layers and gloves. Should we wait out here or should we... snow!"

A snowflake landed on Annabella's nose and quickly evaporated into a poof of shimmer. Jacob and Annabella looked around and noticed just how fast the snow was coming down.

"There is already a thin layer covering everything here. No wonder why Frost was so excited about this," Annabella said before she grabbed Jacob's hand and started spinning around.

"What are you doing?" Jacob asked while he continued to spin.

"I want us to get dizzy so we can fall into it," she said as she continued to jump around. The snow was coming down so thick and fast that the castles fields were completely covered.

"I am already dizzy," Jacob yelled over the sound of the blizzard.

Annabella just laughed before letting go, making both fly backwards and fall into the fluffy snow "Woohoo, that was so fun," she yelled before getting up. Jacob got up himself and laughed before bending over.

"Get on my back, Annabella," Jacob yelled before Annabella laughed and jumped on. Jacob ran around as if she weighed nothing and spun around a few times before jumping into a huge pile of snow.

"This is amazing. Snow back home is so cold and gross. It all melts into water and is too soft to jump into or way too hard. This is perfect," Annabella explained while admiring the density of the snow.

She wasn't paying much attention to anything else when a soft snowball hit her back.

"Oh you are so on," she yelled at Jacob and made a ball of her own before throwing it, completely missing Jacob. It would be a challenging snowball fight with all of the thick snow falling from the sky, but it would be magical. Annabella managed to hit Jacob's arm with a snowball as he ran behind a tree. She ran towards the tree, but was surprised when he threw three of them at her, using his air powers to control where they flew.

"So you want to play it like that, eh?" Annabella smirked as her hands started to glow pink. Ten snowballs formed out of the falling snow and flew to where Jacob was hiding. Annabella laughed as she heard Jacob get hit by each one of them. She decided to quickly climb the tree with a bit of help from the wind.

"I want to do a slow motion jump into that big pile," she said when Jacob looked up at her in a confused way. He smiled at her idea and nodded. Annabella closed her eyes and spread her arms apart, feeling the tingling sensation in her hands before she jumped. Annabella opened her eyes after a few seconds, expecting to almost be at the ground, but much to her surprise was higher up in the air.

"What is this?" Annabella yelled to Jacob. She felt wind rushing around her in the form of a tornado, but she was basically floating inside of it.

"Annabella, try to get down safely. You are not ready for this type of power yet," Jacob yelled from his new position on the ground.

Annabella managed to lower herself, but kept flying around. "This feels great," she laughed and made herself do flips and turns. She even managed to make the snow around her create different shapes. Soon enough, she was beginning to feel drained as she lowered herself even more, not realizing that the tornado had disappeared until she felt herself falling. Jacob quickly ran underneath her and caught her in his arms just in time.

"Are you all right?" he asked, concerned. Annabella nodded before her eyes started to cross and blackness took over her.

"ANNABELLA? ANNABELLA!" Jacob rushed into the castle with Annabella in his arms. "I need the Princess's nurse immediately," he screamed as soon as he entered the castle, running towards the nurse's office. A tall, middle-aged woman ran out of the library after hearing Jacob's call. She ran towards Jacob and directed him into her room before putting on her glasses.

"Thank the heavens you are here. Annabella had a huge power burst today that drained her and caused her to black out," Jacob explained as he gently put Annabella on the bed. The nurse put on her stethoscope and a pair of rubber gloves.

"What type of power was it?" she asked Jacob as she listened to Annabella's heartbeat. Jacob thought back to the event and shook his head.

"I do not know. There was wind for sure, but she created some sort of snow cyclone that carried her around," he explained.

The nurse nodded. "Well her heartbeat is fine. She blacked out from draining her powers all at once. It must have overwhelmed her. I will give her some energy," the nurse said as she went into a cupboard and brought out a plant.

Jacob sat on a stool and didn't take his eyes off of Annabella. *Please be all right,* he thought nervously as he watched her motionless body.

The nurse set the plant down on the nightstand next to Annabella's head, before her hands started glowing. Jacob watched in amazement as he saw a transparent, shimmering golden aura leave the plant and disappear into Annabella's chest. The nurses hands turned into a dark purple colour as the plant started to come back to life.

"How did you do that?" Jacob asked her, completely bewildered at what had just happened. Annabella coughed a few times before slowly opening her eyes.

"Ah, you are awake. Let me formally introduce myself to both of you. My name is Emily. I may look like any normal human, but I am actually half human and half witch. The King hired me to be the family nurse after you were born. You never needed medical attention since you were a very young child, so that is why you are only meeting me now," the nurse explained.

Jacob shook his head. "Half witch? I did not know that those existed, but I suppose it makes sense since you have powers. May I ask what the glow was?" Jacob asked Emily.

Annabella patiently paid attention all while looking extremely confused.

"I was born with healing and land powers. The two work great together since I can heal people using only natural sources. What you saw was just a healing spell I used for the plant. Only I can create those plants. That is why the King hired me on the spot when I demonstrated how good they can be."

Jacob nodded and turned to Annabella "How are you feeling?" he asked her.

Annabella smiled softly at him. "I feel really tired and confused to be honest. What happened? The last thing I remember was me flying in a cool snow tornado and then I woke up here," she explained.

"You had a power blast, a very strong one at that. Even my powers are not strong enough to do that. It was incredible," Jacob said while going over to Annabella's side.

Annabella got up and faced Emily. "Thank you for your help, Emily. It is much appreciated," she said while shaking Emily's hand.

Emily smiled at her. "It was no problem at all, Princess. I will give Jacob a few vials of energy for the next time that this happens because it most likely will. I suggest power training from here on out. From what I have heard your powers are getting incredibly strong and you will need to learn how to keep them under control."

Annabella thanked Emily once again before Jacob helped her out of the nurse's room.

An hour had gone by since Jacob carried Annabella up to her room.

"I come bearing hot chocolate," Jacob announced from the doorway.

Annabella opened her eyes and sat upright on her sofa. "Thank you. Did you remember the marshmallows?"

Jacob laughed and nodded before taking a seat next to her. "I also stopped at the library to pick up a few advanced element books. You are definitely going to need them. Do not worry about reading them all at once, just practice some of the things in them on your own time," Jacob said as he set down three books on the table.

Annabella groaned. " I thought my month break from battle training would be fun. I guess not," she grumbled before taking a sip from her cup.

Jacob laughed. "You have a month break from training with me. You must still practice on your own if you ever want to use that awesome sword you are always eying."

Ever since the beginning of her training, Annabella was drawn towards a certain sword. Jacob said that he would eventually teach her how to use it, but she would have to learn how to use small knives, nunchucks, bows, and other weapons first.

"You will see. When you test me after the new year I will be ready for that sword," Annabella said and stuck out her tongue. Jacob smirked down at her.

"What?" Annabella asked him.

"You have a chocolate moustache," he said before wiping it.

Annabella scowled at him before crossing her arms. "Well, you have no moustache," she retorted in a childish tone.

Jacob chuckled at her before grinning once again. "That is because I am manly and I shave every day," he said while rubbing the stubble that was already showing.

"Well you... you... whatever," Annabella said in defeat as Jacob laughed at her. He smiled as his hands glowed blue. A small fire started to appear in front of Jacob and Annabella, floating in place.

"If I were not so drained I could do that," Annabella said before taking another sip of her hot chocolate.

"I know you could," replied Jacob. "Let us enjoy it while I still have energy. You are going to fall asleep soon, so I will just put you into bed and leave when you do," he said as Annabella snuggled into him for more comfort. Normally she wouldn't do this, but she figured she could get away with it because of what happened.

In a matter of minutes, Annabella was done with her drink and was beginning to drift off while enjoying the warm fire. She smiled at how conformable Jacob's arm, finally letting sleep overcome her. She was still conscious enough to feel Jacob carry her over to her bed and tuck her in. She could barely feel the kiss he gave her forehead before making all of the candles go out, leaving for his own room.

Chapter Thirteen

Christmas morning was absolutely stunning. Annabella woke up to the sound of bells jingling in the distance, and happy Christmas music playing. She quickly got dressed and had Maria put her hair in a bun so she could head over to the village.

"Merry Christmas," Jacob said as he opened the front door of his house.

Annabella jumped on him to give him a big hug. "Merry Christmas. It is so beautiful outside," she mused as Jacob laughed at her energy.

"It is quite lovely," Jacob agreed as he led Annabella inside. The pair sat on the sofa before Jacob made the fire bigger in the fireplace.

"Can I start?" Jacob asked enthusiastically as he rubbed his hands together.

Annabella giggled at his giddiness. "Of course you can."

Jacob reached over the side of the sofa and revealed a small cream coloured box, with a pink satin ribbon wrapped around it. Annabella reached out and gently unwrapped the pretty ribbon, before setting it aside and looking up at Jacob. He smiled at her and gave her a look for her to continue. She took a small breath before opening the box the rest of the way, gasping. Inside of the box was a beautiful white gold necklace, with a cute heart made of the same material. Annabella took the necklace out of the box and held the delicate chain in her hands, looking at it in amazement and familiarity.

"This is beautiful," Annabella said, still in disbelief in how familiar the necklace was to her.

"Here," Jacob said before skidding closer to her. "Let me put it on you." Jacob gently put the necklace around Annabella's neck, clasping the ends together. "I am glad you like it," he said gently, his breath lightly hitting Annabella's neck. Annabella quickly spun around, pushing away the tingling feeling inside of her and gave Jacob a big hug.

"I really love it. Thank you, Jacob. It is really beautiful. Now it is time for your present." Annabella quickly got up and ran towards the kitchen.

"What are you doing there?" Jacob called after her with a confused tone.

"I got your father to hide your present in here so it would not be obvious what it was." Jacob nodded in amusement as Annabella brought a huge box out.

"I really hope you like it," she said as Jacob began to open it. "But..," she interrupted quickly, which made Jacob look up. "... I hope you will not need to use it."

Jacob threw her a puzzled look that made Annabella laugh. As soon as Jacob moved all of the wrapping paper out of the way he froze for a few seconds, before slowly taking the beautiful sword out of the box, admiring it.

"How did you get this? This is so... powerful. Surely you did not simply purchase this."

"I did have to do quite a bit of research, and by that I mean reading and speaking to the King," Annabella admitted. "Since you have powers like I do, but are not from my royal family, my sword would not work for you like it would for me. It took a little while, but with help from many people, we managed to find this one. It is equivalent to my sword, but will only work with you now that you were the first to ever hold it. See, it is glowing the same colour as your aura now."

Jacob looked at the sword as he held it by the handle. It was, in fact, glowing his electric blue aura colour. "This is amazing. I can feel the power it yields," he said before carefully putting it in the scabbard that was already attached to the sash.

"I take it you like it?" Annabella said with a grin.

Jacob threw her a lazy smile before pulling her into a hug. "I absolutely love it. I also too hope I will not have a need for it, but it would surely be handy."

"ANNABELLA, YOU WILL make everyone else late if you do not hurry up," Maria squeaked from outside of the door.

Annabella quickly finished putting on her elbow-length gloves on, exiting her ensuite. "I think I am all ready now," Annabella said with a soft smile.

Maria quickly kissed both of her cheeks before rushing her out of the room. "All the guests have arrived already and are mingling with one another. I will be here all night if you need anything" she explained.

"Do not worry, Maria. Enjoy your night." Annabella wandered off into the main hall and welcomed various guests.

"Annabella," called a girl that looked around Annabella's age.

"Hello?" Annabella smiled awkwardly.

The girl stopped and flipped her white-blonde hair out of the way before she smiled up at Annabella. "You have not forgotten your beautiful cousin Claudia, have you?"

"Of course not," Annabella answered quickly. "How as your trip?"

"It was absolutely dreadful. It is freezing outside and I kept stressing about my skin getting dry. Thankfully my amazing genes would never let that happen," Claudia giggled. Annabella giggled along and faught rolling her eyes. She already wanted Claudia to leave.

"I am going to welcome the other guests. I hope you enjoy the party," Annabella said with a big smile that turned into a scowl as soon as she walked past Claudia. *Talk about a narcissistic Barbie wannabe.*

Annabella continued to welcome guests and receive compliments on her beautiful red dress that suited the event so well.

"Oh, Annabella, you look absolutely stunning," the Queen said as soon as Annabella came into view.

"Thank you, mother. You look very beautiful as well," Annabella said truthfully. The Queen smiled warmly at her before something caught her eye.

"Prince Jeremy. How wonderful it is to see you," the Queen said while motioning him towards them. Annabella quietly cursed before plastering a smile on her face.

"My my, Annabella. You look amazing," Prince Jeremy was smiling warmly at Annabella before he bowed for the Queen. "Pardon my manners, Your Majesty. You look marvellous as well." The Queen smiled at him.

"Thank you, Jeremy. You look very handsome. I will leave you two to catch up," the Queen smiled once more at Annabella, failing to see the worry in her eyes as she left the two alone. Jeremy stuck his arm out for Annabella to take. Annabella unwillingly took it and tried to hide the distaste from her expression.

"Let us watch the gift giving ceremony together," Jeremy announced instead of asking. Annabella smiled and nodded her head before walking with him towards the gigantic Christmas tree that was as tall as the ceiling.

"I gather everyone in The Land of Dreams and visitors here today for this wonderful celebration of Christmas. Here upon this table holds the gifts from my family to yours. I, from the bottom of my heart, sincerely hope you enjoy this magnificent day and your gifts," the King announced from in front of the table.

Children all over the room ran around in search of the gift designated for them. Annabella caught a glimpse of Jacob's siblings taking their presents from the table with huge smiles on their faces. They ran towards Maria and David and that's when Annabella saw Jacob for the first time since the morning.

Jacob was dressed in a nice suit and had a lovely red tie on that made him look extra dashing. He stood with his family, holding a glass of champagne in his left hand as he conversed with everyone. Annabella was analyzing David's suit, wondering if there was a store that sold nodum clothing items, since their legs were so long. It was then that Jacob made eye contact with her. Jacob smiled, but when Annabella waved, Jeremy came into view. Jacob quickly averted his eyes and continued talking to his family.

Jeremy looked down at Annabella in question. "I thought I saw someone wave at me, but I guess it was not meant for me." Jeremy didn't seem to care about what she was saying.

"How about you see my gift to you?" Jeremy put on his most charming smile it seemed.

Annabella nodded. "Is it on the table?"

Jeremy laughed. "Do not worry, my dear. I would not mix a gift to you with the gifts of those commoners."

What a jackass, Annabella thought to herself as she retained the urge to punch Jeremy's pretty face. She was a bit confused when he led her through the back doors of the castle. Of course he had to put his coat on, since his powers weren't as strong as Annabella's or her family, but he didn't seem to be as bothered by the cold as Claudia was earlier.

"Your gift is in here," Jeremy announced when they stopped in front of the stables.

"Is it that big?" she asked him in confusion. Jeremy only kept smiling until Annabella walked inside. At first Annabella saw the few horses she had already met, but when she turned her head to the left, she noticed a new and beautiful white horse.

"Oh wow, she is beautiful" Annabella announced as she approached the horse. However, when she got closer, she noticed something short and pointy emerging from the horse's head.

"You got me a unicorn?" she asked out loud. Jeremy chuckled and came to her side. "Oh my gosh. You got me a unicorn! That is absolutely amazing." Annabella was extremely excited and began patting the animal.

"Actually," Jeremy interrupted, "she is a horned pegasus. Elegant and powerful, just like you."

Annabella's mouth dropped open, but quickly closed back as she turned around to face Jeremy. "A horned pegasus? As in she will be growing wings?" Jeremy let out another chuckle and nodded. Annabella smiled at the pegasus and giggled when she let out a noise.

"She seems to already like you. My father's animal trainer has already trained her for battle. The only thing you would have to do is train on her so you two can get used to each other. This Pegasus has basically been made for you."

It amazed Annabella when Jeremy continued to explain everything about her new pet. Within the next few months to a year, the wings would show up and the horn would be fully-grown. Annabella would only need to get used to riding around on her and using her powers.

"Thank you so much, Jeremy. This is such an amazing gift. I hope that you enjoy your gift, but I know you will not like it as much as I liked this," Annabella told Jeremy with an honest smile for the first time.

Jeremy smiled back at her. "Do not worry, for the best gift is knowing that in less than a year we will be married. Anything you give me will be yours either way." Annabella hated hearing it, but felt glad that her story would be over before they got to any sharing.

"Let us go back inside," Annabella suggested after stroking the pegasus's head once more. Jeremy stuck his arm out for Annabella and the two walked back inside to the party.

AFTER DINNER, THE REAL party was starting. Annabella saw the musicians moving into the ballroom from the corner of her eye as she finished up her drink. Annabella wasn't quite used to drinking alcoholic beverages, but even though it was a magical land she knew, she was becoming tipsy. Jeremy spoke about wedding plans throughout the entire dinner. Annabella had no idea how many shades of beige there were before the conversation, and swore that she would never use them at her real wedding.

"I also think the china I gave you for your birthday would be just lovely if it were displayed in the main hallway. Do you agree, Annabella?"

Annabella quickly looked up, but wasn't paying any attention to what Jeremy had said. "Yes, I agree" she said, knowing that Jeremy was just talking about the wedding again. Annabella excused herself from the table once she was done. Luckily, Jeremy was so engrossed in wedding talk that he didn't even notice her leaving.

"Jacob," Annabella called out when she saw him walking out of the dining halls doors.

Jacob froze and turned around awkwardly. "Hi, Annabella. How was dinner?"

Annabella crossed her arms. "Why did you ignore me earlier?"

Jacob gulped and scratched his head. "I do not know what you are talking about."

Annabella slapped his arm. "Do not lie to me. You completely ignored me."

A sigh of defeat escaped Jacob's lips. "All right. I ignored you once I saw Prince Jeremy. I did not want to interrupt you two and frankly, I do not enjoy his presence."

Annabella frowned. "I do not enjoy his presence either, but at least you are not the one marrying him."

Jacob frowned, but let out a chuckle. "Yes, at least it is not I."

The two walked around and talked about the party. Annabella told Jacob what Jeremy had gifted her.

"Wow, that makes my present seem so dull." Annabella immediately stopped him and spun him around to face her. She pointed to her collarbone.

"Your gift wins any day. Sure, it is a pegasus, but you could have given me any rock off the ground and I would still love it more than any other gift."

Jacob smiled at Annabella when he saw she was telling the truth. "You know, it does really suit you," he said softly.

Annabella smiled and continued conversing with her best friend. An hour had passed before people began announcing that the final dances of the night were going to begin momentarily. Annabella knew she would have to at least dance with Jeremy for one song, so she began making her way towards the ballroom. Giggles coming from a room made Annabella stop in her tracks.

"It is a shame that I will not have a man as handsome as you to be my husband," Claudia's voice spoke.

Annabella stayed on the other side of the wall, trying to concentrate on what was being said.

"Do not worry, my dear. You are absolutely gorgeous, so I am sure you will marry someone handsome. Probably not as handsome as me because let us face it, I am perfect. But you are right. It is a big shame."

Annabella realized it was Jeremy in the room and decided to take a quick look. Claudia was pressed up against the wall and was playing with Jeremy's tie. "The nerve," she said before quickly making her way out of the room.

"Annabella." Annabella turned around to see Jeremy with his tie back in place as if nothing had happened. Claudia was out of sight.

"Yes?" she replied, trying her best not to sound angry. They were in the ballroom.

"I would love if you would give me the honour of having your last dance of the night."

I haven't even had my first, Annabella thought sourly. "I would love to, but I am beginning to feel ill. I think I am going to turn in early. Thank you again for the gift," she said before backing up towards the exit.

Jeremy had a confused expression on his face, but didn't question her before he went on to dance with random girls. Annabella nodded her head to Jacob before completely leaving the room and thankfully he took it as a sign to follow her.

"He what?" Jacob asked after Annabella explained what she had seen and heard.

"That is correct. He is just a lousy player, as you would call it where I come from. He is so full of himself and his looks. He is not even my type. All he cares about is how powerful he will be once we are married and that I live up to his expectations in the looks department," Annabella huffed.

Jacob chuckled. "No way. All of the girls here tonight were drooling over him and his 'luscious white hair' and his 'sparkling blue eyes.' There is no way you are not secretly lusting over him." Annabella scowled at Jacob.

"I admit, he is very attractive, but he is definitely not my type. I like guys with dark hair and eyes on the darker side. I do not care about the actual colour," she said before she felt her face heat up, realizing who she had described.

"Well, I am glad that I am so beautiful," Jacob teased.

"I did not mean it like that. I mean I did. I mean... yes you are incredibly attractive, but... now I... Jacob!" Annabella slapped his arm in the same spot as before when Jacob began laughing hysterically.

"Oh how I love it when I embarrass you," he said in between laughs.

Annabella pouted. "You suck."

Jacob only smirked at her. "You could never stay mad at me."

The sound of people walking made the two quickly took a step back, not realizing how close they were.

"The ball has ended. You should probably go upstairs before people see that you are not really sick. I will see you tomorrow," Jacob said before he gave Annabella a quick kiss on the cheek. Annabella threw a quick smile at him before disappearing to her bedroom.

Annabella was exhausted from her eventful day. She went on auto-pilot and got ready for bed. She was finally in her nightgown with her hair up in a ponytail, ready to sleep, when she noticed an envelope on her bed. Thinking it was a note from her parents or from one of the workers, she quickly opened it to find a long letter.

"Anonymous," Annabella read out loud before proceeding to read what information the letter held. Annabella couldn't even hear her own thoughts as she read. By the time she was completely done she was shaking in fear.

"Oh no," she mumbled under her breath before sticking the letter in her storybook, that now explained what had happened throughout the day in little detail. Annabella double-checked the locks on her windows before settling back into her bed.

"End of spring" Annabella snuggled into her pillow after she repeated the last words from her letter out loud to herself over and over again.

"War at the end of spring."

Chapter Fourteen

The dew in the early hours made the fresh grass glisten under the rays of the rising sun. Birds were happily flying around, singing of April's warm weather while watching the squirrels chase each other. It was quite a beautiful scene, but Annabella barely noticed any of it as she struck the fighting dummy once more.

Annabella's pegasus, who now shared the name Andromeda with the famous mythological creature, ate her morning meal several meters away from the scene. She was very fast and smooth as she landed hit after hit on the dummy that was looking very tattered.

"Whoa there..," Jacob said as he approached Annabella who quickly spun around in a defensive stance.

"Oh, it is just you. Good morning," Annabella greeted in a cheery tone.

Jacob laughed and gave her a hug. "Why are you training so hard? It is barely even spring yet."

Annabella shot Jacob a strange look. "No reason," she said quickly before putting her sword back into its scabbard. Annabella never used her powerful sword to train just because she had a tendency of becoming really focused and feared harming someone.

"Can you help me train on Andromeda today?" Annabella was giving Jacob the puppy eyes she used to make when she wanted something from her real father.

Jacob gave in seconds later when he let out a sigh. "Fine. I will just set her up and we can begin.

After two hours of riding around and hitting different targets, Annabella decided she was done for the day. Jacob had introduced her to a bow, which she learned how to use quickly. In the ninth grade, there was an archery section in gym class that Annabella had aced so it wasn't all that new to her.

"That was amazing. I never would have imagined that in your world you would have learned the art of archery," Jacob was always intrigued while learning things from Annabella's real life.

"It was the only section of that class that I enjoyed. I just need to get the hang of riding without holding on."

"You do not need to. I do not understand why you have been training so much these past few months. There is no need."

Annabella gulped slightly and hoped that Jacob wouldn't notice anything.

"Annabella, please tell me why you are acting so strange. You have been acting like this since the day after Christmas. Is it because of Prince Jeremy?"

Annabella quickly shook her head. "I am not acting strange. Nothing has happened. Please do not worry about it," Annabella said trying to sound calm and not desperate.

Jacob squinted his eyes as if he was thinking, but his facial expression quickly returned to being neutral. "If you say so," he mocked as they walked Andromeda back into the stables.

For the remainder of the day Jacob and Annabella decided to relax and played with the Smokey, the kitten, that Jacob gifted Annabella for her birthday.

"He has grown into a very smart cat," Jacob said as Smokey climbed up his pants to grab his toy.

Annabella giggled at the scene. "He has. I am just happy that he knows what bedtime means. He always wakes me up right on time every morning. I do not even miss my alarm clock." Jacob raised a brow at the last few words.

"Oh, sorry. An alarm clock is like a normal clock, except you can program it to ring at at whatever time you would like. It is just digital," Annabella explained.

"I see," said Jacob who was clearly still confused. The grandfather clock rang signalling that it was eight o'clock. Jacob put Smokey down and helped Annabella up.

"I must get going. Today I am eating dinner with my family. I had a lot of fun today. Would you be up to go riding just for fun tomorrow?"

Annabella didn't want to miss a second of training, but spending time with Jacob made her very happy.

It would also give my muscles more time to heal. "Of course. I will meet you at the stables in the morning at the same time as today. Have a great dinner and say hello to everyone for me," Annabella said before giving Jacob a big hug that he returned just as enthusiastically before leaving the palace.

Annabella decided that she would give herself a bath, but before she could make it to the tub, a strong feeling came over her.

The sounds around Annabella began to fade out along with her sight. She felt frozen inside of her own body before her head began to ache. Sounds of metal clashing came into her head. She heard grunts of men and noises that only a monster could make. She began to see men and familiar creatures fighting other creatures that were unmistakably evil. She couldn't say anything or move. She just watched helplessly as everyone fought around her. Annabella then noticed the King shouting orders before fighting a strange looking creature. She wanted to scream when she saw him killing the creature, but quickly noticed that it was evil when she saw the glow of its red eyes fading away.

Annabella suddenly jolted back to reality. She was lying on her bathroom floor drenched in her own sweat, once again able to see, hear and feel everything around her.

"Oh my God," she whispered as she quickly got up. "That was the war" she realized before she ran into the closet and began searching frantically for an emergency bag she had hidden behind her summer dresses. *I'm not going to let it get to that.*

Annabella returned to her room with a full backpack. She was fully dressed in her battle attire and her hair was pulled back into a French braid. She had snuck into the battle room and retrieved her special sword and shield, along with a few other weapons. On her bed lay a variety of knives, water canteens, and even bandages. She wrapped everything up and put them into the side pocket of her bag before she sat down at her desk. Annabella sat with her eyes closed for several moments, before finally taking out a piece of paper and a quill pen.

'Dear Jacob,' were the first words written on the paper. Annabella continued to write a very lengthy letter to him about how he shouldn't worry about her. She mentioned how much he meant to her and how much she loved him. The entire time she wrote to him she cried on the paper and smudged a few words. She never understood why whenever she cried, it would evaporate in a cloud of sparkling smoke, but she was so focused on writing that she didn't really notice. Annabella told Jacob that she was going after the good witch, but left out the reason why. She told him not to go after her and that she would be fine, saying she feared that something terrible would happen.

When Annabella completed the letter she called for a messenger dove, which quickly arrived at her window. "To Jacob, please," she asked the bird who nodded before it flew off towards the village.

Annabella quickly grabbed her backpack and ran to her outside porch, before jumping down with the help of her wind powers. After a few minutes, Annabella was on Andromeda and they were racing to the other end of the field towards the dark forest. The forest itself

was beautiful, but the air felt eerie, and Annabella could tell that Andromeda was feeling antsy.

Everything was silent at first, but the moment they passed the
protective barrier, Annabella sensed something and immediately
struck out, slashing a creepy looking creature that was about to attack
her.

"Gross," she said with a shudder as the creature fell to the ground.
It wasn't a big one, but it was certainly dangerous. "That wasn't so
bad." Annabella slowly rode deeper into the forest, killing several
similar creatures. She noticed that every time one died, the redness of
its eyes faded away. The further she went in the more creatures there
were. It was getting difficult to fight from on top of Andromeda, but
Annabella wasn't going to give up anytime soon. She slashed a few
more flying creatures, but before she could return her attention to
her surroundings, a big object flew towards her, knocking her off of
the pegasus. Annabella quickly got up on her feet despite the pain at
her side, looking around for what hit her. She was met with silence
before she heard leaves crumbling around her.

"Come out and fight," she screamed before a noise erupted from
a different direction.

She blocked a heavy rock that came flying from her left side before she met the eyes of a very tall monster. "An ogre," she breathed
out as she took in the height of the beast. His under bite held two
long canines that had drool dripping out from between them.
Annabella swung at the beast, who quickly took a step back before
hitting Annabella backwards into a tree. Annabella once again
quickly stood up, but felt very dizzy. She began feeling her adrenaline
building up, so she lashed out at the beast while taking many hits, but
wasn't able to stay uninjured before beheading the ogre.

Right after the ogre's headless body fell backwards into the trees,
Annabella fell to the ground and clutched the side of her head. She

had taken a big hit by a rock and her vision was beginning to blur. *I failed.*

Annabella looked at Andromeda apologetically before she was completely consumed by darkness, but not before feeling body being picked up and carried away. *I'm sorry mom and dad*, she thought to herself. *I'm sorry I couldn't save you.*

ANNABELLA SQUINTED as she woke up. Wherever she was sleeping was very dim and she wasn't alone, judging by the sound of rustling nearby. *Great. Some monster is saving me for dessert*, she thought sourly.

Annabella jumped slightly when she heard the sound of a horse, looking to her right to see Andromeda drinking water. Annabella was confused, but was extremely surprised to see that Andromeda now had wings sticking out of her back.

"And she is alive."

Annabella quickly turned her head around to only clutch it in pain. "Jacob?" she asked out loud before she looked at her hand to see blood on her fingertips. *What the hell is going on?*

"Yes, it is I. Do not worry, Annabella. I followed you into the forest and saw you kill the ogre." He sounded worried, but very angry. "Why would you ever go in there? I told you that it was dangerous Annabella. Why would you risk that? Why would you worry me so much?" Jacob was yelling, clutching Annabella with desperation.

"I'm sorry!" Annabella yelled back with a sob.

Jacob was taken aback and quickly loosened his grip on her shoulders, making her fall back.

"I did not want to worry you. I just wanted to say goodbye in case something happened," Annabella explained almost inaudibly.

"This does not make any sense. You have been acting strangely for such a long time, then I get a strange letter from you saying that you are going after the good witch. Did you want me to have a heart attack? When I saw you fall to the ground I thought I had lost you. If it were not for Andromeda getting her wings, we might not have made it back here alive."

Annabella continued to sob uncontrollably. Jacob quickly embraced her tightly and cried along with her.

"I am sorry for yelling at you and grabbing you. I could not help it. You could have died, Annabella. What would I do if you died? I would not be able to live with myself if I was not able to get you out of there in time," Jacob admitted. "I would be nothing without you," he whispered and looked down in sadness.

"I just wanted to keep you safe," Annabella said quietly. "I have been hiding something from you and everyone else. It is the reason that I was acting strange and went into the dark forest."

Jacob sighed. "Can you please tell me now? I really cannot handle almost losing you again. You have no idea how scared I was back there."

Annabella felt a pang in her heart before taking in a deep breath. "There is going to be a war."

Jacob sat up. "A war? Here?"

Annabella nodded her head slowly to prevent herself from becoming dizzy again. "When I went to bed on Christmas, I found a letter explaining that there would be a war at the end of spring. It was anonymous, but I just know it has to do with the dark forest. Today after you left I had a vision about the war. I do not know why, but I will send it to you." Annabella focused as she let Jacob enter into her mind. She replayed the entire vision as Jacob watched.

"Oh my. That is really bad. Why would you hide this from everyone else and I? You cannot protect this entire Kingdom on your own, Annabella."

Annabella put her head down in shame. "I know. It was foolish of me. I thought I could put an end to this before it truly started. I did not want to risk making the wrong decision in case it was related to the curse. I cannot believe how stupid I was." Another tear streamed down her face, but before it could fall Jacob wiped it away with his thumb.

"You are not stupid. You just acted on your instincts. It is in your blood. I just wish you had told me earlier," Jacob corrected her.

Annabella nodded slowly before softly touching the side of her head once more.

"One second," Jacob said before he got up to fetch a damp cloth. He lightly pressed it against Annabella's wound several times to get rid of the blood.

"You heal fast," he stated as he observed her head.

"That is good," Annabella said with a small smile. *At least something is good.*

"Let us get you into bed. I will stay with you for the night in case anything happens," Jacob said before picking up Annabella and quietly carrying her into the castle so no one would hear.

When Annabella was finally in her bed after having her head patched up by Jacob, he knelt down and faced her. "I want to ask you a serious question."

Annabella lazily nodded and looked at him.

"May I inform the King about this war? I promise to keep this a secret, but I think it would be best in terms of us having a chance to win."

Annabella was feeling uncertain, but she nodded once again. There was something about Jacob that made her feel at ease. She trusted him with her life.

"Thank you. I know this seems hard, but letting him know will only make things easier. Perhaps it is what you are supposed to do. I will sleep on the sofa. Please wake me up if anything happens or if you feel ill," Jacob said as he started to walk away.

Annabella quickly grabbed his hand. "Please stay here. I do not mind. I just do not want to be alone," she said with fear.

Jacob seemed apprehensive, but smiled before lying down on the bed.

Annabella quickly snuggled into him, not caring about what anyone would think if they were to walk in. "Thank you for saving me tonight, Jacob," she said sincerely before letting out a yawn. "I really did mean everything I said in that letter," she said as she dozed off.

Jacob smiled at her sadly before pecking her softly on the cheek.

"That would make me the happiest man in the realm," he replied quietly, Annabella already fast asleep.

Chapter Fifteen

It was an unusually gloomy day in the Land of Dreams as Jacob walked across the main hall and towards the King, who sat in his throne with a very serious expression painted on his face. Jacob's nerves were causing little beads of sweat to form on his forehead and the back of his neck.

"Your Majesty," Jacob said as he bowed down before the King.

"Hello, Jacob. I have received your letter. I have gathered some of my most trustworthy knights in the meeting room. Shall we be on our way?"

Jacob nodded as the King stood up. Both men made their way into a room towards the back of the hall. Jacob recognized this room from when he was recruited to be Annabella's protector. The door had heavy chains around it that could only be opened by the King himself. The walls were completely soundproof so no one could spy from the outside. The mood became somber when Jacob set foot in the room. The King motioned towards a chair next to his own. Jacob nodded and sat down as he analyzed his fellow knights sitting around the large table.

"Fellow knights, we have all been gathered here today for a serious matter. My daughter, Annabella, has received a threatening letter a while back. Jacob has been told of a vision that Annabella received and is here to help us come up with a plan."

Chatter broke out within the room. All of the men had surprised expressions on their faces. It wasn't a surprise to Jacob, the Land of

Dreams was known as very peaceful. A war was the last thing anybody was expecting.

"Do you have the letter with you, son?" the King questioned after the ruckus calmed down. Jacob nodded and took the letter out of his pocket and handed it to the King. The King unfolded the letter before setting it down in front of him on the table. The King read it to himself. "It looks like we are going to war with the dark forest at the end of spring."

"Why is there a war?" a voice chimed in.

"The end of spring?" announced another.

"The forest?" a third joined in.

"That is too soon," another declared.

"Who would want war against our land?" a final voice spoke.

The King looked up slowly from the letter before a flame emitted from his hands. Everyone was stunned into silence at the sudden outburst. The King slowly stalked towards the window with his hands behind his back and looked up at the stormy clouds.

"The warlock."

Jacob abruptly stood up from his seat. "It cannot be. Why would the warlock want to take our land and Princess Annabella?"

The King chuckled in a non-humorous manner. "The warlock does not care about this land. He only cares about Annabella. He cares for her powers. He has no fear, which is why he announced when it will happen."

Jacob's fists clenched at his sides as he began to breathe deeply. "Are you sure he only wants her?"

The King nodded solemnly before resting his hand on Jacob's shoulder. "I am entirely sure of it. Annabella's powers are increasing quickly every day. She could end up being more powerful than the warlock himself, which would make her the most powerful being to walk these lands."

"What if we got help from the good witch?" Jacob questioned.

Several knights looked at him with quizzical expressions.

"She is but a myth. I have never seen her nor have any of my men." explained the King.

Jacob shook his head. "I know it seems crazy, but many claim to have seen her."

One of the knights cut in. "Those are foolish tales."

The King nodded his head, but looked uncertain.

Jacob frowned and shook his head once again. "How would we know? The warlock seems to be real so why not the good witch? Many have claimed visiting her to find their soulmates."

The King sighed. "The dark forest is dark for a reason. The warlock created many monsters that roam around. If the good witch were real do you not think that she would have done something by now? If she really is on the other side of the forest, why has she not sent a sign?"

Jacob closed his mouth. *Had Annabella been wrong? Had she dreamt about the whole thing?* He was beginning to believe that the King could be right. Maybe the good witch was just a tale.

"Maybe she has a good reason. Maybe she is not real. We can never know for sure and there is no time to figure everything out," Jacob said before sitting back down. *The witch has to be real. How could Annabella's storybook be as accurate if she was not? I cannot tell the King. It could ruin Annabella's life.*

The King, Jacob, and all of the knights began to form a plan. They had all decided that neighbouring lands would be contacted to help that same day. The knights were to begin training again and would recruit villagers who wanted to volunteer. They planned on how to protect the villagers and decided on using the castle during the war.

"All right men, you may all go. I will write letters to our neighbouring lands."

The knights, including Jacob, all got up and began to leave, but the King held Jacob back.

"I wanted to tell you something that the other knights do not know about the warlock."

Jacob nodded so the King would carry on.

"He is responsible for my parent's death. He also murdered my grandparents, but that was centuries ago when I was but a child."

Jacob looked down. "I am very sorry to hear that, Your Majesty," he told the King sincerely.

"It was a very long time ago. The wounds from within have healed and stayed in the past. This situation is to be taken very seriously. The warlock is more powerful than you could ever imagine. I do not want my daughter, you, nor my land to suffer."

Jacob nodded at the King. "I understand. I will do my very best," he promised before bowing once more and leaving the room as the King began to write to the neighbouring lands.

ANNABELLA HAD BEEN nervous all morning. All she had done was get ready and take care of Smokey. She knew the meeting would take a while, so she decided to talk a walk around the castle. Annabella walked around for an entire hour before she got a letter from Jacob.

Annabella, the King has come up with a plan, but unfortunately I must work all day so I shall see you tomorrow. I am very sorry I did not tell you in person, but I have been working hard ever since I have arrived at my home. Try not to worry too much and enjoy your day.

"Great," Annabella sighed. She began walking back towards her tower when she decided to walk into the main hall to pay the King a visit. Surely he would say something about the meeting. Annabella walked towards the meeting room that was unlocked, but didn't open the door when she heard the King reading a letter out loud.

"We would love to help your land in the war, but the betrothal must be signed between Princess Annabella and Prince Jeremy. He is on his way as you read this with the papers. I hope all is well and I shall see you in a few weeks."

Annabella felt as if the air had been stolen from her lungs. *Betrothal...* The doors suddenly swung open.

"Oh, it is you, my dear Annabella. I was afraid it was a spy," the King said, relieved by the truth.

"Betrothal," Annabella whispered.

The King's face slowly fell. "Yes, Annabella. You were to marry him either way. This is just a promise that you will marry him after your eighteenth birthday."

Annabella shook her head. "Why so soon? Can I not wait a few years?"

The King shook his head. "We need all of the help that we can get with this war. It is either this, or risk losing everything and maybe even everyone you love."

My parents, Annabella thought. "I understand," she forced herself to say as sweetly as she possibly could. She knew this was supposed to happen in the story, but hearing it become official was not to her liking.

The King smiled brightly and pulled her into a hug. "My wonderful daughter, do not fear marriage. Prince Jeremy is a wonderful young man," he said.

Annabella almost snorted at the thought. *Prince Jeremy wonderful? I'd rather marry a rat.*

"Now," said the King after breaking the hug. "Why do you not take the day to relax? Prince Jeremy will be here in a few hours and I am sure that he would love to spend some time with you."

Annabella nodded and smiled at the King, before making her way back to her room.

"Oh Smokey," she said when the kitten looked up at her from his playhouse. "What am I to do?" Annabella took her storybook from under the pillow and watched as the new words formed on the page.

'The King held a meeting to prepare for the war,' were the only things that were written on the page. The book said nothing about betrothals or Jeremy visiting.

"How will this ever make sense to me if so many details are left out?" Annabella was about to close the book when a few more sentences appeared on the page that made her eyes widen.

The warlock is behind this all? I must destroy him to win this battle.

"PRINCESS ANNABELLA. Looking beautiful as usual," Prince Jeremy said before kissing the back of her hand.

Annabella forced a smile at the beautiful, yet hideous man. "It is very lovely to see you as well, Prince Jeremy."

"Of course it is," he said with a cocky smile that Annabella wanted to wipe off so badly with a swift kick to the face. "I will be leaving later tonight, but I wanted to spend my time here with you. Would you like to go to a restaurant with me?" Jeremy asked.

Annabella wanted to pretend that she was feeling ill, but knew what had to be done.

"That sounds lovely, Jeremy. What time shall we leave?"

Prince Jeremy smirked. "I am ready now and you look acceptable. Let us go at this very moment," he declared before taking Annabella's hand and walking outside of the castle.

Annabella walked quickly to keep up with his pace. *He could at least loosen the grip on my hand,* she thought bitterly as the approached the chariot.

As usual, Prince Jeremy spent the entire time talking about himself and what Annabella should do for the wedding. "Our first child shall be named after myself. I am sure that it would be a great honour to him when he is growing up," Prince Jeremy declared.

"What happens if the first is a girl?" Annabella questioned.

"Oh heaven forbid it." Jeremy looked shocked. "The first child must be a boy if we want them to be a good leader one day."

Annabella scowled. "A female can lead just as well," she added.

Prince Jeremy snorted. "You are quite the joker, Annabella. Do not worry about it. I am sure that it will be a boy. I could not produce anything lesser," he said proudly.

Annabella bit her tongue to keep herself from retaliating. *This dickwad sure is talented at offending people.*

They ate at the same restaurant that Annabella and Jacob had eaten months earlier. Jeremy was extremely rude and didn't let Annabella choose the meal that she wanted because,

"That food was made for the peasants. We shall eat like the royals we are." Jeremy then proceeded to order caviar.

I hate caviar, Annabella thought to herself when the waiter walked away.

The rest of the dinner consisted of Annabella forcing the caviar down her throat without making a face. Jeremy didn't notice her discomfort because he was so busy talking about his "amazing genes" and how their children would be beautiful, but they would never surpass his looks. When they left the restaurant, Annabella thanked the workers.

Jeremy quickly dragged her away. "Do not pay attention to those people. They are nothing but commoners doing their jobs."

Annabella was livid by this point. "They are my friends, Jeremy. I quite enjoy their presence."

Jeremy once again scoffed. "You are much too kind, Annabella. You will make a good queen to the people, but this is why the king is in charge. We cannot let the people of our lands feel like they have more rights. If they become accustomed to kindness from the royals, they will begin to feel like they have power or even worse, feel like they are equal."

Annabella shook her head in dismay. *Thank God I can just go back home after marrying this idiot*, she thought to herself as she walked with her arms crossed below her chest. She didn't realize that it was making her cleavage more prominent.

"Oh, Annabella," Jeremy said dreamily with a look that Annabella didn't recognize. "Sometimes you make me go mad," Jeremy said before squeezing her butt.

"Ow." Annabella instinctively slapped Jeremy's arm with a bit too much force that knocked him back a bit. "Do not dare touch me like that without my consent," she yelled at him, feeling very uncomfortable.

Jeremy looked very angry as he walked back towards Annabella. He grabbed her arm very tightly and held her in place. "You do not dare tell me what I can and cannot do," he hissed. "I am the man in the relationship and you will listen to me."

Annabella was frightened. She did not think that Jeremy would ever yell at her in that way. Her arm was beginning to hurt as his nails dug into her skin.

"You are hurting my arm," Annabella exclaimed before Jeremy let go.

"The papers are signed. You must respect me as your husband," he said as he began walking towards the chariot with Annabella's arm linked to his.

Annabella felt tears threatening to spill out of her eyes. She had never been handled in such a manner before. She had never felt so small. She looked at her arm that was beginning to bruise. A mark from Jeremy's nails was very noticeable she would have to cover until it fully healed.

Just a few more months before this is all over and I can go back to my old life.

Chapter Sixteen

A few weeks had passed since the incident with Jeremy. Annabella considering telling the Queen or King many times, but she couldn't risk her parents' lives because of something so small. Jacob had hugged her the day after her dinner with Jeremy, questioning why her arm was in pain, but she simply lied saying that she fell off of her bed. Of course he didn't believe her, but she made him promise that he would never bring it up again. Later that day, Annabella snuck into the infirmary and used magic to heal her arm of any marks.

Annabella awoke one morning not long after, in a bed that was not her own. Frightened at first, Annabella quickly sat up, but the Queen explained to Annabella that the first set of tests had to be done during her sleep.

"I do not see why you could not have told me this before," Annabella complained.

"I am sorry, Annabella. Your dreams could have reminded you and the tests would not have been as accurate. We must continue testing you on your strength, agility and magic today," the Queen explained after giving Annabella a hug.

"Why am I being tested anyway?" Annabella was very confused at what was going on. A sad look flashed across the Queen's face.

"It is to ensure that you will be safe," Jacob's voice sounded from the door.

Annabella then understood why. The war would be coming soon and she was in the most danger.

"Let us get some food into you so we can continue with the tests," the Queen said as she got up from the bed.

Annabella forced a smile and nodded. "Will Jacob be joining us?"

Jacob nodded. "Of course. I will be helping you with the tests."

When the Queen, Annabella, and Jacob entered the dining hall, Annabella was relieved to see that Jeremy and his father had already eaten and were gone. They had returned earlier in the week and Annabella avoided them like the plague.

"What a shame that Jeremy is not here. He would have loved to watch your testing."

Annabella looked up at the Queen. "He is not here?"

The Queen shook her head. "Jeremy and his father had to run some errands for the day, but will be back in the afternoon."

Annabella sighed internally, relieved that she would not have to deal with him for a few hours. "Let us eat so we can get this done faster," she said quickly before sitting in her usual spot with Jacob beside her.

When Annabella walked into the training room she was met with a strange arrangement. Many knights stood along the wall with notebooks in hand. The King was sitting in a fancy chair that resembled his throne at the far side of the room.

"All right, we will begin with tests of strength," the King announced, which made a few knights emerge from a room with various objects that were all labeled with different numbers. Annabella was beginning to feel nervous of being tested in front of so many people, but having Jacob guide her along made her feel a bit better.

"Go," the King shouted before many of the objects were thrown at Annabella. Even though she was taken by surprise, Annabella managed to deflect the objects before they could harm her.

"Impressive. Now for the more difficult test... Run." Knights of all sizes ran at Annabella. She tackled most of them with much skill, but when they outnumbered her she was on the ground beneath them. A look of disappointment appeared on the King and Queen's faces, but someone gasped. Annabella was able to get out from under the pile of knights without the use of magic.

The King continued to test Annabella's physical strength in many ways. She was tested on her speed, which consisted on many of the knights chasing after her with many obstacles placed in the room which required her to skillfully dodge them. By the end of it, all of the knights were on the ground desperately gasping for air, as Annabella stood nearby with her arms crossed, looking as if she had just been sitting around all day.

"Are we done yet?" she questioned as she made eye contact with the King.

"Well... I uh... we have one more test," the King explained warily.

Annabella noted the strange undertone of his voice, as well as everyone in the room appearing surprised. Jacob, who didn't look nearly as surprised as everyone else, had not joined in the agility challenge since he needed the energy for the magic testing.

"Moving on to the magic testing," announced the King. Everyone moved outside into the back field that had been cleared so nothing would be ruined. "We will start with a land spell. Annabella, I would like you to use the land around you to trap Jacob in the air so that he cannot attack you."

Annabella nodded and Jacob ran at her with a sword. She quickly acted on her instincts as she connected with the land around her. The grass suddenly grew and wrapped around Jacob's feet, making him fall. Jacob began to use his own land magic, but the grass grew to twenty feet, bringing Jacob along and wrapping around his arms.

Annabella heard the Queen gasp and looked her way to see that everyone was shocked. The King motioned for the knights to run at Annabella, but one by one she repeated the same spell, and in about thirty seconds all twelve knights, including Jacob, were tangled in the grass high up in the air.

"How am I doing this?" Annabella questioned loudly. She was both surprised and terrified.

The Queen and King exchanged a look and made their way over to Annabella. "The fact that you are holding the spell without even trying means that your powers have grown immensely," the King explained.

The Queen nodded. "Last time you did a similar spell it was with snow, an easier element to deal with, but then you were not able to hold onto it for a short amount of time before fainting. Are you not feeling the least bit ill?" The Queen was worried and held the back of her hand on Annabella's forehead.

Annabella shook her head. "No, mother. I feel fine," she said, confused.

When the King motioned towards the grass, Annabella made all twelve men come down safely by unraveling the grass and using the air element to float them all down at once.

"Well that takes care of land and air. Now we must test your fire and water abilities," the King announced before leading Annabella towards a big pool of water for the testing to commence.

EVERYONE LEFT ANNABELLA and Jacob alone once the testing came to an end. They were all going to discuss Annabella's process and what would be done for the war. Annabella and Jacob stood in the middle of the battle hall once again.

"I cannot believe this," Annabella said in shock.

Jacob smiled at her and placed a hand on her shoulder. "I can. I always knew you were a very strong woman. It makes me happy to know that you can now defend yourself against many things."

Annabella walked over to her weapons. "Could we train a bit? Eleven knights all trying to fight me at once was one thing, but you are much more skilled," Annabella admitted.

Jacob nodded with a chuckle. "Of course we can. Let us use the rubber weapons," he said before making his way to the cabinet where all of the safety weapons lay.

"How am I not tired?" Annabella questioned.

Jacob turned around and made a noise of confusion. "I really have no idea. I believe it is because you were expecting all of those things and were not as stressed. You may feel tired in a real battle with all of the surprises you could encounter, and from being worried about our people."

Annabella nodded as she took her bow and a few arrows with rubber tips. Jacob grabbed a range of small rubber weapons that he would use to throw at Annabella. When the two started training, Annabella dodged a bunch of fake spears being thrown in her direction. She even managed to catch a few before they made contact with her body. When Jacob went to run behind an obstacle so he could reload one of his weapons, Annabella used the opportunity and shot a rubber arrow at his behind.

"Hey," Jacob yelled. "Keep away from this beautiful bottom. I need it for the ladies."

Annabella burst into laughter. "Ladies? I never knew such a species would be attracted to you," she joked. As she was laughing hysterically, Jacob used a wind spell that quickly transported him behind Annabella. Jacob grabbed her arms and pinned her down on the ground in a position that she could not escape without a spell.

"The women love me," he informed Annabella before he began tickling her sides.

"Stop! You know how ticklish I am. I highly doubt an ugly ogre is going to use that against me in battle," she choked out as she continued to giggle.

Jacob smirked at her. "Ogres may be ugly, but you never know what strategy they will use."

After a several minutes the two decided to give up on battle practice. Jacob lay down next to Annabella and enjoyed the silence.

"Can I ask you something serious?" Annabella asked after a few minutes.

Jacob turned to face her and nodded. "Of course you can, Annabella."

Annabella smiled, but her face returned to a serious one. "Are they going to allow me to fight in the war, or will they keep me trapped inside of the main dungeon room? I know that the war is because of me and to win I need to be alive, but I really cannot stand it if all of my friends are fighting and in danger while I am safe inside."

Jacob frowned at her. "I really do not know. I believe that is something your parents are discussing at the moment. With all of your newfound power they may let you battle, but they may also want you to protect yourself if we lose."

Annabella quickly sat up. "You cannot lose. If you lose that means you die and I cannot lose you," Annabella said on the verge of tears.

Jacob sat up and brushed his right hand on Annabella's cheek to calm her down. "Do not worry, Annabella. We will not lose. I will not let us lose. I can not imagine what would happen if the warlock were to take possession of you."

Annabella nodded and lay down once more as Jacob's hand continued brushing her cheek. They were lying down so close to each other. Their faces were only a few centimetres apart.

When Annabella felt Jacob's other hand brush her face, it began to heat up, but she didn't look away.

"Annabella, there is something that I have been wanting to tell you for a while now," Jacob began.

Annabella felt her heart beat faster and butterflies in her stomach. Both Jacob and Annabella began to lean forward. "You can tell me anything" she said with a smile.

Jacob smiled at her and his expression became more serious.

He's going to kiss me. I can't believe it. He's really going to do it, Annabella thought in her head as they almost reached each other's lips, but the sound of someone stomping away made them both jump slightly.

Jeremy angrily walking out of the battle hall had ruined the moment. Annabella and Jacob exchanged a quick glance before they quickly got up from the floor. "Looks like Jeremy is back," Annabella said sourly.

Jacob scowled. "I guess this means we should get going. The meeting will be done soon and they will be announcing what will happen. I will go shower now," Jacob said before leaving the room quickly.

Once Jacob out of the room Annabella groaned. *God damn it. Why did Jeremy have to ruin the moment. Can't I just enjoy one moment with someone that actually cares about me?* She frowned. *Jacob probably doesn't like me that way though. It was just the moment. It would have just ruined things between us anyway,* she thought sadly before making her way towards her tower.

After giving herself her own bath and putting on a dress, Annabella was called down to discuss everything with the royal council. She walked into the main hall and sat beside the Queen at the long table. Jacob was sitting with the eleven main knights and Jeremy was with his father. The King cleared his throat before he began speaking.

"Today we tested my daughter, Annabella on her fighting, agility, and magic skills. To say the least we were all very surprised at how much power she holds. According to my records Annabella is the most powerful of us all."

Annabella gasped and looked at the King, but didn't say anything.

"She can successfully fight with great reflexes and her powers have grown immensely with control. Before the tests, the plan was to keep Annabella safe in the dungeons, but I fear if something bad were to happen that she would become too concerned to handle a bad situation while blaming herself. Annabella," the King then said, looking right at Annabella. "How would you feel about joining us all in the battle?"

All eyes were on Annabella. She looked around the room and took a few breaths.

"I was hoping that you would ask that. I am prepared for this war and will not stand by and see my loved ones suffer. I will do anything to ensure that we win," Annabella announced.

The Queen smiled warily from beside Annabella, but joined in with the clapping that began. The King smiled and began speaking once again when the room was quiet.

"The village is aware about the war and those who do not wish to fight will be staying in the castle's dungeons as protection. All children and their mothers will be staying in the safest room, which was previously meant for Annabella. We must remember to hold on to our love and honour in this war."

Once the meeting was over Annabella waited outside for Jacob to emerge. "Well that went well," she said with a smile.

Jacob chuckled at how happy she was to go to war. "You know," he began, "most people would not be excited for battle. You are quite a unique one." Jacob was going to say something else, but he was interrupted.

"Ah, just the commoner I was looking for," Jeremy said from behind Annabella.

"Huh?" Jacob looked at him in confusion.

"Do not play dumb with me, commoner. You know very well why I wish to speak with you."

Annabella bit her lip and tried to drag Jacob away, but he wouldn't budge.

"I want you to stay away from my wife-to-be. She does not need you now that I am here. Why would she choose spending time with a mere commoner like you instead of a powerful royal such as myself?" Jeremy had a smirk on his face as soon as he noticed that everyone was now watching and listening.

"You may be royal, but at least I know how to respect a woman," Jacob said back with a smile.

Jeremy scowled and pushed Jacob back.

"Enough," boomed the King. "There will be no unnecessary fighting."

Jeremy smiled slyly. "What about fencing?" he suggested.

Jacob nodded. "Sounds good to me."

Jeremy laughed before his expression returned to annoyance. "You cannot beat a royal fencer such as myself. A simple peasant as yourself could only dream of it."

The room gasped.

Jacob's smile didn't falter at all. "We shall see," is all he said before he made his way towards the battle room.

Annabella quickly followed along with the rest of the room. "Father, you cannot let this happen," she pleaded, but the King only smiled.

"This is the best way to settle an argument. It is to maintain their honour," explained the Queen.

Annabella turned to face Jacob and Jeremy as they began putting on the fencing gear, including their masks. Annabella could still tell who was whom when they were both completely dressed. Jacob's body was much more muscular and his shoulders, as well as the rest of his structure, was broader. He was also a bit taller than Jeremy.

A knight pressed the timer and the battle began. The battle started off slow and peacefully. As the time went on Annabella began feeling anxious. Jeremy was a lot better than she expected at fencing.

"Father, is Jeremy a professional fencer?" Annabella asked the King.

"He is. He has never once lost a battle against any competitor, including ones from other lands."

Annabella's breathing quickened as the battle suddenly sped up. After a few minutes Jacob was beginning to slow down. Jeremy's fencing skills were unbelievable.

Jeremy can't win. Annabella thought to herself before Jeremy almost got a strike on Jacob. Annabella decided to try sending encouraging thoughts to Jacob, including memories of their fun times together. She hoped they were close enough for it to work. *You can do this, Jacob.*

Jacob suddenly started to speed up and fight back harder. The room went completely silent the second that his sword made contact with Jeremy's chest. Jacob took off his mask and wiped the sweat off of his forehead.

Jeremy stood there, stunned at what had just happened. Jacob stepped back and put the fencing sword in the scabbard, sticking out his right hand for Jeremy to shake. Jeremy looked at Jacob's hand and ignored it. He walked by him, pushing Jacob out of the way before walking out of the room.

Annabella looked around before she started cheering. "Yeah, Jacob! You did a great job."

All eleven knights joined in and soon everyone in the room, including Jeremy's father, was clapping. Annabella ran up to Jacob and gave him a big hug.

"Thank you for beating him," she murmured into his chest.

Jacob chuckled and hugged her back. "You are very welcome. How did I even beat him?"

Annabella laughed. "I have no idea, but you did and that is all that matters."

Jacob's fellow knights all came up to pat him on the back and congratulate him. Annabella waved goodbye from the doorway before going back to her room for the night.

"OH SMOKEY," ANNABELLA said as she picked up her kitten. "You've have grown so much. Jacob's sisters will take care of you during the war. I'll make sure you have enough kitty food," Annabella spoke. She enjoyed speaking with Smokey when she was alone, because she didn't need to watch her contractions.

When Annabella walked out of her washroom with only a nightgown on, sirens began to play. Annabella quickly put on a robe, grabbed Smokey, and ran downstairs to the main hall.

"What is going on?" she questioned to one of the guards.

"It is the siren announcing the war. The King has received another letter. The battle begins tomorrow morning," he explained.

Annabella looked around and ran towards Jacob who was with his parents.

"Maria, I am sure you have already sent for your sister and children. I will ensure that they are safe for tomorrow and with you. Would it be all right for you to look after Smokey during the war? I have a bag with enough food for the next month and your water powers are enough to keep him hydrated."

Maria nodded and took the kitten. "I will bring him to our chamber now. Everything is in order. Please be careful, Annabella. Please stay safe and fight with Jacob. You two can do anything if you work together," Maria said with a look of sadness.

Annabella began to tear up and hugged Maria. "I will do everything that I can to make sure Jacob is safe, just like he has done for me. Do not worry. You will see us both again once we win," Annabella said before looking up at David. "Are you sure you want to help in battle?"

David nodded at her with a smile. "I will do everything to protect this land. I love my life here and I want my children to grow up in the same situation that I did. I will see you in the morning," he said before giving Annabella a hug.

Annabella finally turned to Jacob who nodded at her. She smiled and gave him a big hug. "I will see you in the morning. I am just going to sleep now so I can get as much rest as possible and I will meet you at 6 o'clock sharp," she said before squeezing his hand.

Jacob sent her one last smile and wink before walking in the direction of the dungeons with his mother.

After Annabella had Smokey's things brought down, and had everything important locked away, she drank a bit of tea that would help her fall asleep quickly.

I'll do whatever I can to protect everyone. Even if I have to go after the warlock myself, Annabella promised herself as she drifted into a deep sleep.

Chapter Seventeen

The moment the birds began chirping, Annabella shot out of bed and ran to the bathroom to wash her face. It was five o'clock in the morning, which had given her plenty of sleep. She opened her storybook in the hope that something new would show up to help her, but only part of the events from the night before were written on the pages.

In record time, Annabella was bathed and dressed in her battle gear. She had finally figured out how to do a proper French braid on herself, which would keep the hair out of her face. She took off the necklace that Jacob had given her and put it in a secret pocket inside of her clothes. Once she left her room, Annabella casted a locking spell on her door so no one could break in. She made her way down the stairs and into the battle hall where she was to meet Jacob. Surprised, Annabella noticed that Jacob was also early and was already in full gear minus a helmet.

"Oh Jacob," Annabella sighed when she saw the look on his face. She ran up to him and gave him a tight hug.

"Annabella, you have to stay alive no matter what," he whispered into her left ear.

She nodded at him as a tear escaped. "So do you."

The pair got everything together until the others appeared. Annabella had her special sword, magic bow and arrows while Jacob had his knives and powerful sword that Annabella had given him for Christmas. Jacob even showed her the magic arrows that would reappear back in the stash every time it killed a monster.

"What do we do until the battle starts?" Annabella asked. It was seven thirty and everyone was in full battle attire.

"We eat. We must be strong for this battle. Anything could happen."

Fifteen minutes was given for all of the knights and soldiers to eat. The battle would start at nine o'clock, so everyone would have time for the food to settle correctly. Most of the tables were dead silent. Annabella could feel the fear emanating from her own table. A few people at different tables were trying to be happy, and it seemed to make others relax a bit.

"Annabella," the King called.

Annabella turned around and made her way over to him.

"We must get our horses."

Annabella nodded and motioned for Jacob. All of the best knights would be on horses and pegasus' during the battle. When they reached the stables the horses were all set up, Andromeda was wearing special armour custom made to fit her long horn and gigantic wings. Special horseshoes covered her hooves and her white mane was braided. Annabella softly ran her hand on Andromeda's head and gave her a baby carrot.

"You are going to do well," she whispered before hopping onto the horned Pegasus.

The knights were all set up and ready to run into battle. Annabella and Jacob rode on either side of the King as they approached the front line. There was no sign of the warlock or his creatures, which made Annabella hope that the war wouldn't happen after all. Soon after, everyone was set up.

"Are the villagers ready?" Annabella asked the Queen when she rode out on her own pegasus.

The Queen nodded quickly before going to her spot near the stables entrance. The Queen would ensure that the stables would be kept safe from the monsters, so the nurses would be able to heal the wounded soldiers from the Land of Dreams and the Land of Light. The nurses all had earth powers. They had all types of supplies to aid injured soldiers, but unfortunately serious wounds would still take time to heal. They would be working with Annabella's Nurse Emily for the most serious injuries.

The sound of distant growls gained Annabella's attention. "Did you hear that?" she asked to no one in particular.

The King and Jacob nodded along with a bunch of knights.

"They are ready. Attention everyone." The King didn't turn around to face the men, but looked out in the direction of the forest. "They are ready, so be aware and prepared for any surprises." Soon after the King's announcement, the creatures of the dark forest were emerging out of the forest and towards the castle, breaking through the protective barrier as if it didn't exist.

"Charge!" Annabella yelled as the front line began running towards the creatures. In a matter of seconds all of the creatures were destroyed.

"That was easy," Annabella mumbled, knowing it wasn't the end of it.

More creatures ran out of the forest, but this time they were bigger and faster. The elves, who were the best archers in the land, shot out their first set of arrows, killing many creatures instantly. Annabella swung her sword, killing creatures with every hit.

With every death Annabella noticed the red eyes of the evil creatures fading away. *Just like my vision*, she thought to herself.

As the time went on, more and more creatures were running out of the dark forest and into battle. They were also getting much stronger, but nothing complicated seeing as no one from the Land of Dreams had been seriously injured so far. Jacob was effortlessly killing creatures left, right and centre, but failed to notice a flying creature coming right for him.

"Jacob, watch out!" Annabella screamed and killed the creatures with a lightning strike.

"Thank you," Jacob yelled back before continuing the fight.

SEVERAL HOURS HAD GONE by. It was about mid-day when the creatures stopped coming out of the forest. Several were injured, but no one had died. A few with injuries that needed time to heal were transported to the dungeons to be with their families, but most returned to fight. Everyone took the moment of peace to hydrate themselves.

The dark forest puzzled Annabella. Why did the creatures stop coming?

"What is happening?" Annabella asked the King.

The King shook his head as he carefully watched the forest. "I do not know. I cannot hear them. The fairies cannot even sense them near the entrance of the forest."

"Your Majesty, we just sensed many creatures. It is like they came out of thin air," a male fairy frantically screamed.

Annabella and Jacob looked at the King, but he also had a puzzled look on his face. Evil creatures once again began running out of the forest. This time there were many more than before.

"Where are they all coming from?" Jacob yelled as he cut an ogre's head off.

Annabella was wondering the same thing, but a thought ran through her head. *The warlock must be creating them as we fight.* It was confirmed in her mind. Without thinking, she charged further out towards the creatures. She froze several before shattering the ice blocks with her sword. Annabella used her powers to strike a monster with lightning, which created a chain and hurt every creature around it. She shot an orc in the head with an arrow that quickly reappeared with the others in her holder before it fell to the ground.

"As if I am letting you keep that," she scoffed at the dead creature. The sounds of a sword hitting something hard caught Annabella's attention. Jacob was fighting a strange creature she had never seen. She was shocked to see how agile he was. *He's practically dancing around them,* she thought and returned her attention to the forest. She didn't see anyone looking her way, so she took the opportunity to ride out closer to the forest.

Andromeda stood up on her back legs and flapped her wings, refusing to enter the dark forest.

"Let's go," Annabella shouted, but Andromeda wouldn't budge. A troll ran out towards Annabella, but Andromeda swiftly spread her wings, throwing the troll back into a tree, killing it instantly. Annabella jumped off her pegasus and patted her on the side.

"Go protect our people and try not to get hurt," she said to the pegasus, who listened to her order. Annabella glanced around one last time, but failed to notice that Jacob had spotted her before she ran into the forest on her own.

"Annabella!" Jacob yelled, but it was too late. She had already disappeared.

The King rode up to Jacob with worry on his face. "Where is she?" he yelled over the noise desperately.

Jacob slashed another monster before answering, "She went into the forest alone. I can sense her in there. I need to go after her."

The King looked at the darkness of the forest before looking back at Jacob. "Find her and bring her back here."

Jacob shook his head. "I do not think she is going to come out," he said before he began towards the forest. The King calling after Jacob, but was ignored.

Once Jacob made it to the border he jumped off his horse and ran in. Jacob didn't know what direction she had gone, but quickly figured out her path when he noticed her boot markings in the dirt. He ran in her direction, killing several creatures that got in his way.

After several minutes of running the sound of a sword hitting something caught his attention. *Annabella*, he thought as he ran towards her.

Annabella quickly turned around and shot an arrow before realizing it was Jacob. He snatched the arrow out of the air before it hit his face and shot Annabella a knowing look.

"Are you completely insane? Last time you came in here alone you almost died!"

Annabella quickly shot a miniature dragon with a magical arrow and stared at Jacob. There was sweat running down the sides of his face, and blood splattered on his armour.

Annabella sighed and wiped the beads of sweat from her forehead. "I know," she replied. "We will never win this war if the warlock continues creating creatures. We need to destroy him," she said.

Jacob's eyes widened. "Annabella," he yelled as he ran and jumped into the air. The troll that was ready to hit Annabella in the head with a tree trunk was suddenly turned into a block of ice.

"Oh my God. Is that a giant troll?" Annabella said in shock. Annabella knew about trolls, but nowhere in her book of creatures did one that big exist.

Jacob nodded before quickly breaking its head off with his sword. "I have never heard of these, but it is definitely a troll," he replied before looking at Annabella once again. "You do not need to do this. It is not safe," Jacob explained.

Annabella nodded. "I know it is not logical, but I need to save this land so I can get back to my world," she explained.

Jacob nodded. "I understand, which is why I will stay with you to help," he decided.

Annabella smiled and gave Jacob a quick hug before returning her attention to the forest.

"We must move quickly. We will need to find a place to rest before nightfall," Jacob said as he walked by Annabella's side further into the forest. There weren't many creatures deeper into the forest, mostly evil rodents and bats.

"You said that the warlock is creating them. Are they just appearing out of thin air?" Jacob was beginning to feel paranoid with the silence of the forest.

Annabella nodded, "I believe so. I guess the warlock is just making them appear near the entrance of the forest. It explains why the fairies only sensed them that at the last moment."

"I assume he is creating new creatures as well. He must be merging several types together," Jacob realized as he came to a complete stop. Annabella was confused and looked up at him for an explanation. "The soldiers will not be expecting that. If they see a minotaur they will not expect it to breathe fire."

Annabella gasped with her hands covering her mouth. "You are right. We must warn them," she said as she began looking around.

Jacob softly grabbed her arm. "Annabella, there are no messenger doves in the dark forest."

Annabella laughed. "Jacob, we have magic. I can cast a use some on one of the bats to bring a message over to the King," she explained as she used her wind powers to bring a bat closer to her.

Jacob watched, impressed, as Annabella held on to it and chanted a quick spell. "Make the evil act like good, act nice, not fright, like others would," Annabella recited. The bat suddenly stopped struggling and Annabella opened her eyes. "I focused on a messenger dove so hopefully this works out well," she explained before letting the bat fly to a nearby tree trunk.

"Send a mental message to my father, the King," Annabella commanded. The bat flew and landed on her outstretched finger and closed its eyes as Annabella silently thought what she needed the King to hear.

"Thank you," she said before the bat flew in the direction of the castle.

"I am impressed. I would have never thought of that," Jacob admitted as he continued walking again.

"Thank you. I guess being related to a witch and studying all those books can be handy."

By the time the sun was beginning to set, Annabella and Jacob had only fought with four creatures other than the giant troll. They reached a large rock that had a big enough opening for Jacob and Annabella to rest in.

"I will let you sleep for a few hours so you can recharge your energy and powers. After that, I will sleep so we can continue in the morning."

Annabella nodded at Jacob's plan and cast a protection spell on the entrance of the little cave.

"No one will be able to hear, smell, or see us. They also cannot get in," she explained before lying down next to Jacob in a small pile of leaves. She held his hand and looked up at him with a small smile on her face. When Jacob smiled back she squeezed his hand softly.

"Thank you for coming after me. I do not know what I would do without you," she said truthfully.

"Get eaten by an ogre?" Jacob joked and squeezed Annabella's hand back before she closed her eyes and quickly fell asleep.

Chapter Eighteen

Three days had passed since Annabella and Jacob had entered into the dark forest. They spent their days walking through the forest, and their nights resting in different caves. The few monsters that remained were strong, but not a big deal for Annabella and Jacob to deal with.

"Jacob, you have barely slept two hours," Annabella worried. "We are not too far now. I think you should take a nap—at least for another hour."

Jacob shook his head and kept walking. When he tripped over a small stick he looked back at Annabella, who was crossing her arms as he smiled sheepishly.

"I will be fine," he assured.

Annabella walked up to him and held his hand. "Please, Jacob? I do not want anything to happen to you. It is not safe for you to be this tired."

Jacob was apprehensive, but when he noticed Annabella's worried expression he gave in. "Only for an hour," he said before looking around.

"What if we climb up a tree?" Annabella suggested.

Jacob nodded and made his way to a tall tree that wasn't home to any creatures. "We can climb this by using the vines. I see a good spot way up there," he said while pointing to a flatter looking branch.

Annabella nodded and carefully climbed behind him, keeping an open eye for any creatures that may try to attack.

"I am serious, Annabella," Jacob warned. "One hour and we continue on. We need to find a better place to stay during the night."

Annabella nodded and watched as Jacob closed his eyes. She loved the peaceful expression on his face. *He always looks so innocent,* she noticed as his sleep became deeper. Annabella knew Jacob was fully asleep when his breathing became shallow. She gently pushed back the hair covering his eye, leaning into the tree as she looked in the direction they would continue towards.

For the entire hour Annabella kept watch over the area. She even used magic to estimate the distance and located where the good witch's tree was, but it was still a two-day trek away. Annabella was so concentrated on figuring out a plan, that she didn't notice Jacob stirring in his sleep.

When Jacob jolted awake, he slipped off of the edge of the branch and began to fall. Before he could even yell out for help, the wind around him gently brought him down to the ground. Annabella was down a few seconds later by his side.

"Oh my gosh, are you okay?" Annabella worried as she inspected Jacob for injuries.

Jacob caught his breath and looked up at Annabella in shock. "Thank you, Annabella," he breathed out. "If it were not for you I would have fallen to my death," he said as his hands trembled slightly.

Annabella nodded and hugged Jacob. "Do not thank me. I am just glad you are all right," she said before sighing.

After a few moments Jacob looked at her questioningly. "What is it?"

Annabella smiled slightly. "I think the only thing I will not miss about this place is the way you people speak. It is so unnatural and difficult for me. Even in the past people did not speak like this. Can I just speak the way I do back home? Only until we make it back so no one suspects anything. It would make this so much less stressful for me."

Jacob chuckled at Annabella's face. "Of course. It just sounds very strange to me and people would think something is wrong with you. We are out here in the forest so I do not see the harm in it."

Annabella clapped her hands excitedly. "Thank God. I can't even believe I've gone so long speaking like that." Annabella's smile was bright as she yelled out the words.

"I'll even attempt," Jacob said while cringing at the contraction, "To speak like this for fun. It just sounds so... sloppy."

Annabella playfully smacked him on the arm. "Don't worry about speaking that way," she said before helping him up. "Let's get going. We're only about two days away from the good witch's place, which means we're closer than we thought."

After another long six hours of walking, Annabella and Jacob discovered a great location for them to spend the night. There were lots of items that with a lot of patience, and maybe a bit of magic, could be made into weapons. Jacob was in charge of creating the arrows with the rocks and sticks in the area, while Annabella made daggers. The two worked side by side as they created weapons and enchanted them. By the time the sun began to set, Annabella and Jacob had enough daggers and arrows to last them several days.

THE KING WATCHED AS another one of his men took a hit. *This is unbelievable,* he thought to himself as he took on a minotaur with extra horns. Dozens of men from the Land of Dreams and The Land of Light were injured by the strange creations that were only getting faster and stronger.

I am thankful Annabella warned me of these... creations. The King looked around as he continued to fight creatures with his magical sword. The drastic thoughts flew through his mind every time a new monster appeared, or a new soldier was injured. *Come on, Annabella; get out of that forest before it is too late.*

Before he could blink, the King was on the ground watching his horse fall to his death. With the rage inside of him the King let out a strong fire spell that annihilated all of the monsters that were present on the field.

"Your Majesty, you have destroyed them all," David yelled as he approached the King to help him up.

"It seems fighting the evil with fire is not all pointless," the King said as he dusted his pants off. Both men kept their attention at the forest, knowing that there would be more to come.

"If all of us with fire magic work together we can probably destroy the entire forest," David mentioned before his face fell to match the King's expression.

"But we cannot because of our children," the King said for David.

"If they went in the correct direction, they should be near the good witch," said David with a distant look.

The King looked up at his friend before looking back at the forest. "I only fear them not getting out on time. I do not doubt that the both of them together are doing well, but with all of this dark magic there is so much they will not expect," the King worried for his land.

"If the monsters continue getting stronger I fear we will lose this battle," worried David.

The King made a noise in agreement. "We will need to come up with a decision. Because I am the King I cannot be selfish," he said, pacing around. "If worst comes to worst I fear we will need to set fire to the forest, for Annabella and Jacob are two people who might not be saved in comparison to the rest of the land."

David sighed and nodded. "I understand. Our children are smart, they will find a way out of this all. I have faith in them."

"Your Majesty," called a female voice from behind. The King turned around to face the fairy. "We can set a barrier on the forest that should last for a short time. We think you should speak with those who are injured.

Without a second to spare, the King nodded and made his way over to the injured soldiers that were receiving treatment. The King was heart broken. Two of his men had died, and a few required amputations. He thought about their families when he noticed one of his best knights getting his arm bandaged up. It was broken.

"Alexander," the King said as he approached the knight.

"Your Majesty," Alexander replied, standing quickly to bow.

"There is nothing we can do for now to fully heal you, but I will send you in with your family," the King said before closing his eyes.

"Your Majesty, I can still-" Alexander was cut off by the King raising his hand. There was no arguing.

The nurse who was bandaging Alexander took his uninjured arm, and walked him towards the castle for him to be with his family.

The King looked around one last time before returning to the front line.

"ALL DONE," ANNABELLA announced as she put down her last dagger.

Jacob smiled as he sharpened his last arrow with a rock. "They look great. We should have more than enough if more monsters decide to show up. Especially with the magic arrows."

Annabella lit a few floating torches so they could close off the cave for the night, before she found herself struggling to take her shoe off.

"Let me help you with that," Jacob said before he opened the zipper, letting his hand linger on her leg for an extra few seconds.

Annabella blushed when he looked up at her with a strange expression. "Uh... th- thank you," she stuttered as Jacob stood up to face her.

"I do not understand how you can still look so beautiful after all that has happened," Jacob said in amazement.

Annabella's blush deepened at the words. "I probably look like a troll right now, but thank you. You still look really good too," she said looking into his dark eyes.

"You could never look like a troll," Jacob chuckled before surprising Annabella with a hug.

"What was that for?" she laughed.

"You can never show your appreciation for someone too much. I just wanted to thank you again for saving me. It will be hard not having you here once this is all over," Jacob explained.

"I'll still be here," Annabella said. "Well, not me, but the real Princess Annabella. If I'm recreating history she should have a similar personality so nothing will change for you," she explained, feeling sad at her revelation.

"What is wrong?" Jacob asked her.

Annabella sat down against the rock at the back end of their little cave. "It's just that if I remember everything once I get back to my world, it's going to be really hard not having you in my life anymore."

Jacob sat down beside Annabella and put his arm around her for comfort before she leaned her head on his shoulder.

"You will have many people wanting to be your friend," he said.

"I don't have many friends," Annabella admitted, which shocked Jacob. "In my world I'm boring. I've explained this to you before. I'm one of those people that you would walk by and never notice." Annabella felt embarrassed disclosing the information.

"Well than, in that case I really hope I have some alternate version of myself that you can meet one day. Perhaps I will be incredibly handsome in your world," Jacob joked.

Annabella scoffed. "As if it's possible for you to get anymore attractive." She mentally face-palmed herself for letting it slip.

"I am glad you think I am so attractive," Jacob said with a look on his face that Annabella had seen only once before. "Maybe one day I will meet a woman like you," he explained.

"You'll meet someone better than me," Annabella assured him. The sound of a wolf howling in the distance caught their attention.

"I think that's our queue to sleep," Annabella said before lying down in the spot she was sitting in.

Jacob did the same and looked at Annabella as the torches began to dim. "No one in this world could be better than you," he said right before the cave went black.

A FULL DAY AND NIGHT had gone by since the incident. Jacob and Annabella never attempted to climb another tree, but weren't afraid to continue on their journey. If they kept on schedule they would make it out of the forest before nightfall.

"Tell me more about your world," Jacob said suddenly after hours of walking in silence. They had not spotted even one evil creature other than a few rats or bats since the morning of the day before, which gave them hope that it was all over.

"What do you want to know? Give me a subject and I'll explain how it works," Annabella said before ducking to not collide with a tree branch.

Jacob mimicked her actions before answering, "Transportation. Do you also ride chariots?"

Annabella laughed and looked up at Jacob. "Over a century ago people would get around by chariots if they were rich, or just a simple horse and carriage. There are no such things as unicorns or pegasus' back home, but that doesn't really make a difference," Annabella explained as Jacob's expression turned into a surprised one.

Annabella didn't notice and continued on. "Most people travel by cars, busses, trains, or just by walking. If you want to go to different countries most take airplanes or ships."

Jacob suddenly stopped walking and turned to Annabella. "I think you've mentioned cars before. If there is no magic in your world, how do they run?"

The next hour was made up of Annabella explaining various things about her world. She really enjoyed the fact that Jacob was as fascinated about it as she was about the Land of Dreams.

"I wish you could use magic to visit me," Annabella said. "I'd show you around and see if you could make it a day without any magic. It would be hilarious," she joked.

"Haha," Jacob said sarcastically. "You were completely surprised that I pulled a carrot out of my pocket. I feel like I would do better—whoa." Annabella was about to fall, but Jacob caught her. "Are you all right?"

Annabella nodded, but when she looked down to see what caused her to trip, her eyes widened. "Jacob..." she said slowly. "Please tell me that I'm crazy and that tree root isn't moving on its own."

Jacob looked down and suddenly jumped away. "Looks like you are not crazy," he said before grabbing her and running. The tree roots began to move quickly, going after Annabella and Jacob.

"Is there a spell for this?" Annabella screamed as she dodged a tree branch that attempted to stop her.

Jacob dodged many branches trying to grab at him. "I have never seen anything like this before. Nature is not able to do this without the help of magic."

Both Annabella and Jacob continued running hand in hand in hopes to get away from the trees. They ran to an area that seemed to be very open and rested for a bit.

"I think they're gone," Annabella said, panting.

Jacob analyzed his surroundings before sitting down on a rock. "It was only one type of tree that was following us. They are very rare so the warlock must have enchanted them. We need to keep away from darkwood trees."

Annabella nodded. "Are the trunks always completely black?" she asked to which Jacob nodded. "There are a few other trees that are all black, but if you cut these ones they ooze actual black blood. That is what makes them so rare."

Annabella shivered at the thought of bleeding trees. *As if being in an evil forest isn't scary enough.* She began messing around with her hair as she kept an eye out for any other evil trees. She had leaves hanging out of her hair and a few bits of bark.

Jacob chuckled at Annabella's struggle to get a few pieces out. "Let me help you with that," he said as he began gently pulling leaves out of her hair. "You can create a simple spell to see what you look like," Jacob said when he was finished.

Annabella looked up at him in surprise. "Create my own spell? As in I can just make up something and magic will happen?"

When Jacob nodded her mouth dropped in annoyance. "What?" he asked her, confused.

"It might have been helpful if you had told me this months ago," Annabella said before walking towards a spot of dirt. Annabella took out her elastic and shook her head around for a few seconds before flipping her hair back. She crouched down and used a stick to draw a rectangular shape on the ground.

Mirror, mirror, in the ground, show me what I look like now, Annabella thought in her head before deciding it was good enough. The rectangle became reflective like a mirror. "How is it even possible that my hair can look this good by just shaking it around?" Annabella wondered out loud as she ran her fingers through her once again silky hair.

Jacob cracked a smile at Annabella's fascination. "Good genes? Your mother...the Queen," he corrected, "has the same hair as you."

Annabella once again created a French braid to keep her hair out of her face. While doing so the arm of her battle suit slid down her arm, revealing her shoulder.

"Whoa," Jacob said as he looked at her arm.

"What is it?" Annabella asked before she looked at her arm and gasped. There was a large gash on close to her shoulder.

"Why is your battle suit not ripped?" Jacob asked he held Annabella's arm lightly.

"Your mother said that this body suit is made of a special material that mends itself back together and doesn't let liquid pass through. I think it was one of the tree branches," Annabella explained.

"Does it hurt?" Jacob asked her, worried.

Annabella shook her head, but then quickly nodded. "I didn't feel it before. I think looking at it makes it hurt more."

Jacob nodded and walked towards a pile of leaves before inspecting them. He picked one up from the ground and held it up for Annabella to see.

"Is that one of those healing leaves?" she asked Jacob, who nodded.

"A calactula leaf," he corrected her.

"Wait, why is that here? This is the dark forest," Annabella wondered.

"I guess you have not gotten to the history of the dark forest. It used to be a normal forest before the big war. The warlock turned the dark forest to evil along with its creatures. I guess this leaf was not attached to the tree when the magic happened. It is the only explanation that would make sense," Jacob explained.

"Are there any more? Annabella asked him.

Jacob shook his head. "This is the only one I have seen so far. If you see any make sure to pick them up in case."

Annabella nodded and held out her arm for Jacob. As soon as the leaf wrapped itself around her arm the healing began. Annabella pulled the sleeve back up.

Jacob looked up at the sun before turning back to Annabella. "We should go now. We can still make it out before the sun begins to set."

Annabella readjusted her gear and caught up to Jacob. "I can almost smell the freedom," she said as they walked towards what looked like the exit of the forest.

Jacob opened his mouth to reply, but was pulled back so quickly that only a slight squeak was heard.

"Jacob!" Annabella screamed as she ran after him. A large tree was holding Jacob up in the air by its roots that were completely wrapped around him. "Put him down," Annabella screamed as she charged at the tree with her sword out. She dodged various branches that were swinging at her and even cut a few off, which made the tree let out a terrifying screeching noise.

"You have to stab through it," Jacob yelled before another branch wrapped around his mouth, keeping him from talking.

Annabella continued to cut off branches that were attacking her before stabbing her sword into the tree. The tree let out another horrible screech, but kept fighting.

"My sword isn't long enough to reach the center," Annabella realized before pulling her sword out. The tree threw her back into the ground with a lot of force. Jacob tried to scream, but only muffles were heard.

"That's it," Annabella screamed in pure rage before yelling out a powerful fire spell that made the tree fling Jacob away.

Jacob yelled in pain out when he landed on a stick that punctured through his left leg.

"Jacob," Annabella screamed before the tree disintegrated, leaving nothing but smoke behind. Annabella ran to Jacob who was clutching his leg in pain. "Let me pull it out," she said as soon as she saw the large stick poking through both sides.

"Do it quickly," Jacob said through clenched teeth as sweat poured down his face like a waterfall.

Annabella grabbed the bottom end of the stick and quickly pulled it out, which made Jacob to let out another painful scream.

"I'm so sorry," she said as blood poured out of his leg. "Oh my God," she said before frantically looking around. "I need to put pressure on it so you don't lose too much blood."

Jacob nodded quickly as his eyes stayed closed from the pain. Annabella looked down at her skirt and quickly ripped it off, leaving her in her body suit, wrapping it around Jacob's leg tightly as he let out groans of pain.

"I'm so sorry, Jacob," she said as she stood him up quickly and put his arm around her shoulder. "I'm getting you out of here," she said as she attempted to run with Jacob hobbling on his one good leg. When they made it out of the forest Annabella didn't think twice and brought Jacob into a cave and laid him down gently.

"Are you all right?" Annabella worried as she noticed that Jacob was still in immense pain.

"It... it punctured my... femoral... femoral artery," Jacob managed to get out before letting out another scream of pain.

Annabella looked down at his injured leg and noticed that the blood was seeping all around the fabric. "Oh my God," she said as she noticed that Jacob was turning pale. "No. You can't do this to me," she said before standing him up again. "There has to be something that I can do," she sobbed. *I should've left the stick in.*

"I am sorry," Jacob said quietly as Annabella dragged him deeper into the cave. She noticed light peaking through a rock and used her powers to break through. On the other side was a beautiful field with a huge lake that held sparkling water.

Annabella dragged Jacob to the edge of the water and attempted to heal him with spells. Each time nothing would happen, which made her panic even more. She looked at the water and splashed some on Jacob in hopes to calm down the excessive sweating.

"No no no no no no no," Annabella mumbled as Jacob's breathing became more and more shallow. "Don't die, Jacob. You can't leave me here," she sobbed before looking at the water once again. She quickly collected some and threw it at the huge gash in Jacob's leg in hopes to clean it up a bit. When she went to dab the area, Annabella noticed that the cuts on her hands were disappearing.

"Oh my God." Annabella realized what was happening. "The water is magic."

Annabella swivelled Jacob around to let his injured leg hang over the edge and into the water. She took out her water jug and filled it up with the magical water before forcing it into Jacob's mouth. "Please work," she begged after Jacob weakly swallowed the water. She held onto his hands tightly and continued to cry at the sight of Jacob life fading away. She drank some water to try and calm herself down.

"Jacob, please wake up. You can't die," Annabella cried. "You're my best friend. I don't know what I'd do without you. Jacob, I love you," she said as she tightened her grip on his hand. "I love you so freaking much and I can't believe I'm just realizing it now." She felt like an idiot for not giving into her feelings sooner.

"I'm in love with you, Jacob," she whispered before sobbing all over again. "You can't go now. You really can't. Especially now that I know that I'm in love with you. I'll do anything if you wake up, Jacob. Just please don't leave me. I can't handle losing someone else," she said as the tears streamed down her face. When nothing happened another sob escaped Annabella's lips. *He's dead,* Annabella thought as she lost all hope.

Suddenly Jacob's eyes opened widely and he began to cough and Annabella was frozen in her place, surprised by what was happening. "Jacob?" Annabella inspected him and noticed that his leg was completely healed. She quickly sat him up and wrapped her arms around him as tightly as she possibly could.

"You're alive," she cried into his shoulder when he finally returned the hug.

"I am," Jacob replied, his voice sounding much better.

Annabella's heart was beating fast and she wasn't thinking when she pulled Jacob into a kiss for a few moments. She finally realized what she was doing and quickly pulled away.

"Oh my God. I'm so sorry," she said quickly as Jacob's expression became unreadable. "I was just so worried and thought that you died and I don't know what I was thinking I just-"

Jacob put a finger up to Annabella's mouth, cutting her off. "I am in love with you too," Jacob said suddenly.

"What?" she asked in confusion.

"I heard everything you said. I was just too weak to reply. I tried telling you this before, but I am also in love with you," Jacob said before pulling Annabella into a passionate kiss.

The kiss was like nothing Annabella had ever experienced before. She felt pure joy in that moment. Her heart felt full. Suddenly, Annabella pulled away when memories began to resurface.

"This isn't how it's supposed to happen," Annabella realized. When Jacob raised a brow she shook her head. "I'm not supposed to be in love with you. I'm supposed to live the life story of Princess Annabella. I remember now, none of this was supposed to happen. I was supposed to stay in battle and we would've won." Annabella was starting to hyperventilate.

"What are you talking about?" Jacob asked her.

"My storybook. I remember now. I messed everything up," she cried.

"We can still win this," Jacob said, trying to comfort her.

"No we can't. I'm such an idiot. There's no way we can fight the warlock on our own. What was I thinking?"

"You were thinking about the safety of our land," Jacob explained. "We can go back. We can find the good witch and go back home and finish the battle the way we were supposed to," Jacob explained.

"All right," Annabella said before a small smile made its way onto her face. She felt a bit calmer and wiped the tears from her face. "Everything I said was true," she explained. "I'd rather die than let that happen again. You deserve to live a long amazing life, Jacob."

Jacob shook his head. "Please do not say that, Annabella. I am just a villager that works for the royal family. You are a princess who deserves the best prince in all of the lands," he said.

"No. I don't want the best prince. I don't want any prince. I want *you*. You're the only person in this world that makes me this happy. You're the greatest man I have ever met. You're extremely intelligent, handsome, caring and you know how to make me feel better. I feel safe with you. You make me want to stay here forever," Annabella admitted.

Jacob looked into Annabella's eyes and saw nothing but the truth. "Than be with me tonight," he said as he lightly pulled her closer.

Annabella continued to look into his eyes before she nodded, understanding his request. "There is nothing that I want more," she said before kissing Jacob with all of the passion inside of her, before they experienced everything feeling right for the first time in a long while.

Chapter Nineteen

The sun rose slowly and reflected on the shimmering water of the magical lake. Birds were happily chirping as Annabella opened her eyes. She blinked a few times before yawning and sitting up. When she realized that she was sleeping on Jacob's naked chest, memories from the night before flooded her mind.

"Good morning, Annabella," Jacob said with a lazy smile as he also sat up.

Annabella returned the smile, but could feel her face heating up. As soon as she noticed her battle suit thrown off to the side, she felt unconscious and quickly covered up.

"I am going to go in the lake for a bath and drink from the waterfall. Care to join me?" Jacob said, still completely naked.

Oh God oh God oh God oh God, Annabella thought to herself before cracking out a response. "Yeah, that'd be awesome," she said, cringing at her own words. *Way to be cool, Annabella. Way to be cool.*

Both Annabella and Jacob jumped into the magical water. The temperature seemed perfect. It was cold, but in a refreshing rather than uncomfortable way. Annabella was thankful that the water near the waterfall was bubbly enough to hide. Jacob didn't seem to mind being so open in front of Annabella. *It must be a guy thing.*

Once they were both done bathing, Jacob decided to explore the nearby field for something to eat. Annabella took her chance to quickly scrub her battle clothing in the water. With the help of her air powers, she dried her body suit in a matter of minutes before putting it back on. The water somehow cleaned the blood off of her skirt, so she clipped it back on as well.

"Thank God for that," she mumbled to herself before doing her hair.

Jacob still hadn't returned with breakfast, so Annabella decided to take the extra time to think. She thought about the war and how it was going, how the King and Queen were doing, and whether the good witch would be able to help them or not. But most of all, Annabella thought about the night before. She thought about how Jacob made her feel comfortable, how he made sure it was special. She thought about how much she hated herself afterwards for thinking that, if she got trapped in the Land of Dreams, she wouldn't be all that upset because it meant she would have Jacob with her *literally* forever. It would probably change the future as well, so there was a chance her parents wouldn't face the same fate.

"I am back and I have eggs, fruit and nuts," Jacob's voice cut through Annabella's thoughts.

"Great," Annabella quickly searched for a long and flat rock and rinsed it in the lake. When she returned, she sat it down in front of her and motioned for Jacob to give her the eggs. With her fire magic, Annabella touched the rock to quickly warm it up and fry the eggs. Jacob helped by washing the fruit off and filling all of their water canteens with the magical water.

"We can just use our magic for regular drinking water," Annabella explained as Jacob put the water canteens inside of his battle gear.

"I know," he said still with a happy tone of voice. "This is just in case either of us gets injured," he said casually before walking back to the water with a miniature toothbrush.

Annabella quickly grabbed her own toothbrush from her emergency satchel and joined Jacob. Once they were done, Jacob determined that they would make it to the good witch's tree within an hour if they moved quickly.

"Do you have everything?" Jacob asked as he stood near the exit that led back into the cave. Annabella nodded and put her sword into her scabbard, before quietly walking ahead. When Jacob grabbed her arm and pulled her into a deep and passionate kiss, she felt like melting.

"I know what we did was completely crazy, but I just wanted to let you know that last night was the best night of my life. If I do not make it out alive I will not mind because my life is now complete," Jacob said while staring into Annabella's eyes. When a small sob escaped Annabella's lips, he quickly pulled her into a tight hug and rubbed her back.

"I feel the same way Jacob," she admitted while holding the hug. "I really do. Even though it may change the course of things, I would do it all again a million times."

Jacob pulled away and kissed Annabella on the head. "We have a witch to get to."

"WE'RE ALMOST THERE," Annabella explained as they approached a brown tree covered in moss and vines. She remembered seeing it from the witch's balcony months before. In a matter of minutes they arrived. No monsters or darkwood trees were in sight, which was a relief to the pair.

Annabella had failed to notice that there was an entrance at the base of the tree, but she knew it didn't lead to anything. *This must've been here before the good witch was brought here as a prisoner.* When she looked up, she was surprised at how tall the actual tree was.

"How are we supposed to get up there?" Jacob asked her.

"Wind?" Annabella questioned.

Jacob shook his head. "We cannot get up that high. We are going to have to climb," he groaned before looking around.

Annabella continued looking up at the tree when she noticed a vine growing up its height. "Jacob," she called out.

When Jacob looked back at Annabella, she motioned towards the vine. The smirk on Jacob's face calmed her down. They both approached the vine and grabbed it before they closed their eyes.

"Grow," they commanded the vine to grow at the same time. Both held onto the vine as it lifted them up the giant tree.

"Jump to the left right after me," Annabella said before jumping down. Jacob followed and seemed relieved when they landed on a balcony. Annabella looked around at the forest. Everything looked and sounded so calm, which saddened her because she knew that all of the creatures were currently trying to destroy the kingdom. Jacob pulled Annabella into a comforting hug after wiping away a stray tear from her face. After a few moments passed, Annabella broke away and pulled Jacob along. She was relieved to see that the door was once again open. Without a moment of hesitation Annabella pulled Jacob into the room and closed the door behind them.

"Caroline?" Annabella called out. When the woman identical to her grandmother appeared from the other side of the room, Annabella couldn't help but run over to her and give her a hug.

"Oh Caroline," Annabella cried. "I've made such a big mistake. I didn't follow the story and stupidly tried to go after the warlock. What am I going to do now?"

Caroline patted Annabella's back before looking at her. "I do not know, my child," Caroline admitted sadly. "Like I said before, the extra tears could have completely altered the story. I cannot tell you what you have to do. You will need to do it on your own and follow your heart," she explained before noticing Jacob awkwardly standing against the wall.

"Jacob," Caroline said as she began to approach him.

Jacob nervously swallowed before sticking out his hand. "I- It is a p- pleasure to meet you," he said shakily.

Caroline laughed at his expression and turned to Annabella. "I cannot believe Jacob is afraid of a powerless old woman such as myself," she laughed.

"Powerless?" Jacob echoed in surprise. "How did you know my name?"

When Caroline turned around with a smirk on her face, Jacob pressed himself deeper into the wall. "I remember your father," she explained. Jacob relaxed slightly, staring intently for Caroline to go on.

"When he came here in search for answers about whether or not he had a soulmate, he told me of his dreams. He dreamt of working for the royal family, finding the love of his life, naming his firstborn son... Jacob," she said with a smile.

"So he was not lying when he said he came here," Jacob said to himself before looking down at Caroline once again. "What can you do?"

Caroline smirked once again and looked back at Annabella, analyzing her for a few moments. "I can still read people's emotions. Anger, happiness, annoyance, lust," she said before winking at Annabella, slowly turning back to Jacob who was scratching his neck and trying to hide a blush. "I can also usually tell certain aspects of the future and determine who has or does not have a soulmate. In this case since it deals with the storybook, which I know you are aware of, I cannot tell you what is going to happen. What I can tell you is, is that we need to get back to the castle as soon as possible."

Annabella looked at Caroline in shock. "We? I thought you were trapped here?" she questioned.

Caroline looked outside of the window before turning to Annabella and Jacob. "The warlock is not concerned with me at the moment. He has stripped even more of my powers, including the ability to transport you, which has also taken away the protection spell keeping me in here. We need to get back to the castle as quickly as we possibly can. But first," Caroline said as she walked towards her bookcase. "We must read up on a few... *special* spells."

THE MONSTERS WERE INCREDIBLY fast and the King was beginning to panic. "David," he called out loudly. The tall man turned around and kicked an ogre with his extremely long legs. "They are winning. It has been too long. If they are not out of the forest by now they are probably dead," the King yelled out as he continued to fight the vast amounts of monsters. When David nodded, the King worked up his anger and once again let out another strong fire spell, instantly destroying all of the enemies that were surrounding him.

"It has been too long. If they survived they would have made it out of the forest by now. We cannot keep waiting," a knight shouted from the King's right side.

"Silence," the King demanded angrily. The knight quickly turned away in fear before the King noticed David staring at him. "What is it?" he snapped.

David sighed and ran a hand over his face. "I love my son very much, but this war is getting out of hand. We are losing. Too many are injured or dead and at this rate we will lose many more."

The King's expression remained the same. "You think I should end this?" the King stated. When David nodded slowly the King sighed. "You are right. I am the King and I need to do what is right for my land. Gather all of the men with fire and wind powers," the King ordered.

When David ran off to recruit all of the men they would require, the King stared out into the forest.

"My dear Annabella, I hope that you made it out. I do not want to lose you, but I know you would understand." After a few minutes had passed, dozens of men from The Land of Dreams and The Land of Light stood by the King.

"We are ready," David announced to the King who then began walking towards the forest.

"All of the fire men must team up with wind men. This way we can spread the fire deep into the forest as quickly as possible," the King explained.

Once all of the men were paired up, the King focused his anger on the forest.

"On a count of three we will do this together. Remember to focus all of your anger on destroying the forest." The King took in a deep breath before counting. "Three... two... one... fire!"

"ARE YOU SURE YOU ALREADY know these?" Caroline asked in confusion. Annabella and Jacob nodded quickly.

"They are all in the castle's library," Jacob explained.

"Well this is not good," Caroline mumbled.

"The sun is beginning to set. We have to figure something out quickly or spend the night here," Annabella said.

"Then we must leave in the morning and journey back to the castle," Jacob decided.

Annabella and Caroline nodded and closed the books in front of them. As they were cleaning up, an incredibly strong blast of wind blew through them, knocking Caroline down.

"What was that?" Annabella questioned as she helped the good witch stand back up.

"It must have been magic," she replied before dusting off her dress.

Jacob moved towards the window and when he paused there, both Caroline and Annabella became concerned.

"Jacob? Is everything all right?"

When he turned around with a shocked expression Annabella quickly ran towards the window to see for herself. "The forest is on fire! It's spreading really fast," she yelled before pacing around.

"We must escape from here. The fire will only come up and burn this tree down now that there isn't a protection spell on it." Caroline said before walking out onto the balcony. Annabella and Jacob followed, but noticed the fire had spread enough for them to not be able to see the ground.

"Our powers are not enough for this," Jacob yelled over the sound of the wind and fire destroying everything.

"We're going to die," Annabella worried. She looked down at Caroline, but became more concerned when she noticed that Caroline had a confused expression on.

"I do not know what we can do now," Caroline said calmly as she looked over the forest sadly.

Annabella tried various times to use her water powers, but they wouldn't it work. The fire was making the air too dry.

"The smoke is too close. We will not make it much longer," Jacob said in-between coughs.

Tears were running down Annabella's face when she grabbed Jacob and Caroline's hands. "I'm so sorry. This is all my fault," she cried.

When both squeezed her hand, Annabella suddenly remembered something from months ago.

'How do I call you?'

'If you need us you will figure it out.'

"Hoot and Tom!" Annabella exclaimed, which made Caroline's eyes widen in excitement.

"You are right. I remember now. I think the warlock erased certain aspects of my memory," Caroline said.

Jacob looked at both women in confusion, but didn't question them.

Annabella closed her eyes and focused on the owl and the gryphon. She said their names over and over again in her head and out loud, imagining them coming for her. When she opened her eyes and saw nothing she let out a breath, but when she heard the sharp sound of an eagle's call she smiled.

"We are saved," Caroline announced happily.

When Tom arrived, Annabella quickly jumped onto his paw and climbed up onto his back. "You have no idea how happy I am to see you," Annabella said before looking back at Jacob and Caroline. "Jump on his paw. He'll help you up here and so will I."

Jacob held onto Caroline's hand before jumping on the gryphon. Once he made it behind Annabella, he wrapped the tassel around him and Caroline so they wouldn't fall off.

"Did you miss me?" Another familiar voice said.

"Hoot!" Annabella exclaimed once again when the owl appeared in front of her.

"I am glad that you remembered to call us," he said as Tom flew higher up in the sky to escape the smoke.

"We were afraid you would not figure out how, but we kept close by to this area," Tom said as he began flying in the direction of the castle.

"Wait, you guys can talk?" Jacob suddenly spoke up. When Annabella and Caroline laughed he frowned. "I remember you telling me about them, but you never said that they could speak," he complained.

"I didn't have much time to explain that," Annabella defended herself.

For the entire flight Jacob held onto Annabella tightly. She tried to get him to loosen up, but she figured out that he was just afraid of how high up and fast they were going. She focused on relaxing during the trip so she could reenergize her powers. She knew that she would need the energy to fight off the remaining monsters when they made it back.

Annabella smiled at the thought of the dark forest being destroyed, but something deep inside of her said that it wouldn't be the end of their troubles just yet.

Chapter Twenty

"We are almost there," Tom announced to everyone. Annabella looked into the distance and saw the outline of the castle. "Thank goodness," she said as she sat up straight. "We're going to leave you somewhere safe," she said to Caroline who nodded.

"Annabella, you should go back to speaking like we do. You do not want anyone to suspect anything. Especially not during the war," Jacob explained.

Annabella sighed and nodded. "You are right. It was great while it lasted."

Tom let out a loud eagle call as they descended towards the castle. The knights and soldiers all looked up in awe as the gryphon slowly came closer.

"Annabella," the King shouted in glee.

"Jacob," David shouted simultaneously.

Annabella waved happily, but noticed a monster running towards them. "Look out," she shouted as she quickly grabbed an arrow, shooting the monster right in the center of his forehead.

"Nice shot," Jacob commented with a smirk, which made Annabella nudge him.

Caroline jumped onto the castle's balcony as soon as they were close enough. "Thank you. All of you."

Tom descended to the ground and used his tail to throw back all of the monsters that surrounded him, before he let Annabella and Jacob down.

"Thank you," Annabella said to Tom and Hoot. "I will never forget you."

"No problem. Remember to call us if you ever need us again," Hoot said before Tom jumped up into the air and flew away.

"Annabella," the King shouted once again, before running to her and embracing her in a tight hug.

"Father, I am all right," Annabella assured the King, while David hugged Jacob.

"Who is that on the balcony?" The King squinted as he looked up, but Caroline had backed away for safety.

"The good witch," Annabella replied before focusing on the forest that was completely destroyed. "Let us destroy the remaining monsters," she said as she began walking back towards the action.

Annabella noticed the amount of blood on the grass as she approached the front line. *They will pay*, she promised herself, before quickly pulling her sword out of the scabbard and running towards the action.

Within seconds Annabella had destroyed three monsters. Knights all around watched her in amazement as she effortlessly fought the enemy. When Jacob joined in, everyone returned their full attention to the battle.

From the corner of Annabella's eye she noticed Jeremy fighting an evil centaur. Jeremy's white-blonde hair was stained with blood that either belonged to him or a monster. Annabella quickly decided that it was probably his since it was a regular red colour.

The sky was getting darker by the time the monsters were almost gone. The nature fairies confirmed that the entire forest had finished burning down and that there was no sign of life within.

"I do not like this," the King said as he put a hand on Annabella's shoulder.

"It is too quiet," Annabella agreed.

The King looked around the battlegrounds and quickly lit up the entire area when he noticed the good witch running towards him.

"Hello there, it is very nice to finally meet you," the King said while bowing. Surprised, the King felt the good witch hug him.

"Oh Joseph," the good witch cried.

The King moved back in shock. "You know my name," he stated.

The good witch looked up at him as tears continued to fall. "You do not remember me, do you?"

The King observed the strange lady in front of him for a few minutes, but shook his head. "No, I am afraid I do not."

The good witch nodded sadly, but quickly smiled again. "Do you remember who taught you your first gardening spell?"

The King smiled. "But of course. It was so many years ago, but my... my grandmother... no. That is not possible. My grandmother died in the great war."

The good witch shook her head at the King. "I did not. The warlock locked me away at the other end of the dark forest. For years I waited for someone to come save me, but I only received a few visitors who did not know who I was." The good witch looked at David quickly before returning her attention to the King.

"For years I waited for you to become curious about a soulmate so you would visit me, but you did not need me. You found her on your own."

The King looked confused. "Why did you not send me a message?" he interrupted her.

"I tried. Oh how I tried. For years and years I wrote letters, but I never heard back. The warlock always found a way to keep me from contacting you all, but several months ago an owl landed on my balcony—an owl from this land. He felt an unknown need to come to me with his friend Tom, the gryphon you just saw. That is how we escaped my tree safely."

The King silently looked down at the good witch. "And now you are here with me again," he said before bending down to give her a proper hug.

"If you feel strange, feel free to call me Caroline," she explained to which the King nodded. "That would be wonderful."

Annabella looked between the two in awe. "Wait... I did not know any of this," she said to Jacob who also looked confused.

"It only makes sense," he said quietly back. "If your real grand-mother is an identical reincarnation of her, and the King looks some-what similar to your father, than of course it makes sense that she is the King's grandmother."

Annabella looked at Jacob in confusion. "That makes sense, but why do I look so different? I am chubby, have boring hair and my eyes are not nearly as bright. I do not have clear skin either back home," Annabella explained sadly.

Jacob lightly squeezed her shoulder. "I really wish I could see you. I am sure that you do not look that different. You probably see your-self differently than what you really are," he said while smiling down at Annabella.

"It would be nice if I went back looking like this," she sighed be-fore a large boom sounded in the distance.

"What was that?" the King asked aloud.

The knights and soldiers looked at each other and around the field, but did not see anything. Annabella quickly grabbed Jacob's hand and nervously looked around herself.

"It is the warlock. He is here," Caroline said warily before a large flame appeared, revealing a man. Everyone suddenly backed away and raised their weapons as they looked at the warlock in fear. Many, including Annabella, were shocked to see that he looked like a regu-lar man in his forties.

"Charge!" the King yelled before he and many soldiers ran at the warlock.

The King stopped running when several soldiers flew back after they seemed to have bounced off an invisible force. The warlock shook his head and laughed at the scene before him.

"You are just like your father. You think a few commoners can injure me? You are all idiots. I am the most powerful warlock in all the lands. No one can destroy me," the warlock yelled at everyone as his eyes glowed red.

Annabella gasped when she noticed. "You are that wolf that I saw in the Forest of Light," she yelled towards him.

"Indeed I am, Princess Annabella. You seem smarter than the rest of these fools," the warlock replied before sticking his hand out. "Join me. If you do you will survive and become the most powerful being in the world other than myself."

Annabella stared at his hand for a few seconds before slowly approaching the warlock. Jacob tried to grab her, but she shook his hand off. When Annabella was a few meters away from the warlock she looked at his hand before looking at him straight in the eye and spitting on the ground in front of him.

"You disgust me," she spat before backing up once again. The warlock chuckled for a moment before lightning struck in the darkening skies above him.

"You foolish little girl. I guess you will all have to die. What a shame," the warlock said before he began floating in the air.

Before anyone could blink Annabella blocked a spell thrown at her by the warlock. They magical beings began to throw their own spells at the warlock, but he either blocked them or took very little damage.

"Nothing is working," Annabella worried out as she threw an earth spell at the warlock.

Roots exploded from the ground and wrapped themselves around the warlock, but in seconds they melted off leaving the evil man on his feet, smirking.

"He is much too powerful for us," Jacob said after throwing a lightning bolt.

Annabella looked back to see Caroline watching the warlock with a face of confusion. "Caroline," Annabella called out. When Caroline looked up, Annabella quickly moved towards her. "What are you thinking?"

Caroline inhaled deeply. "I think I remember a spell from years ago that could help, but is very dangerous."

A fireball flew by them that made Annabella duck. She looked back down at Caroline and bit her lip.

"I feel like dangerous is our best bet at winning," Annabella said before throwing a few more spells at the warlock. "What would we need to do?" she asked while still focusing on the battle.

"All royals would have to join hands and focus on taking away his powers by absorbing them. It could overwhelm some, if not all, but it is the only way."

Another loud bang sounded from the battle before Annabella nodded desperately. She sent mental messages to Jacob and the King to call in all of the royals. Annabella ran around recruiting all of those of royal blood when Jeremy came into her view once again. *Why,* she mentally groaned before approaching him.

"We have a spell that can destroy him, but we need all of the royals to work together," she stated.

Jeremy smirked at him before crossing his arms smugly. "The helpless Annabella needs me. Oh what a sight this is," he chuckled.

Annabella raised a finger before poking his chest strongly. "Now listen here you little piece of sh-" she began, but was interrupted by the King.

"Jeremy, you understand that you will die without us. Annabella is much more powerful than you will ever be, but we cannot risk everyone's death. You either help or die," he explained while towering over Jeremy.

Jeremy gulped and nodded before following the King and Annabella to center field.

"Join hands," Caroline shouted.

All of the royals did as they were told and focused on the warlock. As the seconds flew by the warlock screamed in agony. He looked much weaker and the barrier keeping him safe was beginning to break.

"Why is he not dying?" Annabella screamed after a few minutes. Many of the royals were in pain from the power and she knew they would die if they continued on much longer.

"It is not royals we need. It is true power and a pure heart. Jacob, join hands with Annabella," Caroline yelled with a new look on her face.

Jacob quickly held onto Annabella's hand before an electric blue aura surrounded them, knocking back some of the royals. Annabella could feel the power running through her veins. When both focused on the warlock he screamed louder than ever. He fell to his knees and held onto his head as he began convulsing.

"It is working," Annabella yelled before she moved closer, bringing Jacob along. When the warlock stopped shaking and laid still, Annabella let go of Jacob's hand and relaxed. She turned around to smile at everyone, but before her expression could change a loud screeching noise that she had never heard sounded behind her.

Jacob instantly flew several meters back towards the rest of the men. Annabella quickly turned around to see that the warlock was gone, but a gigantic red dragon had taken his place.

"Annabella, be careful. He is now in his true form," Caroline yelled from the crowd. The warlock burst into flames as he spit out balls of fire into the field, killing a few villagers in the blink of an eye.

"I am not letting you win," Annabella screamed in rage before she started shaking from her adrenalin. Within milliseconds Annabella was in the air surrounded by a blizzard. "Die!" she screamed with a voice that surprised everyone as it was not her own. It sounded so powerful and frightening, yet magical and soothing. Her eyes were now glowing the colour of her aura as she glared at the warlock.

The warlock in his dragon form flew around while throwing fireballs at Annabella, but she would block them every time with snow and ice. The knights and soldiers below watched as Annabella turned into a blur and engulfed the dragon in her powers. The entire field was covered in snow and looked like Christmas day, but no one was paying attention to anything other than the wretched noise the dragon made before exploding into a large flame and leaving its ashes behind.

Annabella watched as the smoked cleared up, but she quickly felt her energy disappear before she began falling into darkness.

"Annabella," Jacob shouted as he noticed her flying towards the ground at a great speed. He quickly used his wind powers to slow her down a bit, but she was going at a speed so fast that he couldn't stop her from getting hurt. As soon as Annabella landed in a large pile of snow, Jacob ran towards her and gathered her in his arms.

"I need a nurse," he yelled as he began running towards the castle. "She is not breathing and I cannot feel a pulse."

The soldiers were still in shock from what had just happened. They were happy that they had won the battle, but worried that Annabella had died saving them. Caroline quickly grabbed the King's hand and ran after Jacob while David and others followed behind.

Chapter Twenty-One

Jacob sat at Annabella's side once again looking disheveled. Emily, Annabella's personal nurse, approached Jacob before putting a calming hand on his shoulder. "Jacob," she said softly to get his attention. When he looked up she smiled down at him. "It has been several days. Go bathe yourself," she ordered him.

"I know, but-" he began before Emily shushed him.

"She will not wake up within the time that you take a bath."

Jacob sighed and looked at Annabella before softly running his thumb along her cheek. He looked back at Emily with a worried expression. "Please tell me if anything happens" he pleaded.

Emily messed up his hair even more before pushing him in the direction of the other room. "For the last three months that you have been asking me that. I always tell you that I will, even if it means seeing you naked. Just go bathe—you are really starting to stink."

When Jacob reluctantly disappeared into the other room Emily began making her potions. The half-human half-witch carefully added the proper ingredients to the mixture. Once they were complete, they glowed the same bright purple as her aura did. "Perfect," she said while setting the vials back in their holders. All three containers stood next to each other, labeled so Jacob would know when to give them to Annabella.

"All done," Jacob said while entering the room with his hair still wet. Emily crossed her arms and gave Jacob a disapproving look. "What?" he defended himself immediately.

"You have wind powers. An extra two minutes would not hurt."

Jacob sighed and sat back down next to Annabella. "I do not want to risk anything. I also volunteered to be the one to give her the medication and energy."

Emily frowned and kneeled in front of him before holding his hands. "Jacob you have not left these two rooms since the incident."

Jacob kept looking at Annabella as he spoke. "I let in the fresh air," he complained.

"Look," Emily started. "Annabella would not want to see you like this. She would want you to enjoy yourself once in a while. Go take a walk around the castle and do it outside. I will give her the first potion for the day. I am sure that your mother and father would be pleased to see you bathed and out of this room for a few minutes."

Jacob looked at Annabella who was still sleeping as she had been for the last three months. "All right," he sighed while getting up. He quickly turned to Emily and opened his mouth, but was quickly interrupted.

"I will," Emily said, which made him let out a breath.

"Thank you," he said before looking back once again at Annabella and leaving the room.

Jacob decided to walk around outside so he could enjoy his few minutes of free time a little more. Everything seemed so foreign to him. The garden looked different, as did the newly reconstructed stables. Jacob decided to quickly check on Andromeda to make sure that she was fully healed from the battle.

"Jacob," the voice he hated most spoke from his side.

"Good morning, Prince Jeremy," he replied without stopping.

Once he was in the stables Jeremy walked in after him. "How is my lovely fiancée doing?"

Jacob clenched his jaw and closed his eyes. "You know, it would not kill you to spend some time with her. You are going to be her husband after all," he replied as calmly as he could.

"But that is what *friends* are for," Jeremy said with a smirk.

Jacob turned around and looked at Jeremy who stood a few inches shorter. "Which is why you are no friend of mine."

Jeremy let out a bark of laughter. "I would never be friends with a commoner such as yourself. I do not see why you complain of me not spending time with Annabella. It is pointless to spend time with someone who is unconscious. I mean, she will not feel the difference," Jeremy said before leaving the barn.

Jacob mumbled various vulgar words before looking for Andromeda. He was glad to see that the horned pegasus was looking spotless. Her wings were fluffy with feathers, her horn sharp like a lethal weapon.

"I am glad you are all right. When Annabella wakes up, she will be happy to see you once again," Jacob said before patting the Pegasus and leaving the stables.

Upon her return to the infirmary Jacob ran into his father.

"Ah, Jacob. It is good to see you walking around," David said to his son.

Jacob smiled up at the nodum. "How is everyone doing?"

David smiled sadly at Jacob. "Your siblings are doing all right, but they do miss you dearly. I was thinking about bringing them over to visit you soon," David explained.

Jacob smiled. "I would like that very much. Tell them that I miss them too. If you see mother, could you tell her that I finally left the room? I am sure it will make her happy."

David smiled and nodded before Jacob began walking once again. As soon as he opened the door Emily stood up from his seat.

"Everything is the same. Just give her the potion at three and nine o'clock and remember to call for me if anything happens," she explained to Jacob who nodded and sat down in his seat when she left.

"Oh Annabella." Jacob suddenly began to cry. "You do not understand how much it breaks my heart to see you like this. I know I have said this a million times, but I really miss seeing you laugh. I miss talking to you about random things. I miss seeing you happy. Even when you wake up I know you will not be happy marrying that... that jerk. But you will be happy once you return to your family and that is all that matters."

Jacob reached under Annabella's pillow and took out the storybook that he hadn't touched in months. He read everything that had happened since the last time they checked, and was surprised to see that the book hadn't written anything about the night they had spent together. The book only spoke of the battle, Princess Annabella and Jacob's journey into the dark forest, and the Princess destroying the warlock with Prince Jeremy's help. The book did not even talk about Caroline being the King's grandmother, or Annabella's coma.

"This does not do justice to how amazing and strong you are," Jacob continued to cry. He quickly closed the book and set it on the nightstand when he noticed that he was wetting the pages with his tears. "Please wake up, Annabella. I beg of you. I need you and I miss you. Please," he cried as he held Annabella's hands.

Annabella felt herself waking up, but she couldn't see anything or move. She tried to speak, but she couldn't even move her mouth. *Jacob,* she thought, but she knew he didn't hear it when he didn't say anything. Jacob continued to cry and plead Annabella to wake up, but she couldn't do anything but listen. *Come on* Annabella begged herself as she tried to open her eyes and move, but she kept failing. She began to feel the tingle in her fingers from Jacob's hand touching hers, but she couldn't feel herself trying to move her fingers.

"Annabella," Jacob suddenly said. "I swear I felt your hand move. Do it again," he said.

Annabella didn't know what had happened, but she continued trying to move. When Jacob gasped she knew that something had happened. "You shocked me and your finger is glowing pink. Emily," Jacob called before Annabella heard him running. She heard the sound of a door opening before Jacob kept yelling for Emily to come.

"What happened?" A voice Annabella vaguely recognized slightly came into range.

"She shocked me with her electric powers. I felt her finger move and when I told her to do it again she shocked me," Jacob explained quickly.

"She must be waking up now," Emily said.

My nurse, Annabella realized. The sound of movement surrounded Annabella as it became more clear.

"What are you doing?" Jacob asked while sitting back down.

"I am making a potion that will fully wake her. She can probably hear everything, but cannot open her eyes or speak. This will quicken the process," Emily explained.

When a small "poof" sound reached Annabella's ears she knew it was because the potion was complete.

"We must give this to her through her mouth. Annabella, if you can hear me try your best to swallow this—even if you have to imagine doing it. I just need this to go down all the way," Emily said before she placed the vial on Annabella's lips and tilted it upwards.

Annabella could feel the liquid and did as she was told. She tried her best to swallow, but couldn't tell if it had happened until she felt the liquid begin to move farther down her throat.

"Guard," Emily called out. Annabella heard someone run into the room. "Call for the King and Queen. Tell them that Annabella is waking up."

The footsteps quickly moved away before the door once again closed. After a few minutes, Annabella suddenly felt a tingling sensation spreading through her body. She tried to move her hand again and this time felt it. Out of nowhere she began having a coughing fit and then suddenly opened her eyes to groan and close them again.

"Close the window," Emily said quickly.

Jacob used his wind powers to close the blinds. "Annabella," he said before lifting her and bringing her into a hug.

As soon as Annabella stopped coughing she weakly hugged Jacob back. "Jacob," she said quietly and opened her eyes slowly. Emily fixed the pillows so Annabella could sit up comfortably. When Jacob pulled away, Annabella looked to see tear stains on his cheeks. She slowly raised her arm and tried to wipe them away, but her arm dropped once again.

"Annabella," the Queen gasped from the door before running to the other side of the bed to hug her daughter.

"I am so glad that you are awake," the King said as he approached Annabella.

Caroline walked in after and made her way next to Jacob. "My dear great granddaughter," she said while lightly stroking Annabella's cheeks.

"How long have I been out?" Annabella finally asked with a scratchy voice.

Jacob looked at her sadly. "It has been three months. You have been in a coma all this time," he explained.

Annabella quickly sucked in air. "Three months?" she echoed. "The last thing I remember was seeing the warlock disintegrate. Did I really do that?"

Jacob nodded.

"Indeed you did," the King replied. "You single handedly destroyed the most powerful being known in existence, which means you have replaced him."

Annabella looked at everybody in shock. "Wow," was all she was able to say to that. "Wait," she spoke up after a few seconds. "What happened to everyone who took shelter in the castle? Are they ok?"

The Queen shushed the King so she could explain herself. "Many parts of the castle were destroyed, but no one inside was injured. Everyone, including Smokey, was fine when your father and the rest of the soldiers came to announce that we had won."

Annabella nodded in relief before her eyes widened. "Oh my gosh, Andromeda," she said before quickly trying to get up.

"Careful now," Jacob said while holding her shoulders. "She is perfectly all right. I checked on her for you. You are the only one we should be worried about right now."

Annabella sighed and sat back against the pillows. "How did I survive?"

This time it was Emily who answered. "Jacob gave you magical water as soon as we brought you in here. You would have likely died if it were not for that."

Annabella looked up at Jacob and smiled at him. "Thank you," she whispered while squeezing his hand.

"IT IS BEST TO ANNOUNCE it now," Annabella heard from outside the door. She had just finished eating soup with Jacob's help. Jacob spent hours catching her up on everything that had happened in the last three months, both the good and the bad news. Soon after someone knocked.

"Come in," Annabella said. She was surprised to see both Kings walking into the room with Jeremy trailing behind.

"Your Majesty," Annabella greeted while Jacob half bowed in his sitting position.

"Good day Annabella and err..." The King of the Land of Light truly looked confused.

Jacob coughed. "Jacob."

"Ah, yes. Jacob actually, we need to talk to Annabella in private so would you excuse us?"

Jacob nodded, but Annabella stopped him from getting up. "I want him to stay," Annabella said.

The King of the Land of Light threw a confused look at her, but nodded. "Hmm yes. Very well then. Your father, Jeremy and I all came to talk to you about the wedding."

Annabella tensed.

"Since you have awaken from your coma and you are healing rather quickly, the wedding will still occur on the same day," the King of the Land of Light continued.

"Is that all?" Annabella asked.

King Joseph, her father, then put a hand on her shoulder. "Basically. Other than that you will need to work on healing. Your great grandmother has gotten all of her powers back so she will be able to help you."

"I actually have to go," Jacob said suddenly. Annabella looked at him confused. "I uh... I told my father that I would visit my siblings as soon as you were better. They have not seen me for a long time," he explained before hugging Annabella awkwardly.

"All right," she said still confused. "I will see you tomorrow," she said before he could walk out the door.

Jacob paused and turned his head to look at Annabella, but his expression was sombre.

He turned back to look into the hallway and said, "yeah, I will see you tomorrow," sadly, before walking out and leaving Annabella confused and alone with the royals.

Chapter Twenty-Two

Annabella had been nothing but determined during the two weeks after she woke up from her coma. She wasn't allowed to leave the infirmary without Nurse Emily or any of the castles workers, but during the nighttime she would sneak out to work on walking.

Annabella was thankful that Jacob saved her life with the magical sparkling water, but she hadn't been seeing very much of him ever since she woke up. She assumed that Jacob wasn't there because she woke up. She had learned from him that he spent every single day for three months straight by her side, so it would only make sense that he would be running errands and spending time with his family.

This night was different. Annabella's walking had gotten much better. She still felt pain, but it wasn't going to stop her from seeing Smokey. Maria had been taking care of him since the war began, but Annabella truly missed him. She sucked in her breath when a guard almost spotted her. She quickly hid behind the corner when he turned around to investigate. After a few moments of silence the guard turned around and returned to patrolling.

"Perfect," Annabella said before she attempted to jog over to her tower's stairs.

The candles leading up the spiral stairs were all out, but one by one Annabella lit them with her powers that were slowly growing again. After a long fifteen minutes of hobbling up the steps, Annabella finally reached her room. She stared at the door for awhile before tentatively reaching out for the knob. Once she turned the knob, she

quickly walked in and lit the chandelier before spotting Smokey laying on his back in his bed.

"Smokey," Annabella said with a growing smile before the cat
woke up. Smokey analyzed her for a few moments with uncertainty.
He doesn't remember me, Annabella thought as she shifted uncom-
fortably.

Smokey slowly got up and walked towards her. He cautiously circled Annabella a few times while sniffing her nightgown. Suddenly,
Smokey leaped in the air.

"Humph," was what came out of Annabella's mouth when
Smokey landed in her arms. "You have gotten so big," she mused
as the cat purred affectionately. "I wish you could come down with
me, but you are a little tyrant and would probably break everything,"
she joked. Annabella cuddled with Smokey for a few minutes before
putting him down in his bed.

"I will visit you again soon," she said before opening the door.
Annabella wasn't paying attention when she turned to walk out of
her room and crashed right into someone. Before she could fall Jacob
caught hold of her and helped her straighten up.

"Jacob," Annabella said with a smile. Jacob flipped his messy hair
that hadn't been cut in months and coughed.

"What are you doing out of the infirmary?"

Annabella's smile faded into a frown when she noticed he didn't
seem happy to see her.

"I just wanted to see Smokey," she explained. She watched Jacob
nod slowly. "Wait, why are you here?" she asked.

"I heard some noises from my room so I went to investigate.
There was one candle on in your stairwell so I thought someone
might still be up here," Jacob explained.

Annabella nodded and closed the door behind her. She began
walking next to Jacob, but really struggled going down the stairs.

"Here," Jacob said with his arm out.

Annabella nodded and smiled before taking his arm to help her down. When they got to the bottom of the stairs, Annabella looked up at Jacob and opened her mouth to say something.

"Well, goodnight," he said quickly before he began walking away.

"Wait," Annabella called after him. She was feeling extremely frustrated.

Jacob stopped walking, but didn't turn around to face her. Annabella walked a few steps, but stopped when Jacob kept his back to her.

"Jacob, why are you acting like this?"

Jacob didn't move a muscle. "I do not understand."

Annabella frowned. "I have not seen you in two weeks, and now you are ignoring me."

"I am not. I have simply been doing my job. You are safe in the infirmary so I am tending to other things," Jacob defended himself.

"Yes, you are doing your job, but you have not been acting like yourself. We always spend hours talking about the simplest things. Now that we are talking you are avoiding me," Annabella debated.

Jacob turned around and looked down at Annabella. "I am doing my job," he said again.

When Annabella shook her head in dismay Jacob let out a breath. "Look, I went three months without doing any work. I am simply catching up on it. You are also busy with wedding planning, so there really is no point to wasting time with fun, Princess."

Annabella looked at Jacob angrily. "Do not even try to lie to me. You called me 'Princess.' You have only called me by my name since the first time I asked you to. This is something else, Jacob. Why can you not be my friend?" Annabella didn't care that she was yelling or that tears were running down her face.

"You want to know why?" Jacob yelled back.

"Yes, I do," Annabella barked.

Jacob licked his lips and shook his head. "Because there is no point anymore. How can you not understand this? This is not real for you. You are going to get married to that... that poor excuse of a Prince and be crowned as queen to wake up and be back to your real life. You are going to forget about me and everything else. I do not want to waste my time with something that is not even real."

"Shut up," Annabella demanded quickly. "No one can know about this."

Jacob looked around and rubbed a hand over his face. "I put a spell on the room. No one can hear us."

Annabella nodded. "Good. But that does not change this. You think I want to marry that asshole? A man who is not afraid of hurting me? A coward? No. I do not want to and I do not want to be queen. All I want is for my life to work out for once and if I do not marry him my parents will die, Jacob. You have your parents and that will not change, ever. But if I do what I want my parents are gone forever. They do not get to live on for centuries. I will not get to live probably will not live to see a century, but that does not matter because I am forced to lose something I love either way. And here you are acting like a jerk because of it." Tears were streaming down Annabella's face, but she refused to wipe them away.

"You think I want your parents to die? I do not. But when you are gone, Princess Annabella will still be here, and I know she will not be the same person you are. Reincarnation or alternate version or whatever you are, you are not the same person. I will lose you and I would rather distance myself so it will not hurt as much," Jacob said as his own tears escaped. His face suddenly hardened. "Wait... he hurt you?" he demanded.

Annabella shook her head. "He just grabbed my arm really hard and threatened me. It left a few bruises, but it was nothing serious," she said quietly. "I lied to you and said that I had hurt it falling out of bed."

Jacob shook his head. "This does not make sense. Why should you have to marry a man like that? Why does your storybook leave out those details? It is not fair."

Without thinking, Annabella ran up to Jacob, despite her sore legs, and hugged him. "I do not want to lose you. I will never be able to forget you Jacob. I do not want to waste any time left that I have with you," she cried.

Jacob didn't look down or return the hug.

Annabella looked up and grabbed his face. "We can forget about what happened in the forest. I just want you to be my friend until this is all over," she begged.

Jacob swallowed and looked into her eyes. "I would love to, but it would break my heart even more than it has already broken," he said before walking away, leaving Annabella standing alone in the dark hall.

"IS THIS COLOUR NOT just the most beautiful thing you have ever seen?" the Queen asked as she held up a piece of fabric. Annabella nodded without looking at the light blue silk. Her arm was supporting her head and she wanted nothing more than to leave. The Queen and many workers sat at the large dining table with various fabrics, colour samples, cutlery and everything else that could help with décor for the wedding.

"Oh just look at the finishing of these plates," the Queen's assistant, Irene, said as she admired a white Victorian-looking plate. The Queen clapped her hands together and had a look of such happiness on her face. "Oh Annabella, my little Princess. You have grown up so quickly," the Queen cooed.

Annabella looked at her and forced a smile. "I guess I have," she said before enduring the rest of the meeting. The wedding was only a few days away, and by the end of the meeting, all of the final touches were complete. All Annabella had to do was stay out of her room and spend extra time relaxing, as Nurse Emily worked hard to finish healing her.

"Nervous?" the King asked as he walked into the infirmary. Annabella stood up and spun around.

"I am not nervous. But I am feeling much better and bet that I could run around the castle a few times."

The King chuckled and hugged his daughter. "I am so proud of you, Annabella. You have always been such a polite girl growing up. You have always hated being called "Princess" and treat all people the same, royalty or not. You even saved The Land of Dreams. I do not think it is possible to be any prouder of you and your decisions, but you know what they say. Nothing is impossible," he said before walking away.

Annabella stood in the same place in confusion at what the King had just said. "Wait," she called after him. When the King turned around, she took a step forward. "You are going so soon?"

The King chuckled. "I came to check up on you quickly before going to a meeting with Jeremy's father. We are deciding on the changes now that our lands will be combined into one," he explained.

"Oh, all right. I will see you at dinner," Annabella said before he left the room. She returned to her bed and called for Maria to help with her bath since her powers were not completely back.

Maria seemed quiet to Annabella, but she didn't question it. No one other than the Queen and her workers seemed truly happy anymore. Even dinner was quiet. Both royal families ate together and the only person to say something was Jeremy, talking about how Annabella was going to love the way he was going to look in his wedding attire.

When it was time for bed, Annabella felt like a robot going through her nighttime routine. She no longer looked forward to a day of freedom, as it would give her too much time to think.

Annabella finally sat down on her bed and went to flip her pillow upside down and noticed her storybook. She picked it up and analyzed the front before angrily stuffing it into her nightstand.

Annabella knew that it would be another night of her crying herself to sleep. She missed Jacob dearly and was angry with him for being reasonable, but she was even angrier with herself for letting things go too far between them and being selfish.

Annabella blew out the candle on her nightstand—deciding to save up all of the magical energy she had—before finally laying down. She knew it would be a better night because there would be no talk about the wedding until the day of, which made her feel a bit better before she felt tears welling up in her eyes yet again.

Chapter Twenty-Three

Annabella woke up on her wedding day hoping that the weather would be horrible so the it could be postponed. Keeping herself from using unnecessary magic, she decided to physically open her blinds to reveal the outside world. Her smile dropped as soon as her bright green eyes met the beautiful weather.

"Wonderful," she muttered before closing the blinds and hiding under the covers once again. An annoyed groan came out of Annabella's mouth when the birds began chirping with glee. Knowing that there was no use to attempt to go back to sleep, she decided to feed Smokey and make her bed. She let out another groan when she heard the sound of heels walking up the stairs.

"Annabella, what are you still doing in here? We must start working on the room." Annabella sighed and grabbed her bag. "Yes mother," she said before leaving the room with the wedding planner.

The Queen decided that she would have Annabella's room completely redecorated so the newlyweds could enjoy their night before the honeymoon. As soon as Annabella walked out of her room the door shut behind her. Letting out another sigh of defeat, she walked down the stairs only to find a bunch of middle-aged woman waiting to greet her.

"Quickly, we must prep your nails while you eat," a woman Annabella didn't know well said.

"Would it not be better to wait until after I bathe?"

The three women quickly shook their heads before pulling Annabella into the dining hall. Annabella attempted to eat her breakfast, but having to eat with one hand while the other two women worked on her feet was hard enough. After the uncomfortable breakfast, Annabella was brought straight into the castles beauty room that she liked to call the salon. For the first time that morning, Annabella was finally able to relax. After being bathed she lay on a massage table, face mask and all, while the masseuse worked her magic on her *very* tense muscles.

After a couple of hours, Annabella was released. Walking down the halls never seemed harder for her and it wasn't because of the hair rollers making her scalp itch. The Land of Dreams had become Annabella's home for the year and she would miss it dearly. As she took in every detail of the hall she attempted to find the room she would be staying in until it was time for her to get dressed. Although it had been a year, she still struggled to find rooms. Each hallway she had been in had at least twenty different doors that looked identical.

Maybe it's this one, Annabella thought before reaching for the doorknob. The door opened slightly instead, revealing a small part of the bed. Annabella quickly backed away when she noticed that two people were on it. She let out a sigh of relief when she realized that they hadn't noticed her. *That would've been embarrassing.*

Before she continued on looking for her room, she heard Princess Annabella's cousin Claudia's voice coming from that very room.

"I can't believe... Get to have fun." Annabella didn't want to use a hearing spell, but she could understand what was going on by the heavy breathing and moaning. She once again peeked in to get a better look.

"Do not worry... Annabella is away.... Peasants we can still have our fun."

As Annabella suspected, it was Jeremy that was with Claudia. "Unbelievable," she muttered before going back to searching for her room. She was annoyed that this was who the Princess was stuck with, but if the real Annabella was ok with Jeremy's behaviour, she couldn't care less. Maybe Princess Annabella wasn't who she thought she was, considering the storybook left so much information out.

As soon as Annabella walked into her temporary room she hopped onto the bed. The curlers were in so tight that she doubted that her hair would be ruined if she laid down. As soon as her head touched the pillow, she sat back up and pulled out her storybook.

"Why are you following me," she said to the book in frustration before opening it. Annabella quickly shut the book when she saw that it made everything sound so positive.

The book skipped over everything that had happened with Jacob and her, Jeremy's unfaithfulness, making Annabella sound like the happiest girl in the world. *If only this were like that movie where I could write the future,* she thought before putting the book back under the pillow.

Annabella spent the remainder of her time daydreaming about all of the good things she experienced in the Land of Dreams. When someone knocked on the door, she jumped a bit and wiped the tears she not noticed were on her face. "Come in," she said once she was sitting up.

"Time to put on your dress," the Queen sang.

Annabella forced a smile, but the Queen was to busy being excited to notice that she wasn't happy. "After we get this on your makeup will be done and then you can finish up with your hair. After that you should be ready to walk down the aisle."

Annabella stood up straight as the women dressed her. She had to admit that the dress was beautiful, but it was too fancy for her liking. A dress like that could only cost a fortune. Annabella looked down at the lace detailing of the dress. The design was so simple and elegant, but it didn't surprise her—she was royalty after all.

Annabella caught a glimpse of the necklace Jacob had given her for Christmas and tucked it into her dress to keep it safe, refusing to take it off even though he wasn't talking to her.

"Make a kissy face," the new makeup artist ordered.

Annabella quickly made a face that resembled that of a scared puffer fish before lipstick began running over her lips. The one thing that Annabella was happy about was that her eyebrows were naturally shaped nicely so there was no need for painful plucking.

"I think we are done," said the makeup artist before all of the women backed away.

When Annabella stood up all of the women in the room stared at her with smiles on their faces.

The Queen walked up to Annabella and held her hands softly. "My Princess has grown up. You look absolutely amazing," she said as tears began to fill her eyes.

"Thank you, mother. You look amazing as well. You always do," was Annabella's honest reply. She had her best smile on.

The Queen finally seemed to notice Annabella's discomfort. "Do not worry, Bella. I too was very nervous on my wedding day."

Annabella flinched at the nickname. Her own mother would always shorten her name while trying to comfort her. A knock sounded at the door, which made Annabella feel even more anxious.

"It is time for the bride to take her waiting location," David's voice spoke from the hallway.

The Queen gently hugged Annabella and gave her one last smile before they all left the room. Annabella took a deep breath in and slowly let it out before she herself could leave the room.

"Is something wrong?" David asked with genuine concern.

Annabella quickly shook her head and forced a quick smile, but David sent her a look that she knew all too well.

"You are lying. You can tell me what is wrong. I promise to not tell Jacob," he said.

Annabella sighed and looked up at him. "I do not love him," she answered simply.

David nodded as he continued walking. "If Prince Jeremy is a good person you will learn to love him. I can tell that you love my son, but you are royalty and he is not. I guess life is not fair even for the most powerful beings," he explained.

"How is Jacob doing? I am assuming that you know about how we are not talking to one another," Annabella asked, which made David sigh.

"Jacob is a strong man who can convince others that he is all right, but I can tell from the lack of shine in his eyes and the way he walks that he is depressed. Perhaps it will go away with time, or maybe he will have the luck of meeting his soulmate if he has one. But as I said before; Jacob is a strong person. He will get through this."

When David stopped in front of a room with a beautiful golden handle Annabella hugged him.

"Thank you for being so good to me, David. You deserve all the best," Annabella told him honestly as he hugged her back.

"I have nothing but the best thanks to your family and my own. You will be a great Queen," he said before opening the door for Annabella, revealing the King sitting on a sofa.

"Annabella," said the King as he straightened up and smiled. "You look absolutely stunning."

Annabella smiled back and walked towards him. "Thank you, father. It means a lot to me," she responded before the King stood up to hug her.

"It is hard for me to comprehend that my little Princess is getting married. If I could, I would keep you my baby forever, but sadly I cannot do that," he said with his eyes watering.

Annabella bit her cheek to keep herself from crying. The King's eyes were similar to her real father's and it hurt her to see him sad.

"I will never leave you and mother. I will always be your little Princess" Annabella told him, believing that the real Princess Annabella loved them dearly.

"We have a half hour before we walk down the aisle. Let us relax until then," the King decided before sitting down and patting the spot next to him. Annabella smiled and was relieved to sit down. She rested her head gently on the King's shoulder and tried to daydream about something other than the wedding so she could have a few minutes of happiness.

The famous "Canon in "D began playing and Annabella could hear it through the doors. *I guess Pachelbel also exists in this dimension,* she thought. She peeked outside of the window that revealed hundreds of guests sitting in their chairs. The wedding was outdoors due to the beautiful weather and fresh air, but Annabella felt as if breathing was the last thing that she could do. Jeremy was standing at the other side of the long red carpet along with the minister.

When the King called, Annabella quickly looped her arm through his and forced herself to relax. The large French doors opened, revealing Annabella to all of the guests. Annabella was thankful that her veil would cover her up until she got to the other side of the carpet, but her legs were trembling as she held onto the King's arm with her dear life.

Step by step, Annabella and the King walked down the aisle. All of the guests had huge smiles on their faces as they watched her, but when Annabella spotted Caroline, she was confused. Caroline had a serious look on her face. It looked almost determined.

Annabella then noticed Jacob standing next to Maria and David. Watching Jacob look so miserable broke her heart. She could tell that he was holding back his tears. All she wanted to do was run up to him and give him a hug.

When Annabella and the King reached the front, he gave her a kiss on the cheek over her veil and shook Jeremy's hand, before sitting next to the Queen and Caroline in the front row. Annabella turned to Jeremy who had a huge smile on his face. Anyone else would've thought that Jeremy was honestly excited and in love with them, but Annabella knew better. He was excited for the power and wealth.

"You look absolutely beautiful," Jeremy said once he lifted the veil and pushed it back.

Annabella forced a smile at him. "Thanks," she said, not returning the compliment that he was obviously craving.

"Dearly beloved, we are gathered here today..." the minister started.

Annabella kept running things through her head the entire time he spoke. She couldn't care less about it. It didn't mean a thing to her—especially since she wouldn't actually be married in a few weeks. When one of Jeremy's little cousins came up with the rings, Annabella forced herself to return her attention to her ceremony.

"Prince Jeremy, do you take Princess Annabella to be your wedded wife?" Jeremy smiled down at her lovingly and slid the ring onto her finger. "I do."

Annabella grabbed the other ring and placed it on the tip of Jeremy's finger.

"Princess Annabella, do you take Prince Jeremy to be you wedded husband?" Annabella gulped and looked out into the crowd. Jacob was looking down at his feet, while the Queen looked overjoyed. The King had a pensive look on his face, while Caroline still looked serious. Annabella kept looking at Caroline and felt worried.

When Caroline mouthed the word "soulmate," Annabella felt as if time had frozen. She quickly glanced at Jacob and back to Caroline, who then nodded. Annabella faced Jeremy and looked down at the ring before looking back up at his face, which looked a bit confused.

"I cannot do this." Annabella flinched slightly when the crowd made surprised sounds.

Jeremy laughed sarcastically and looked at Annabella. "You are such a joker," he said.

Annabella shook her head. "No, I am serious. I cannot marry you."

Jeremy looked angry. "But we are betrothed. There is no way out of this one."

Annabella looked into the crowd of chattering people and saw Jacob looking confused. "I have a soulmate," she announced loudly.

Jacob's mouth was hanging open in shock. Annabella motioned towards Caroline who had a small smile on her face. Jacob seemed to understand, but he continued to look confused and now very concerned.

"This is absurd," Jeremy said before turning to the minister. "We are betrothed. There is not a way out of it, correct?"

Annabella looked at the minister. "Can you please check? I heard that having a soulmate may change this," she pleaded.

The minister sighed and began flipping through his large book. As everyone waited for the minister to decide if the betrothal was breakable or not, Annabella sat at the bottom of the stairs.

"Why would you do that?"

Annabella looked up to see Jacob hovering over her.

"I cannot marry him when I am in love with you," she said. Jacob closed his eyes and breathed in before sitting down next to her.

"Your parents, Annabella. You cannot go back if you do not go through with this," Jacob explained. "*You* are in love with me, but the real Princess is not," he whispered.

Annabella shook her head. "I know. I know I cannot go back, but I do not want to anymore. If I am here, then there is no Annabella back there, and the real one would be stuck with a monster for a husband while being in love with you. It would be as if I never existed and my family never existed. It would probably change the past completely. And you are her soulmate either way. That would not change."

Jacob grabbed her hand. "You will never see your real parents ever again," Jacob explained.

Annabella nodded and swallowed. She felt like a horrible person, but knew her heart would be broken to not be with Jacob. "They technically do not exist right now, so I would be fine with it. If this would cause them to die than I would marry him, but since I am stuck here, nothing that has ever happened in my old life would be real anymore. I am prepared for that. I just want to be happy with you and if I returned to that world with my memories, it would kill me to not see you ever again," she explained. Jacob smiled slightly, but was interrupted before he could say anything.

"Princess Annabella, this betrothal is legally binding. Having a soulmate cannot change the situation," the minister explained. It was like Annabella's world was shattering around her. She felt as if someone had ripped her heart out of her chest, leaving her with a void that would stay there forever.

"There is nothing that can be done?" Jacob asked when he noticed Annabella couldn't speak.

"You heard him, commoner. There is nothing that can be done," Jeremy said smugly.

"Well," the priest started. Everyone quieted down instantly and listened closely. "The only way that the betrothal can be broken, is if either you or Jeremy was unfaithful after it was signed. And by unfaithful I mean the act of fornication with someone whom is not involved in the agreement."

Annabella's eyes lit up. "Jacob and I slept together."

Once again the crowd gasped and began chattering. People from Jeremy's kingdom looked angry as they shouted insults at Annabella, but she didn't care and waved them off.

"How could you? I love you. I thought you loved me," Jeremy said in a convincing manner.

"Oh can it, asshole," Annabella snapped at him. "I saw you and Claudia having sex this morning so you are just as guilty as I am."

Jeremy's eyes widened as the crowd gasped yet again. "We did no such thing. I would never betray the love of my life. I would commit an act of such dishonesty."

Annabella laughed at that. "Everyone listen up," she shouted to the crowd. Many people stopped talking, but many were still yelling at her. Jacob whistled loudly which shut everyone else right up.

"Close your eyes and watch for yourselves," Annabella said before sending everyone the mental images she had retained from walking in on Jeremy and Claudia. She also included the memory from the Christmas celebration when Annabella first discovered the two, as well as the time that Jeremy had manhandled her.

When the flashback ended Annabella felt light-headed from using too much power, and sat back down.

"Are you all right?" Jacob asked her.

Annabella nodded. "It was because of the power I used to show everyone. The headache should be gone in a few minutes," she explained before a strange woman stood up.

"You bastard," she shouted and pointed at Jeremy.

Annabella couldn't help but smirk at the look on Jeremy's face. She there was nothing that he could do about it. He got caught red handed and now he was going to pay. Annabella quickly got up and ran off the little stage with Jacob behind her. The minister was sitting down and looked flustered.

Annabella stopped and turned back to look at Jeremy. "Fetch," she said before throwing her diamond wedding band as far as she could. Jeremy glared at her and shook his head before he ran off to frantically search for it with a crowd of people yelling insults after him.

"You made the right decision," the King told Annabella before bringing her into a tight hug.

"It was a stupid risk, but it was worth it," the Queen added on before she looked at Jacob. "Welcome to the family, Jacob. I will be looking forward to calling you my Annabella's boyfriend."

Annabella looked at the crowd that was beginning to get smaller. Most of the people from Jeremy's kingdom had left, while the villagers from the Land of Dreams stayed seated.

"I am very sorry for my son's behaviour. I assure you that we will not be bothering you again unless you need our help," King Ronald, Jeremy's father, apologized. "If I had known of Jeremy's behaviour, I would not have agreed to requesting the official betrothal. I truly hope that you will forgive my land and we can continue on as allies," King Ronald finished before returning to his wife and leaving the field.

"That feels a lot better," Annabella said before holding Jacob's hand, and resting her head on his shoulder as the King and Queen spoke to the guests who had decided to stay. Jacob kissed Annabella on the head and smiled.

"It really does."

Chapter Twenty-Four

Annabella was unconsciously smiling as the Queen spoke with a few guests. The feeling of Jacob's warm fingers wrapped around her own soothed her as random thoughts flew around in her head. When she noticed the minister packing up, Annabella ran over to him without thinking twice.

"Can you marry Jacob and I? No need for the fancy stuff," Annabella asked.

The minister rolled his eyes and sighed. "This has by far been the strangest day of my life, but I can do it," he replied. "But," he started again, "you will need rings to make it official."

Annabella looked at him and began to worry once again.

"Annabella, are you sure you want to do this? We can wait a few weeks or even a few days so you can have the wedding you want. It would also give me a chance to get you a ring," Jacob said.

Annabella shook her head. "I would marry you in the rain while wearing my nightgown," she said before an idea popped into her head. Annabella focused on the little vines that wrapped around the gazebo. With her hands glowing pink she watched as the vines extended to wrap around her finger, and then Jacob's, snapping them off and leaving what looked like green rings behind. Annabella took hers off carefully and handed it to Jacob.

"This will have to do for now," she laughed.

The minister looked between the two lovers and shook his head. "Call both of your parents. You will not want them to miss this," he said before both Annabella and Jacob ran to where their parents were conversing.

"We are getting married," Jacob announced at the same time as Annabella.

The King and Queen looked at Maria and David with confusion, but Maria and the Queen quickly started jumping with excitement.

"When do you want to get married?" the King asked Annabella.

"Right now actually. The minister said that he could do it. We even have temporary rings," Annabella said as she held up the little vine rings.

"I have a better idea," the King said before reaching inside of his suit. He pulled out a silver chain that had two rings hanging on it. "These rings belonged to my parents. When they were killed, the rings survived and ever since I have kept them on this chain. I think you two could use these more than I."

Annabella looked at Jacob and smiled.

"Thank you, Your Majesty," said Jacob before he took the rings off of the chain and handed it back to the King.

The minister walked over to the group once Annabella motioned for him. Several people from the Land of Dreams stayed in their seats and smiled when Annabella and Jacob stood at the front holding hands, facing each other.

"Dearly beloved, we are gathered here today... again... to welcome the lovely Princess Annabella and the well respected knight, Sir Jacob, on their special day," the minister began.

Annabella was trying to pay attention, but she didn't want to stop looking at Jacob. She could finally do what made her happy. Even though she would never see her real parents again, Annabella knew that most would not be presented with the same opportunity as her, and that there was no guarantee that completing the story would even save them. The King and Queen were technically

Annabella's parents and they were similar enough, and she was happy to be with Jacob.

"Do you, Sir Jacob, take Princess Annabella to be your wedded wife?"

Jacob's smile grew even wider. "I do," he replied as he slightly tightened his grip before Annabella slid the ring onto his finger. The ring glowed Jacob's aura colour and magically changed to fit his finger.

"And do you," the minister said before facing Annabella, "Princess Annabella, take Sir Jacob to be your wedded husband?"

Annabella nodded quickly. "Of course I do," she said before Jacob slid her ring down the rest of her finger. Her ring did the same, but it glowed her pink aura colour instead.

"Congratulations," the minister said with relief. "I now pronounce you husband and wife."

Before the minister could say the remaining line Annabella quickly wrapped her arms around Jacob's neck and kissed him. Jacob's arms wrapped around Annabella's waist and held her closer as the crowd began clapping and cheering.

Annabella, broke away and laughed. "We are married," she told Jacob.

Jacob laughed himself. "I guess we are. This day turned out very differently from what I thought it would be."

ANNABELLA WATCHED AS the last person left to return to the village. She glanced down at her ring and smiled to herself. Jacob was conversing with his parents and siblings when the King walked towards Annabella.

"Can we speak?"

Annabella nodded and walked with the King towards the seats in the middle.

"I knew you would make the right decision. Well, I did not know, but I had a strange feeling that something would happen."

Annabella looked up at the King with confusion. "What do you mean? Did something happen that I do not know of?"

The King chuckled and shook his head. "Something that happened a very long time ago. Much before you were born. You see, when my parents died, these rings were not the only things they left me." King Joseph motioned towards Annabella's ring finger. "They also left me a letter."

Annabella kept her attention on the King. *If he's telling me this he may know about everything,* she thought. Now that she was staying in this world, Annabella knew she would have to do everything she could to be Princess Annabella.

"They told me that you would have a soulmate. Naturally, I was very excited to know that I would have a daughter, but this was long before I even met your mother. I soon began to doubt the letter. I did not understand why they kept this from me. I still do not understand how they knew. Your great grandmother, Caroline, brought this up to me earlier today. She was aware that my parents knew something, but she did not know what it was exactly. When I told her about the letter she told me that it was true, that you indeed do have a soulmate."

Annabella smiled sadly. "Wow. Was that all that the letter said?"

The King shook his head. "No. The letter explained that I would bring your soulmate into your life. When I hired Jacob I knew there was something special about him. Not only did I know that he was more powerful than any of the other knights, but he has powers that usually only those of royal blood possess, such as the ability to create spells. He had blood that runs only through the veins of someone who is destined to be royal. If I had believed more, I would never have chosen Jeremy. I should have known that you were meant to be with Jacob. If it were not for the war and my fear of losing, I would have never decided to make that betrothal official. If I had waited, I could have told you this months ago and you would have been happier. I am truly sorry, Annabella."

Annabella was confused by what she had just heard. *Did I ruin the story so badly that this is happening now?* She quickly formed a smile. "It is all right. Everyone makes mistakes, and I am very lucky that I got out of the betrothal. I wish I had confided in you and mother before. I hated Jeremy since the first day I met him. All he wanted was to have the power of being the king of such great lands." Annabella's eyes widened. " Now that I am not married to a king, who is going to take your place?"

The King smiled at Annabella. "Like I said, mortals that have magic like Jacob are not usual. They are meant to be royalty. This means that you are not married to a commoner, but to Jacob, future King of the Land of Dreams."

Annabella's smile grew. "He will be an amazing king,"she promised.

"That I know," replied the King. "But since things have changed, your mother and I have decided to rule the land for a few more years. You and Jacob have been through so much this year that it would only be fair. Enjoy being newlyweds, Annabella. We want to relieve you of any royal responsibilities for a while. After all you will not have this much free time until your own child becomes King or Queen."

Annabella hugged the King. "I love you, daddy," she said as a tear ran down her face.

She truly meant it. She knew her father wasn't a reincarnation of the King, but his eyes and smile were very similar. *Once Jacob and I are back from our honeymoon I'll speak with Caroline to figure out everything else*, she promised herself before running towards Jacob.

"I am so happy you two are together. I could not ask for a better daughter-in-law," Maria said before hugging Annabella.

"Thank you, Maria. I will look forward to seeing you more often as family," Annabella said honestly before turning to Jacob who was already looking at her.

"Shall we prepare for the dinner?" Jacob's grin grew before he took Annabella's hand into his own and waved to his parents.

"You know," Jacob started, "We still have to talk about all of this."

Annabella sighed. "I know, but can we talk about it later? I am starving."

Jacob nodded and wrapped his arm around his wife's waist as they happily walked into castle.

"HAVE FUN ON YOUR HONEYMOON. I am sure that you two will enjoy the Land of Stars. If you ever get lost, all you need to do is follow the brightest star back to their village," the Queen explained before hugging Annabella and Jacob for the last time. The dining hall was empty except for the tables and plates. The workers would be coming in to clean everything up and restore the castle within a few hours. Normally everything would be cleaned up by now, but they had also taken part in the celebration at Annabella's request.

"I will send letters," Annabella promised before the Queen disappeared. The feeling of someone staring made her turn around and look up at Jacob's smirking face.

"What?" Annabella asked when she saw his expression. Jacob's smirk grew wider as he circled his hands around her waist.

"You know," he began before pulling her closer and moving a strand of hair behind her ear. "It *is* the night of our wedding," he whispered before lightly placing a kiss on Annabella's neck.

Annabella shivered as she felt the best kind of goosebumps forming before wrapping her arms around Jacob's neck. "I am well aware of that," she said quietly before Jacob quickly picked her up bridal style. Annabella giggled at how big the smile on his face was as he carried her up the stairs in her tower.

When Jacob opened the door to Annabella's room they were both surprised. The room wasn't too overdone, but actually looked really nice. With a glowing snap of a finger, candles all over the room were lit, creating a beautiful soft glow throughout the room. Annabella looked up at Jacob before he walked her over to the bed and lay her down.

"Do you want to talk about everything now?" Jacob asked.

Annabella shook her head slowly and pulled him closer to her. "I just want you now," she said as she began unbuttoning his dress shirt. "We *literally* have all of the time in the world to talk."

Jacob smiled and quickly caught her lips. "I love you," he whispered before waving his hand to lock the door.

"I love you too," Annabella responded before pulling him in.

Chapter Twenty-Five

The slight breeze flew into the room making Annabella's hair tickle her face. The smell of fresh grass helped her wake up slowly. She had a small smile on her face as she opened her eyes.

I'm married, Annabella thought to herself before letting out a yawn. After softly rubbing the sleep from her eyes, Annabella turned to her right to face Jacob.

The night before had been magical. Annabella had made the biggest decision of her life when she decided against marrying Jeremy to save her parents. Sure, she would be stuck in the Land of Dreams forever and would never see her real parents again, but she would still be changing the future, because the 'real' Annabella Tompkins would be born with a different soul, or wouldn't exist at all.

"Jacob?" Annabella spoke when she noticed he wasn't in bed next to her. When she looked up she quickly sat up in her bed. The bedding was a different colour and felt different as well.

"This can't be happening," she said when she realized that she was in her room—her *old* room. Annabella frantically looked around in search of something, anything that could give her answers. That's when she spotted a familiar police officer sitting on her futon.

"Oh no..." Annabella said quietly as her heart started to beat faster. "No!" she screamed as tears quickly began to flow down her face.

Officer Patterson jolted awake. "Oh Annabella, I'm so sorry. I must've fallen asleep for a few moments," she said and looked down at her watch with a confused expression. "The time hasn't changed at all. That's weird," Officer Patterson said as she got up and slowly made her way towards Annabella's bed.

"They're dead," Annabella choked between sobs when she looked up at Officer Patterson.

The police officer nodded sadly. "They are, sweetie. I'm so sorry. I guess it's finally hit you now."

Annabella sucked in a long, shaky breath and wiped her face with her sheets. "I failed them," she realized.

"Oh sweetie, it wasn't your fault. You couldn't have done anything to prevent it," Officer Patterson said, trying to convince Annabella, but she knew better.

I let them die so I could marry Jacob, and now all of us are losing. Annabella thought about the shock Jacob would have when he woke up next to the real Princess Annabella. "They died because I was too selfish to complete the story the right way."

Officer Patterson looked confused. "What do you mean?"

Annabella grabbed her storybook and flipped it to the last page before handing it to the police officer. "I married Jacob instead of Jeremy. I wasn't supposed to do that. Now they're gone," she explained.

Officer Patterson read the page and looked down on Annabella looking even more confused. "It says that the Princess denied Jeremy and married a knight named Jacob instead and lived happily ever after."

Annabella quickly grabbed the book back from Officer Patterson and scanned the page. "What? That can't be right," she said before quickly flipping through the storybook's pages.

Officer Patterson put her hand on Annabella's. "Sweetie, it's ok. I'm sure there's an explanation for this. You didn't believe me before, but I want to ask you one more time. Do you want to come with my partner and I to the hospital to see them?"

Annabella really didn't want to go, but she couldn't handle the feeling of her guilt getting any stronger. She nodded her head and let Officer Patterson help her out of the bed. Annabella's legs felt like jelly as she slowly made her way down the stairs. She spotted Officer Blake sitting on the living room couch that she thought she'd never see again.

"I'll start the car," Officer Blake said, seeming to understand what was happening.

Annabella absorbed everything going on around her. She had forgotten the colour that her living room was painted, but what really got to her was the realization that she no longer had magic. Annabella had tried flicking off the lights with the wave of her finger, but when Officer Patterson flicked the light switch off, she remembered that electricity is what lit up the room instead of magic-controlled candles.

Even though it was summer, a light breeze blew through the night air and Annabella felt goosebumps forming on her arms. She shivered and wished she were back in the Land of Dreams where she couldn't feel the cold as much.

Annabella was helped into the back of the police car, which felt fitting with her guilt. The officers were trying to talk to her, but she just nodded and looked out the window at the curious neighbours as they drove towards the hospital.

THE HOSPITAL WAS AWFUL for Annabella. She had to answer several questions before finally being allowed into the morgue, signing forms to take possession of her parent's belongings. When it was finally time to see them, Annabella's eyes were dry. Seeing their bodies made her feel sick. Annabella felt so much anger inside of her and couldn't handle it much longer. She had grieved in the Land of Dreams, but now she just felt numb. *Let's just get this over with.*

The doctor explained that they were able to save a few organs since both of her parents signed up to be donors.

At least something good came out of this.

The next steps were for Annabella to wait and meet with a lawyer who would explain what she had to do next. She still had another year left of high school, so she needed a guardian for the time being, and then the legal documentation for the house would have to be signed over into her name.

"This is going to suck," Annabella mumbled while looking at herself in the bathroom mirror. Her hair was back to looking bland and her eyes looked more hazel than green and lacked vibrancy. She was also slightly bigger and no longer had perfectly clear skin.

Annabella jumped when she felt something vibrating in her pocket. "What the..." she began as she pulled her cellphone out of her pocket. *I forgot about these,* she thought before reading the name on the screen. "Holy shit," she said before tapping the green circle on the screen.

"Mrs. Carter?" Annabella asked.

"Oh thank goodness you picked up, Annabella. We heard about everything and took an emergency flight out. We just landed at the airport and are on our way to pick you up from the hospital," Mrs. Carter rushed out.

What is she talking about? Annabella's eyes widened in realization. *Zach and his parents are moving back.* "Uh ok. I'll wait here" she said awkwardly.

"I'm so sorry about this, honey. I'll see you soon," Mrs. Carter said before hanging up.

"This week is really going to be all over the place." Annabella sighed and once again took a seat.

Annabella thanked Officers Patterson and Blake and apologized for how she had acted before. They seemed happy that she was feeling better, but she knew they didn't believe her about the Land of

Dreams. Annabella was starting to doubt herself, but it felt too real to be a dream. At the same time, her imagination had always been wild and the shock from suddenly losing her parents could've caused it. What didn't make sense to her was the new ending.

I've been reading it all my life, she thought. *They're probably right. I might just be crazy.*

It took an hour for Mrs. Carter to arrive. Annabella barely recognized her, but when she was enveloped into a hug, she knew it was her.

"Oh Annabella," Mrs. Carter cried. "I can't believe this has happened. I'm so sorry that you have to go through this."

Annabella felt as if she were hugging a very close friend. The feeling was familiar, but she knew she was vulnerable and it was affecting her. "Thank you. I don't know what I'm going to do without them. It's going to be so hard to get used to being alone."

"Oh sweetie, you won't be alone. That's something you don't have to worry about. We had a long chat on the flight over and agreed that you can stay with us. We know your grandmother lives a too far, and it wouldn't be fair to take you away from your house. If you don't want to be there we can find somewhere else to live," Mrs. Carter explained.

Annabella smiled genuinely for the first time since arriving back from the Land of Dreams. "Thank you, Mrs. Carter. I would love to stay." Annabella knew it would be tough, but she had mourned for a year knowing that there was a good chance that she couldn't save her parents. *I guess the tears truly did change the story.*

"Where are Zach and Mr. Carter?" Annabella questioned.

Mrs. Carter smiled at her. "They're at our hotel room. We weren't sure of the decision that you would make so we got a room. They'll be ok for the night, but I was wondering if you wanted to go back to the hotel or go home? I can go home with you if you'd like."

Annabella nodded. "Home would be wonderful. I have a bunch of paperwork to go through and would love your help. I kind of know what they had in terms of life insurance and in their will, but I don't even know where to start."

"Please don't worry about that for today. You've just experienced tragedy and should relax and think about yourself. How about we have a bit of a girls night and pamper ourselves before bed?" Mrs. Carter was smiling up at Annabella.

Annabella nodded. "That would be lovely."

ALTHOUGH IT WAS ALREADY the middle of the night, Mrs. Carter made sure to entertain Annabella. She told embarrassing stories about Zach and questioned her about boys.

"You're not lying to me, are you?" she questioned Annabella.

"No, I swear. I don't have a boyfriend. I haven't had one since the ninth grade and I wouldn't even consider that one a real boyfriend. The most we ever did was hold hands and that only lasted for a few weeks," Annabella laughed. *I can't exactly tell her that I did have a husband for a night.*

"I can't believe that. You are such a smart and beautiful girl," Mrs. Carter marvelled.

Annabella shrugged. "Tell that to the boys at my school." They both laughed.

Annabella took a long shower that steamed up the entire washroom. She missed having her water powers, but her shower was nice enough.

"Damn it," Annabella cursed when she wiped the mirror. The humidity had made her hair a bit damp and it looked like a mess.

"Are you ok in there, sweetie? I'm heading over to your room if you don't need anything," Mrs. Carter called from outside the washroom.

"I'm fine," Annabella yelled back. "My hair is just a mess. I'll be out in two." Annabella put on her pajamas and brushed her teeth before making her way back towards her room. On the way, Annabella stopped at her parents' room and peeked inside. Everything looked the exact same as it did before they left for their trip. The bed was perfectly made and looked like it was straight out of a furniture advertisement. It was a very cozy room.

"I'll miss you guys," Annabella whispered and wiped a tear away. She knew it would be very difficult forgiving herself for what had happened, but she also knew that the situation was unique and no one else would've been provided with the small chance.

"There you are. I don't see what's wrong with your hair," Mrs. Carter said.

"It got a bit wet with all of the shower steam. It's going to look gross in the morning."

Mrs. Carter clapped her hands excitedly. "I can help you with that. Come, sit right here in front of me," she said while patting the empty spot on the bed. Annabella shrugged and made her way over. She sat down facing away from Mrs. Carter and crossed her legs for comfort.

"I've always loved doing french braids on my friends. I unfortunately never ended up having a girl, but if I did I would've done these all the time," Mrs. Carter explained excitedly.

Annabella smiled to herself. "I know someone who loves doing the as well. I love how they look so that would be lovely."

Mrs. Carter grabbed a brush from the nightstand and began styling Annabella's hair. "You know," she started, "I always did these on your mother. She used to love them, but after doing them a few hundred times she started to get sick of them," Mrs. Carter suddenly stopped moving her hands. "I'm sorry. You probably don't want me to talk about them."

Annabella turned her head and smiled. "Don't worry, I don't mind. I think it's better to talk about them. It's nice learning new things about them. It'll help their memory live on."

Mrs. Carter smiled and hugged Annabella again. "You were such a strong little girl. I can see that hasn't changed one bit."

After Annabella's hair was in a perfect French braid she was ready to sleep.

"Are you sure you don't want me to sleep on the futon?" Mrs. Carter asked for the third time.

Annabella laughed. "I'm sure. You and Mr. Carter can stay in my parents room from now on. I really don't mind. It's much better than it being empty."

Mrs. Carter smiled at her and gave her one last hug. "Goodnight sweetie. Zach and his father will be here in the afternoon after we get some of the time-sensitive stuff out of the way. Please don't hesitate to wake me up if you need anything, and I mean anything at all."

Annabella nodded. "I promise I will, but I'm sure it'll be ok. Goodnight, Mrs. Carter, and thank you again."

Annabella was finally in bed and ready to sleep. Her storybook was sitting on her nightstand and she was tempted to go through it, but knew it would only make her miss Jacob even more. *I can't believe I'll never see you again.* She turned off her table lamp and rolled onto her side before crying herself to sleep thinking about her parents, but most of all, Jacob.

THE NEXT DAY SEEMED to drag on forever. Annabella and Mrs. Carter had sat down to talk about the will. Annabella already knew that everything would be left to her, but she had to sign a few documents to ensure the life insurance would properly reach her. The life insurance would've paid off the rest of the mortgage and probably cover a new one, so Annabella planned on keeping the house around at least until her final year of high-school was over. The insurance money would cover the bills and would pay for university.

They also had to go to the bank and set up a few different accounts. Things needed to be transferred to Annabella, and she even set up an account that would give her a set amount of money every few months to live off of.

Mom and Dad really thought this through, she thought. It seemed like everything would be taken care of. Even the funeral arrangements were straight-forward. Annabella knew her parents wanted to be cremated, and Annabella planned on getting jewellery made so she could always have a part of them with her.

Annabella and Mrs. Carter were relieved to finally be out of the last meeting.

"I just texted them to pick pizza up on the way over to your house," Mrs. Carter said, referring to Mr. Carter and Zach.

Annabella couldn't help but smile. "I'm really excited to see Zach again. I can't believe it's finally time."

Mrs. Carter smiled at her and began to drive. "He's really excited to see you too. He hasn't shut up about it for the past several months."

Annabella felt oddly happy about that. She still really missed the Land of Dreams, but was finally accepting the fact that it was just a dream. The doctors had explained that going through a traumatic experience could lead to confusion and even memory loss. *Maybe my story always did end that way.*

After arriving at home Annabella decided to take another shower. She didn't want to smell like a funeral home when finally seeing Zach and Mr. Carter again.

Gosh you're acting like it's a date, Annabella thought to herself and frowned. She felt guilty for being excited about seeing him.

I miss the Land of Dreams, Annabella thought before she let out a sarcastic laugh. The guilt quickly turned to anger. *The freaking land of actual dreams that isn't even real.* Annabella shook her head and decided to stop thinking about it. "It was just a dream and I need to move on from it," she decided before making her way towards her room to get ready for dinner. Zach and Mr. Carter would be arriving soon, and she wanted to make a good impression.

Chapter Twenty-Six

With all of the meetings, Annabella had forgotten that there was only one day left before her seventeenth birthday. She was looking forward to seeing everyone again and starting her new life. She was pacing around waiting for the doorbell to ring when she felt her phone vibrating.

"Hello?" Annabella answered, forgetting to check the name on the screen.

"Hey, Annabella. Happy almost birthday."

"Zach, hey! Thank you," Annabella answered excitedly. She was so excited to see Zach again after twelve years, and knowing that she would have him back at any moment was unbelievable to her.

"I really wish we could've been there for you yesterday. We're still on our way, but thankfully there isn't much traffic so we should be there in under an hour," Zach explained. Annabella smiled as she paced around.

"I'm so excited to have you back. And I'm excited to finally see how you've changed. Can you at least tell me how tall you are?" Zach laughed from his end of the phone.

"No can do. But you'll see me soon so it doesn't matter."

Annabella could hear shuffling downstairs and wondered what Mrs. Carter was doing.

"Hello?" Zach said.

Annabella snapped back to the conversation. "Oh sorry, your mom cooking distracted me. But I am very excited. It's crazy to think that so many years have gone by," she mused.

Before Zach could reply, Annabella heard a knock on the door.

"I think someone is here. I'm going to go answer the door. Text me when you're close so I can go downstairs," Annabella said.

Zach laughed and said goodbye before Annabella hung up and made her way to the door. The moment it swung open Annabella's mouth dropped.

"Jacob?" she gasped as the Jacob from her dream stood in front of her. His dark messy hair was the same along with his height, build, face and the rest of his features. The only difference was the modern clothing.

"I guess you can call me that if you really want to, but I'd prefer if you called me Zach like you did a few seconds ago," Zach said before pulling Annabella into a tight hug.

She quickly hugged back and fought back the tears. *This has to be Jacob,* she thought before opening her eyes. Standing next to Annabella's tree in the front lawn was her grandmother. Annabella continued to stare at the woman she hadn't seen in years, but didn't say anything. *I guess she got the call about Mom and Dad,* she thought, but her grandmother had a determined look on her face. When her grandmother mouthed the words "soulmate" she knew that Zach was in fact the Jacob from storybook and it had all been real. Annabella shut her eyes for a few moments and when she opened them her grandmother was gone.

"Oh my God," Annabella said, which made Zach step back from the hug and send her a worried look.

"What's wrong?" he asked her. Annabella looked around and shook her head before smiling up at him. "Nothing. It's just... I can't believe you're really here. I was beginning to think it was all a dream."

Zach smiled before pressing his index finger to his lips. Annabella looked behind him to see his father in a parked car on the other side of the street.

"But how are you here?" Annabella whispered as she looked at Zach in confusion.

"It's complicated, but we can talk about that later," he said with a smile. The sound of car door shutting made Zach straighten up.

"Well," he started in a louder voice, "you're a little shorty, but don't worry, you've definitely aged well," he said. "Nice necklace, by the way."

Annabella looked down at her necklace and smiled at Zach before giving him another hug. "You have no idea how happy I am that you're here with me again."

Zach tightened the hug. "Correction. You have no idea how happy I am now that I'm back with you, Princess Annabella," he said which made her smile grow even wider.

I knew it wasn't a dream, Annabella thought before the Mr. Carter's voice yelling her name brought her back to reality. Zach quickly winked at Annabella after they shared a knowing look.

"Mr. Carter, I've missed you," Annabella said as she approached the man that felt like a second father to her. After they hugged after he gave Zach the pizza box and conversed for a bit

Annabella ran back to Zach. "Please come inside. There's tons of food and cake and I can't wait to dig into that pizza," she said before Zach and his father walked in.

Before she shut the door, Annabella looked at the tree once more to see no one there. She smiled to herself, and sighed before closing the front door behind her as if she was closing her storybook for the final time.

About the Author

Amy is a Young Adult Fantasy author of Brazilian descent, but grew up in Toronto, Ontario. Amy started posting her stories online at just 11 years old and several years later discovered Wattpad, where she has accumulated over 3 million reads. Her other hobbies include Greek mythology, beauty blogging and petting dogs.

For new releases, freebies, and more about Amy Sousa, sign up for her newsletter on her blog!

Read more at www.amysousa.blogspot.com.

About the Publisher

Patchwork Press is an indie publishing collective that strives to combine the creative freedom of independent publishing with the benefits of traditional publishing. With a focus on producing quality, professional-grade books, Patchwork Press has nearly thirty titles to its list. More information about the press, its authors and services can be found elsewhere on the site: www.patchwork-press.com